DOUBLE JEOPARDY

Book II of the Blue Shift Trilogy

The Terrible Time of Waiting for Possible Annihilation as the Ghost Star Passes Near Earth

by

Howard Johnson

To order additional copies of this book, contact:
Senesis Word
PHONE: 904-687-1865 - **CELL:** 579-265-3386
Website: www.hojowriter.com (Not up yet)
Email: Senesisword@yahoo.com
BS2-txt-16D27S

The Cover Photo

This massive, young stellar grouping, called R136, is only a few million years old and resides in the 30 Doradus Nebula, a turbulent star-birth region in the Large Magellanic Cloud, a satellite galaxy of the Milky Way. There is no known star-forming region in the Milky Way Galaxy as large or as prolific as 30 Doradus.

Many of the diamond-like icy blue stars are among the most massive stars known. Several of them are 100 times more massive than our sun. These hefty stars are destined to pop off, like a string of firecrackers, as supernovas in a few million years.

The image, taken in ultraviolet, visible and red light by Hubble's Wide Field Camera 3, spans about 100 light-years. The nebula is close enough to Earth that Hubble can resolve individual stars, giving astronomers important information about the stars' birth and evolution.

The brilliant stars are carving deep cavities in the surrounding material by unleashing a torrent of ultraviolet light, and hurricane-force stellar winds (streams of charged particles), which are etching away the enveloping hydrogen gas cloud in which the stars were born. The image reveals a fantasy landscape of pillars, ridges, and valleys, as well as a dark region in the center that roughly looks like the outline of a holiday tree. Besides sculpting the gaseous terrain, the brilliant stars can also help create a successive generation of offspring. When the winds hit dense walls of gas, they create shocks, which may be generating a new wave of star birth.

These observations were taken Oct. 20-27, 2009. The blue color is light from the hottest, most massive stars; the green from the glow of oxygen; the red from fluorescing hydrogen.

Image Credit: NASA, ESA, and F. Paresce (INAF-IASF, Bologna, Italy), R. O'Connell (University of Virginia, Charlottesville), and the Wide Field Camera 3 Science Oversight Committee

Last Updated: May 16, 2015

Editor: NASA Administrator

CONTENTS

PROLOGUE:

A menace and a threat are not the same thing. A threat is the mere possibility of danger or something without danger that may appear as danger for a time. It can be dealt with or avoided by clever counter action. A menace, on the other hand, is a real danger and must be dealt with. Its occurrence is as certain as the rising of the sun.

As the jet rumbled down the LAX runway toward its scheduled path to Hawaii, Dr. Charles Botkin's mind raced through the multitude of new questions triggered by recent events at the Gemini Observatory in Hawaii. *Crazy Charlie*, as he was known to his friends, was drawn into the inner circle of those with knowledge of the menacing star when the director of the Gemini Project, John Carroll, asked him for help. He was asked to provide computer simulations of the effects of a star passing through the solar system at 90% of the speed of light. What began as a simple theoretical question became a terrifying reality when Gemini Astronomer, Angus Thomas, admitted the reality of the situation. The quest then turned into a search at the cutting edges of current science into application of relativity, quantum physics, and quantum cosmology theory to this unusual star. Just the concept of such an object half the mass of our sun, moving at such a phenomenal velocity, was mind boggling. To consider it might plow right through the solar system in 2031 was far worse and menacing as well.

What would be the result if this unusual star named, *The Ghost*, passes through the solar system as current projections of its path indicate? At its unprecedented velocity, would the star's gravity disrupt the orbits of the planets and possibly fling the earth out into the oblivion of interstellar space? How did this star attain such an unprecedented speed in the first place? This was a speed attained by only the tiniest of objects such as those particles Dr. Botkin researched and taught about at Cal Tech in Pasadena. Initially, understanding this phenomenon defied even his brilliant mind. He would be witnessing real events never before considered by any scientist. A whole new field of theory, together with the possibility of practical experience, was opening before his eyes. Would powerful gravitational waves be generated by the rapid movement of the mass of the star? Would these powerful waves tear apart the planets, including earth, or would they pass without effect because of their speed? Would the inertia of the planets resist the gravitational effects because of the rapid movement of the star? These questions were unknown and not even speculated about before, because they were outside the realm of possibility before the discovery. As his plane hurtled through the sky, his mind continued swimming through the morass of ever expanding unanswered questions. He began remembering his first visit to the Gemini telescope on the big island of Hawaii and of all the new people now so involved in his life.

IN BOOK I OF THE BLUE SHIFT TRILOGY

Using the new Gemini telescope on the island of Hawaii, astronomer Angus Thomas discovers a wayward star on a course toward Earth which might threaten to destroy all life when it races past the earth in about thirty years. Discovery of this inescapable menace unleashes snowballing events that batter the former all-pro running back, his beautiful assistant, Lani Namahoe, their families and friends. This determined group of people battle ignorance, internal enemies, and government agents as they deal with the discovery of this irresistible, unavoidable menace man is powerless to change or escape. Then they face the awesome responsibility of announcing to the public the possible end of life on the earth while struggling against powerful forces trying to prevent them from doing so. After the initial shock and reaction to such unnerving news quieted down, people throughout the world settled back to their normal life activities as before with a few exceptions. Most of these centered around those who would try to determine what would happen, and those who would use the knowledge and the associated emotional reactions for their own benefit. These people and organizations often acted against the welfare of the general population.

1

A Search for New Knowledge Begins

Tuesday, August 14, 2001,Tuesday, August 14, 2001, John Carroll, director of the Gemini telescope on the big island of Hawaii, called Dr. Angus Thomas, an astronomer working at Gemini, with some important news. Charlie Botkin called to say he prepared some preliminary results of the simulations of the effects of the Ghost star passing near or through the solar system, and wanted to deliver them in person. Charlie told him he needed to unwind for a few days and was taking him up on his earlier invitation. He would arrive in Hilo Wednesday afternoon and at Gemini by three. He declined to answer any questions about the simulations over the phone.

By three o'clock the next day, Angus and John were in the lobby of the Gemini Northern Operations Center in Hilo awaiting Charlie's arrival. He called to say his plane landed a bit early so he would take a cab.

A cab drove up and disgorged a tall, slender man in tattered jeans and a ponytail. He wore a garish Hawaiian shirt and carried a stuffed duffel bag. No one would ever expect this character to be a serious, world-famous scientist.

As soon as John introduced Angus, Charlie commented, "You worked with Pat Yamaguchi at Arizona, didn't you? I understand you found an unusual new star."

Surprised, Angus took a moment to answer, "Why . . . yes, but how are you aware of my work with Pat?"

Charlie laughed. "Pat worked with me at Cal Tech during our graduate studies before he moved to the University of Arizona. We still get together occasionally. I called him for some input on the problem you gave me. He was helpful."

John and Angus glanced at each other in dismay, their minds racing. This was an unexpected development. "What did he say about the problem?" John asked, as he regained his composure.

"He said it was impossible. Nothing could cause a star to reach such speed." Charlie answered in a matter-of-fact voice. Then he asked, "Is the girl at the reception desk Jenny?"

"Yes, do you know her?" John Asked.

"No. I asked her to marry me once, and now I'd like to meet her."

John and Angus looked at each other as John explained, "See now why they call him Crazy Charlie?"

Charlie sauntered over to the reception desk smiling brightly. "Are you Jenny?"

"Why yes. How can I help you?"

"We spoke on the phone a while back. I'm Charlie Botkin from Cal-Tech. Do you remember?"

"How could I forget a man who proposed to me over the phone the first time we talked? You are crazy."

"Right! Crazy Charlie, my friends call me. I just wanted to meet you in person. Incidentally, you are even prettier than you sounded over the phone."

Jenny tried desperately to maintain a professional attitude under this onslaught of complimentary remarks. "What can I do for you?" she struggled to say.

"Nothing right now, but I may have a question or two for you later, so be forewarned." Charlie said as he turned to rejoin John and Angus.

✳ Thursday, August 16, 2001 ✳

Just before noon, Dr. Charles Botkin drove up in a newly rented car and walked into the lobby of the Gemini Op Center in Hilo. Crazy Charlie was dressed neatly in slacks and a conservative shirt. Both were crisp and new. He stopped at the desk and spoke to Jenny, the receptionist, in his most proper fashion. "I've kidded you a bit before, but I'd like to ask a serious question. Do you have a steady boyfriend?"

Jenny, who recently terminated a relationship, was wary. She picked up a pencil from the desk and drummed it steadily. "You call asking me to marry you the first time we spoke on the phone a little kidding? And now you're being quite nosey."

Charlie conjured up his most innocent look. "That was for laughs. This is serious. I was wondering if you could show me around after you finish work. My request wouldn't be appropriate if you had a steady boyfriend."

"I don't have a boyfriend, but still, I don't know you at all. I'm a bit wary about going out with you." Jenny continued drumming the pencil nervously. She still didn't know quite how to take him.

"I'll provide references. How about Dr. Angus Thomas or his assistant, Lani? Or even your chief honcho, Dr. Carroll? They would vouch for me." He placed his extended thumbs in the armpits of his shirt. "I even bought a new outfit this morning just for you. I don't always dress as casually as I did yesterday when I arrived from LA."

"I don't date men I meet here at Gemini. It's not a good idea." Her coy smile betrayed her.

Charlie smiled as he caught the encouraging contradiction. "This is my first time here and will most likely be my last, a friendly visit here with my old friend, Dr. Carroll. I promise you fun, companionship and no wrestling matches. I'd like to tour this place with someone younger than my parents and you're the only one I met. Please?" Charlie was using all his considerable boyish charm.

Jenny smiled, hesitated, then carefully placed the pencil on the desktop. "I suppose going out with you will be okay,"

"Then how's six o'clock? You pick the place to eat. I'll rely on your judgement, but remember, I like expensive food."

Jenny pulled a Hilo map from her desk, placed it on the counter and marked a spot on the map. "Right here's where I live. I'll write the address and phone number on the map. Think you can find your way?"

Charlie broke into a wide grin. "No problem. See you at six. And thanks."

❋   6:00 **p.m.**   ❋

At six on the dot, Jenny bounced through her apartment to answer the door for Charlie. "Are you always so on time?"

"Are you always so ready? You seem all set to go."

Jenny spun once around. Her pleated pale blue skirt flounced jauntily. "How do you like the dress? My sis bought it for me. She said it made her think of me."

"It brings out the blue of your eyes and is quite pretty."

"It's not Hawaiian, but I like it." She led him across the room and pointed to a chair. "Let's take time to sit for a while."

Charlie was silent for a moment, searching for something to say. "You're not from the islands, that's obvious. I'd say somewhere in the Southwest."

"How clever. I grew up in Albuquerque. Do I detect a slight Midwestern tinge to your words?"

"Right on. I'm an Indiana farm boy."

"Right! And with a BS from Purdue at age 17, a PhD from Cal Tech, and a string of awards and achievements as long as your arm. The top dog in the USA in particle physics. Just a humble farm boy? Ha!"

"How do you know all that?" Charlie was genuinely puzzled.

Jenny laughed. "It's part of my job, silly. I get a detailed rundown on almost every VIP that comes to my desk. As soon as I find one is coming, I check them out in our visitor's book. What I don't learn in our book, I search for on the internet. You'd be surprised at how much you can find out about a person in just a few minutes on the net."

Charlie leaned back in his chair, mouth in a broad grin, hands behind his head. "In other words, you put me at a distinct disadvantage. All I learned about you is you are a pleasant, pretty-as-a-picture, young lady from Albuquerque."

"Thank you kind sir." Jenny transformed from coy to matter-of-fact as she stood up. "It's time we headed out for dinner. We can trade personal histories over dinner."

"Where are we going'?"

"You suggested expensive which would also mean stuffy, formal atmosphere. I would suggest we concentrate on good food and a lively place. What do you say?"

"Not one of those places where you can't hear yourself think?"

Jenny laughed. "Of course not. My favorite eatery is a comfortable place to talk and listen to quiet music."

"Sounds romantic."

"Good food, pleasant atmosphere, but not romantic. The ambiance is encouraging to pleasant conversation."

"Sounds okay! Let's go."

As they stepped into the car Jenny pointed in the general direction of the university. "Head over in that direction. I'll show you a few things on our way."

After a short instructive tour of the university grounds, Jenny guided them to a low building almost hidden with huge plants. Near the entrance to a busy parking lot stood a large tasteful sign with a volcano and the words, "Pele's Pit."

"The Pit's popular with university faculty members and many professionals. Few frills but delicious food and fast service."

Charlie stepped around the car and opened the door for her. "Sounds like our kind of place."

Jenny beamed as they walked toward the restaurant. "My goodness. I never before had a man open a car door for me, never."

"You can't be serious? You're not offended are you."

"Of course not. I'm pleasantly surprised. To quote from an old song, I enjoy being a girl."

They stepped inside and were seated within a few minutes. Tables surrounded central islands. One was a large grille with a copper hood, the other a colorful Hawaiian salad and desert bar.

Jenny pointed to the grille. "The grill is Pele's Pit. I'm sure you learned about Pele."

"Goddess of the volcano's fire, right?"

"So, you've done your homework." Jenny smiled, glanced around, pointed out several people, and provided their names.

"I don't know a soul here and you've brought me among all you friends?"

Jenny laughed. "I know about them just like I do about you. They each visited Gemini at one time or another. They haven't the foggiest idea who I am."

"Okay then, tell me about yourself. I'd like to know more about this pleasant person with whom I'm spending the evening."

"I'm afraid my past is not very exciting, nor am I."

"Let me guess. You've been to the hot air balloon festival. You are a college undergrad. Your interest in astronomy led to your job at Gemini. You ran away from home after high school, met a man who brought you to Hawaii and then dumped you penniless, and you work nights as a stripper to make money to further your education and pay for your way back home."

Jenny howled with laughter. "Okay, I get the message, but how'd you find out I worked as a stripper?"

Charlie's had his turn to laugh. "Touché! I see I'd better watch my step."

"Just keeping you on your toes." Jenny's face shifted gears. "Funny, your description hit on some realities. I did leave home after high school and came here with a man."

"I knew you were a bit wild and crazy."

"The man was my father."

"Oh!"

"My dad is a specialist on weird concrete buildings and foundations. He was involved in the construction of the foundations for several of the telescopes on Mauna Kea. He brought me along when he was working on the Keck and then the Gemini foundations. I enrolled in Hilo University and decided to stay when his work on the Gemini project was finished and he went off to another project. I needed a job so when Gemini started I applied for and got this job. I still go to the university part time and should finish my degree next year."

"What's your major?"

"What fits? Astronomy of course."

"Logical."

After they ordered dinner, Jenny talked about her family and the home where she grew up. "Other than the effects of a world traveler father and a wonderful creative mother, my life has been uneventful so far."

"You mentioned a sister. Were there others?"

"A younger brother, Max, and an older sister, Eileen. My sister Susan gave me this dress. She's just a year older than I and we're close. We look so much alike we often pass for twins. We're all quite close. Max is five years younger and still in high school and Eileen is four years older then Susan. She's married and already has two little guys. They're adorable and full of mischief. I don't see them enough since they moved east to Philadelphia."

"Those things happen when children grow up and move away."

"True, but I still miss seeing them."

"I hear just what you are saying."

"Susan came out here for a year at the university. We had some wonderful times rooming together. Then she decided to go back to Stanford for her degree. She won a scholarship she just couldn't pass up. She left two years ago and though we see each other quite often, I still miss her being here."

"Sounds like yours is a close family."

"Yeah. They're wonderful. We were all close when we lived at home, except for Max when he was younger."

"Your brother? Why was he an exception?"

"Max and I fought almost as far back as I remember. He was always such a pain, the typical mean little brother. I wasn't nice to him either. Then an incident changed our relationship, interesting how it happened. Several of my high school girl friends were over after school. We were standing talking in our yard when two boys from school showed up. They were nasty so I asked them to leave. During the ensuing argument, one boy pushed me to the ground. Suddenly, thirteen-year-old Max came from nowhere and flew into him, fists flying, and bloodied his nose. In spite of their larger size, the two of them ran out of the yard. They wanted nothing to do with such a small fury."

"He was protecting his family, a strong instinct."

"True, but his action was special to me and changed the way I related to Max. Our relationship changed dramatically for the better. He turned out to be a dear brother."

"See. He wasn't so bad after all."

"What happened improved his standing in the whole family. Maybe it was just me and my attitude, but the family benefitted. Now we've all pretty much gone our separate ways. It's kinda sad. I hate to think of it, but my folks are probably going to sell their big house and move into an apartment. They won't need the big house after next year when Max goes off to college. After they move, our house will be home no longer."

Charlie stared into space for a moment."Passages - Life is filled with passages."

"I understand what you mean—kinda. You spend several years in a familiar place with familiar people, then suddenly, you find yourself in a new place with a whole new group of people. Sometimes they're your friends, sometimes not. I remember when I went from middle school to high school it was like that."

"My big one was from military school to the university. That was traumatic."

"Tell me. I'd like to know more about the real person behind all those big letters."

"Surely you don't want my entire life history."

"Graduating from any university with two degrees at age seventeen says you lived an unusual childhood. Tell me about growing up and about your family."

Charlie shook his head. "You mean it?"

"Positively."

"Well, okay, but please stop me if I am too boring."

"Don't worry, I will. Did you really grow up on a farm?"

"Yep, a small family farm in northern Indiana. My mom, a schoolteacher, noted my insatiable curiosity and began tutoring me quite early. Right from the gitgo she knew I was different. When I started public school at age six, they did not know what to do with me. Then, I was tested and placed at the fifth grade level. Within a few months, Mom and my fifth grade teacher decided the public schools in our rural area couldn't provide what I needed. After a search of a few weeks they found a boy's military school with a program for gifted children. I was lucky and qualified for a grant from a wealthy family who provided money for the education of kids like me. Otherwise the tuition would cost much more than my parents could afford.

"I remember how scared I was to be going away from home so young. Mom decided to come and stay with me while I started at the school. I soon fit in well with my classmates and not long after we arrived, Mom was able to leave and return home. I went home only during holidays and spent each summer helping on the family farm. I came to treasure those summers at home. Other than my schooling, I was a normal kid. I enjoyed playing with other children my age. I didn't see myself as different."

"I'd say you were most fortunate. So many prodigies become little monsters."

"Between my parents and the military training by teachers at the school, there was little chance of that. Another thing, those teachers let me learn at my own pace. They moved me ahead and provided advanced assignments as soon as I mastered the subjects. I loved math, physics, and engineering. During my last two years I was taking courses in those subjects at a nearby college. I enjoyed those college courses in spite of the occasional kidding from much older classmates at the university. The military discipline was the hardest thing for me to handle. I followed what I couldn't avoid, but remained a maverick until graduation from high school at thirteen."

"I can't see you squelching your independent spirit. It sticks out like a sore thumb in all I've seen of you."

Charlie grinned and stared straight at her. "Believe it or not, I can be quite conventional. I just can't be conventional when it makes no sense to be. If that makes me a maverick, so be it."

Their meal interrupted Charlie's tale. "How about I park my life story tour-bus so we can concentrate on dinner?"

Jenny smiled in agreement. "Sounds like a plan."

✳   ✳   ✳

As he finished the last of his steak, Charlie leaned back, shook his head slowly and expressed satisfaction. "Mmmmm . . . You were quite right about the food. It's fantastic. Now, a comfortable, not-quite-stuffed feeling makes me feel satisfied. I'll pass on desert."

"How about a little fresh pineapple, fried? It won't stuff you and it's supposed to aid digestion."

"I'll bet you're repeating propaganda started by the pineapple growers, but I'll go along with your suggestion."

Jenny stared intently at Charlie as the waitress took the order for the pineapple. "It's scrumptious. You'll see." Charlie loved how Jenny's eyes crinkled at the corners and sparkled with excitement when she spoke.

"I was a senior before I became aware of good restaurant food. Good old fashioned Indiana farm fare was all I ever wanted, until I was taken to a popular Chicago restaurant by one of our professors during a visit to the University of Chicago. This first time I tasted rare meat and French sauces hooked me. I still recall those first marvelous tastes."

"Doing so must have been a heady experience for a teen age farm boy. To back up a bit and return to your story, why Purdue? Surely some high-powered eastern schools were after you."

"You're right. Several of them pursued my family relentlessly. We jointly decided on Purdue University because of their excellent math and physics program as well as engineering. The fact it was only a couple of hours from home was another reason. In spite of entering at the sophomore level I spent a full four years at Purdue. With her schoolteacher's instincts, my mom convinced me to take many courses outside my major subjects. I will always thank her for such wonderful advice."

"Such a fantastic mother. You were lucky. I'll bet she was supportive."

"And loving and caring and dependable. My dad is quiet, the strong silent type, not demonstrative. Still, he cared in his own way. I am one lucky guy."

"I'm lucky too. My dad's work took him away from home for long periods, but he would be home for weeks at a time between projects. He was special to me those times he was home." The sparkle left Jenny's eyes for an instant when she changed the subject. "I read you graduated with honors and degrees in both math and physics."

"I'll bet you didn't read what I did with my summers while I was at Purdue."

"Research at the university?"

Charlie grinned. "Nope. I went home and worked on the farm every summer, just as I did before. Working the land provides something almost spiritual. I treasured those days in the heat, dust and dirt. The last summer I worked on the farm was the one after I graduated. I savored each and every sight, smell, and experience of summer, knowing this would be my last. The work was sheer pleasure, deliciously intoxicating. I loved the land and knew I would never return for another summer's work. I've missed working the lands big time ever since."

Jenny's face slacked into a pensive expression. Her shoulders drooped slightly as she sighed. "That's the way with life. It moves on, often away from things we value."

Charlie looked at his hands, wistfully. "You never stop caring for those people, places or experiences you love. You remember often and sometimes you cry."

They exchanged sad, knowing glances and sat silent for a moment. Now in full melancholia, Charlie told of the sad parting when the family drove him to the airport in Chicago as he left for Cal Tech and grad school. "I never took a sadder trip. Few words were spoken by anyone during the three-hour trip. Even my uncle Charlie, Mom's older brother, was quiet and he always had something to say. Mom wanted to go to Pasadena with me, but I wouldn't let her. I wanted to break the silver cord and start my new life on my own. C, the whole family calls my uncle Charlie, 'C.' C told her, 'Let the bird try his new wings. He'll do just fine.' I'll tell you about C some time."

"Partings can be so emotional."

"I don't think my father understood the pain. All he could do was say, 'I'll miss you.' My mother did understand and hugged me for a long time at the gate. I cried more during the flight than ever before or since. I was a sorry sight when I arrived in Pasadena. Christmas came around before I could face going home."

"You didn't mention any brothers or sisters."

"No, I was a spoiled only child."

"I don't think you were spoiled."

"I suppose you're right. I was lucky on that count as well. My family gave me lots of love and the opportunity to be my own person. I still did chores and toed the line my parents set. Farm work teaches lots of self discipline. It also taught me to respect and to earn respect as well."

"What happened at Cal Tech?"

"I always say I came to Cal Tech a neat, clean, short haired Midwestern boy in pressed slacks and left a long-haired, rock musician in tattered jeans. I call that progress."

"Some transition!"

"Not long after my arrival my roommate gave me an old guitar. That ratty instrument opened up the world of music for me. I always enjoyed music, but the old guitar turned me into a madman. After playing for friends at parties for a few months I started with a local rock group. After a year, I started my own rock band which stayed together until I finished my doctoral thesis. I also worked hard at my studies. I retired that old guitar long ago when I hung it on the wall of my bedroom where it still hangs. The music was an outlet for frustrations and provided balance to my life. The kids we played for began calling me 'Crazy Charlie' and our band became 'Crazy Charlie's.' Even my friends at Cal Tech began calling me 'Crazy Charlie.' I doubt anyone in our audiences believed I was a serious physicist."

"I can see you in that role. So you stayed on at Cal Tech."

"Yeh. I mixed rock music and teaching with doing research in particle physics."

Jenny smiled as she finished her pineapple and pushed back her plate. "Do you still play your guitar?"

"I love my work, my family, my independence, and my rock band. Those different things result in some weird conflicts. The recognition has its good and bad sides. I tend to downplay it as much as I can. Except for uncle C, my entire family was shocked when I showed up for Christmas with my long hair, jeans and guitar. The big difference from when I left almost four months earlier took them a while to understand. They soon found I was the old Charlie beneath the much changed appearance. My music shocked them as well, but when they listened they heard a moral message in the words. I feel intense about personal morals, drugs, alcohol and tobacco and my music screams out against them and against what I call 'moral stupidity.'"

"I understand what you're saying, but what does it mean to you?"

"I'm lukewarm about religion and not much of a church goer, but I think morality is paramount. To me, all this peer promotion of drugs, alcohol and sex goes against common sense. They call it *moral freedom*. I call it *moral stupidity*. It destroys character, will, and personal futures along with individuals, marriages and families. It's all kinda like smoking cigarettes. The few benefits are so far outweighed by the deadly dangers, it just makes no sense."

"A unique viewpoint for sure."

"I despise stupidity. I feel sorry for those injured, but I despise the stupid, easily avoidable actions causing those injuries."

"Wow. You feel intense about that don't you?"

"Yes, I do. Maybe it's because it's so remote from my work. My music with those messages on morality brought me more and more concerts sponsored by churches and religious organizations. At one of these performances, a woman from a detention home for troubled youths came to me and asked if I would play, sing and then talk to these youths. She thought I could be a positive role model and might be able to reach some of the youths."

"And did you?"

"I hope so. My first one was quite an experience. After my concert and talk were finished, one young man challenged my stand on about everything from drugs to sex. I remember the verbal exchange quite well, along with what happened after.

"'Why should I give up girls, booze and gettin' high on dope? I like bein' bad with them all. Might as well be dead if I quit.'

"His fellow prisoners laughed and repeated his comment.

"Things started to be a bit testy and I replied, 'Well, for one thing, being bad as you say, got you in here in the first place. I don't call it bad, just stupid! Do you like being in this place?'

"'Course not. I won't be caught next time,' he replied to a chorus of 'yeahs' from his friends.

"'Real punishment does not require you to be caught. If you're so stupid, you'll punish yourself. Visit the drug rehab section at a prison hospital. It's filled with guys like you just a few years older. No one should be forced to go through the hell they put themselves through and that's right where you're headed. How about the drunk tank at the local jail? Does the smell of vomit and stale urine please you? You guys are trapped by your own ignorance. Pleasure and then pain, pleasure and more pain, over and over again until you die. If you like getting high, try something to help you, not harm you, something you can never OD on.'

"'What the hell is that? I'll try some,' came from one voice from the group.

"I lit into them then.

"'I call it getting smart, being your own man, being in control of yourself and not being a patsy for guys making a fortune from your stupidity. You guys are like pigs being led to the slaughterhouse. You have no idea where you're going, but everybody else is headed in a similar direction, so you'll just go with the flow. You've given up on leading your own lives and doing your own thinking. You let the guys with the drugs and booze tell you what to do and then you do it. They used to call that slavery and fought a war to abolish it!'

"After an angry response from the young inmates, I kept it up.

"'Good! You should be angry! Ask yourselves if you're angry at the truth and at me for speaking the truth, which is what I just gave you. Or are you angry at yourselves for being so stupid as to obey the controls of those making money on your stupidity? Go look at the face in your mirror. Do you see a pig on the way to slaughter or a man who can think for himself? Think about it! Your life depends on your choices alone. Are you a pig or a man? Only you can answer and you will, one way or another!'

"After the confrontation and the angry comments were over, I challenged them to consider their future. Soon, I was talking to the young men about the highs of learning about new things. I decided if I ever spoke to a group like this again, I would polish my presentation to receive a less angry response. I envisioned a larger group losing control of their anger. It was not a pretty picture.

"As I was leaving, the woman who invited me said she thought my message went over quite well. I told her I was afraid I stepped on their toes a little too hard.

"She replied, 'They needed a jolt to hold their attention. They were not as close to losing control as you might think. A lot of displays of anger represent posturing to impress fellow inmates. We keep a tight lid on things here. I'd like for you to come back in a few months. Their response will tell us a lot about the effectiveness of your message.'

"I agreed to return. I saw those young men as such a waste. It's a shame to waste even one human life. I was invited to many other youth groups, detention homes and prisons in the years to follow. It was rewarding to hear my music and talks were credited with turning quite a few lives around."

Jenny shook her head in amazement. "That information wasn't included in my notes about you, but it should be. You are a special person."

Charlie stood up as they started to leave. "You're a special person yourself."

Warm thoughts and feelings toward this pretty little lady in the pale blue dress coursed through the young man from Indiana. A significant silence followed them as they walked to the car. Soft images occupied both their minds. When Charlie opened the door, he managed a few intelligible words through the warm fuzzy fog clouding his thoughts.

"Well, where to now, little tour guide?"

Jenny sat down and stared straight ahead. Her mind refused to function. Her voice simply would not respond. Charlie started the car and sat without moving. Suddenly their eyes met and locked them in an endless trance-like state. A bright flash from the lights of a car turning in front of them broke their common trance and reality returned. Jenny snapped back to action.

"Wow, what - oh yes, where are we going?"

"I think that's what I just asked. Did we go through a time warp or something?"

"Could be! Let's head out before it hits us again."

"Which way?"

"We'd better call it a night. Friday's always a big day for me at Gemini. I must prepare visitation tables for all the VIPs coming next week. You are scheduled for a full day with Drs. Thomas and Carroll and their group so you'll need to be sharp yourself. If I'm to show you much of the island on Saturday, we'll head out early, say six-thirty?"

Charlie headed for Jenny's apartment a few minutes away. "I didn't realize how late it was. I'm still functioning on part California time so it won't be too early for me."

"Breakfast will be ready when you get here. Then we can hit the road right away."

"Great!"

"What would you like for breakfast?"

"I'm sure whatever you fix will be fine."

They pulled up to Jenny's door and Charlie stepped out and opened the door to walk her to her door. "You needn't walk me home. It's a short distance."

"Yes, but it is quite important for me. If my mom ever heard I didn't walk a young lady to her door, she'd never speak to me again."

A walk to the door, a courteous good night, and Charlie headed for his hotel.

2

Crazy Charlie Really Goes Crazy
✳ Saturday, Aug 18, 2001 ✳

Saturday morning after breakfast they headed out for their tour. Jenny packed a basket of fruit, snacks, and half a dozen sandwiches, "In case we decide to stop somewhere and picnic."

After things were in the car, Charlie started the engine. "Where to boss?"

"We've seen the university and most of Hilo. How about a visit to the lava flow?"

"The one that buried Kalapana?"

"Yes, it's the only active one, and has been erupting for years. I believe it's the longest continuous eruption on record, about twenty years."

"Sounds like a good place to start."

Charlie marveled at the black wall of lava rising above the roadway. Frozen now, it still seemed ominous where the road disappeared underneath. They walked out on the lava all the way to where steam rose from the ocean as red-hot lava poured out of the black wall into the surf.

Jenny pointed down. "Does it make you nervous knowing hot, liquid lava is flowing a few feet beneath our feet?"

"As a matter of fact, yes, it does. I hope we don't break through."

"There are a few places with 'windows' in the surface where you can see the lava flowing. Barricades are placed around those to keep people from getting too close."

"I'll stay far from those 'windows.' What about any other dangers?"

"Occasionally a shelf of lava will break off and tumble into the sea. One like the place below where we are now standing."

"Hadn't we better step back a bit?"

Jenny laughed. "Where we are is safe enough. See the flat area below us?"

"Yes. You mean where those people are taking pictures?"

"Yes. A few years ago, a similar shelf collapsed into the sea and several people drowned or were otherwise killed. Since then they check the edges regularly and put up barricades when they suspect danger of an accident."

"I still feel a bit nervous."

"You mean you won't walk down with me?"

"You're kidding. You're not going down, are you?"

"Sis and I went down on the same shelf many times. It's safe enough."

"Okay! My life is in your hands."

From the lower area they could clearly see the bright red lava pouring into the sea. Steaming pieces of lava were thrown up on the black beach as each wave came in. "Those steaming pieces are created when the hot lava explodes on the surface. Our famous black beaches are formed from lava. Isn't it exciting?"

"I don't think I'd want to walk on that beach."

"Later today I'll take you to a broad, black sand beach you can walk on. It's like no other sandy beach, soft and moveable. You'll know what I mean."

After leaving the lava flow and the remains of Kalapana they headed up to see Volcano Park and the huge caldera. They stopped many times to walk and see the sights during the day as they drove all the way around the island. During this time they shared much with each other about their past and families. Jenny decided there was much more to this gentle man than titles and letters. He was a real, down-to-earth person. They picked up some bottles of tea at a little deli in Waimea before heading for the north shore highway. By the time they were driving down the north shore, the sun was near the western horizon.

Jenny pointed to a small park between the road and the beach. "Stop here! We can eat at one of those tables. I'm starved."

"I thought you'd never ask. Were you here before?"

"Sis and I took the tour we did today when she first came to the islands. We're only about twenty miles from Hilo. We came to this little park several times to picnic and swim."

"It's nice and only a few people are here. Is it ever crowded?"

"During the day it can be more crowded, But by evening it's like this, quiet and peaceful."

"Too bad we didn't bring bathing suits. It looks like a nice place to swim."

Jenny picked a small bag from the trunk along with her picnic basket. "And what do you suppose is in here?"

"Your bathing suit?"

"I thought we might end up here so I picked one out for you on my way home from work. I hope it fits."

"You brought one for me, too? You're quite clever miss Corso."

"Thank you for the compliment, Dr. Botkin."

"Let's go swimming and then eat. I may be hungry, but I'd like a swim first."

"Okay. See the little building?" Jenny pointed to a low, brick building near the beach. "We can change in the locker room and shower with fresh water after our swim."

She took a bright Hawaiian suit out of her case, handed it to him and started running for the building shouting, "Last one in the water is a rotten egg."

Charlie won but barely. They swam, walked down the beach, and swam again before heading in to shower and dress. By time they reached the table and took out their lunch, the sun was sinking behind Mauna Loa. They ate and talked for an hour. A mere hint of light showed on the horizon to the west when they picked things up and put them in the car.

Jenny stopped by the car and turned toward Charlie with his hand on the door. "Let's take another walk on the beach. I don't want to leave yet. You are going to leave tomorrow and I may never see you again."

Charlie smiled knowing no chance would this be their last time together. He decided earlier in the day to come back to visit this delightful little lady who made him feel so warm and comfortable. "I'd love another walk on the beach, where I may share a secret."

"What's the secret?"

"I decided to come back to visit you and your beautiful island again. As soon as I can manage it."

Jenny felt the same warm, fuzzy feeling she pushed out of her thoughts earlier. "Do you mean it?"

"If you'd like me to."

"I want you to."

They were silent at first as they walked on the beach. Each was afraid to succumb to the emotional pressures bubbling beneath the surface of their thoughts. When they did began to talk it was small talk. The warm ocean breeze, the sounds of the waves on the beach, all the magic of a tropic night were scrupulously avoided in their conversation. Fear of the fuzzy, mind befuddling sensation trying to engulf them made it so. They spoke of family, friends, their work, and other mundane subjects while avoiding the spectacular starry sky above. They walked up and down the beach in a state of suspended excitement for an hour.

Jenny could stand it no longer. She spun around and stood facing Charlie, her hair flowing softly across her face in the breeze. "Are you really coming back to see me? I'd love it if you did but will you?"

"Unless you'd rather I didn't . . . No. I would still come back to visit you even if you said no. I'd want to change your mind."

Slightly shaken and still wary, Jenny waited a long time before speaking. "I'm not sure. We've only been together for a day and yet, at this moment, I don't want you to leave. It would be impossible for me to say no."

Charlie began to feel a bit more comfortable. "Suppose we find out it's perilous? I mean this thing between us."

"It may be kinda chancy and intense but surely not perilous."

"You mean it doesn't scare you?"

"I am terrified."

"Me too."

Charlie shifted his feet in the sand and tried to concentrate on the small mounds he pushed up. His heart seemed about to jump out of his chest. His powers of speech left him.

Jenny gazed straight in his eyes and reached out with her arms. "Why don't you put your arms around me?"

Charlie's arms seemed paralyzed as he looked back at Jenny. Then they slowly reached out, circled Jenny's waist and drew her to him. Arms entwined, they stood in silence as the night sounds and sights worked their magic. After a long, silent wait, Charlie found his hand brushing against Jenny's soft cheek as once more their eyes locked. Then, like the snap of a soft, tender trap, their mouths sought and found each other - again and again. Thus, they stood without a hint of letting go for a long time.

✳ Sunday, August 19, 2001 ✳

Charlie awoke at seven sharp. Jenny was to pick him up at eight-thirty for breakfast and then they were to go to her church. It had been a long time since Charlie went to a Sunday church service and he was a bit apprehensive. After a short night's sleep, the cold water he continued to splash on his face brought him slowly to life. His thoughts kept rushing through the wondrous time with Jenny. He was terminally smitten and he knew it and it frightened him. This was not in his life's plan and Charlie always worked with a plan. Laughs are great, but this was deadly serious.

As he stepped out of his room, Jenny drove up. "Ready?" She asked with her cheery smile.

"Me, ready? I hope your church is ready for me," Charlie said with a smile.

✳   ✳   ✳

After breakfast and church they had three hours before Charlie's plane left from Kailua on the other side of the mountain. Jenny did not want him to drive his rental car to the airport. "Can't you drop it off here? I'd like to take you to the airport so we can spend more time together."

Charlie took out his rental contract. "Here, it says I can drop it off in Hilo. How fortunate."

"Now we will be together for a few more hours."

After checking out, putting his luggage in Jenny's car and returning the rental, they headed over the mountain toward Kailua.

As they left Hilo, Charlie waved out the window. "Don't worry Hilo. I'll be back."

"I don't suppose you have any idea when, do you?"

"Right now, no. From here I'm going clear back to Indiana to visit my folks and my uncle C for a week. I need to talk to C about a new problem. Over the years he's come up with some unbelievable answers to tough problems."

"You were going to tell me about C, remember? You talked about everyone else in your family but him. Since we'll be on the road for a couple of hours, can you tell me now?"

"Sure! There's so much to tell, I don't know where to start."

"You only told me he's your mother's older brother and he means a lot to you, nothing more."

"Well, everyone outside the family describes him as an eccentric old man with a checkered past. It hurts when I hear people say those things about him.

They understand nothing about him, nothing at all. Even some in the family consider him a real nut and an unlikely source of acceptable knowledge. Mom, Dad, my aunt Matty, and I are almost the only ones who respect him. I think he likes it that way. No one bothers him much and he can do as he likes most of the time."

"Sounds like he's independent."

"A true free spirit is a better description. A free spirit in the best sense of the word, and one with a brilliant mind few people ever recognize."

"I'll bet he treasures your opinion of him."

"No more than I do his opinion of me. He's a kind, wonderful, wise man who respects life and lives it to the hilt. I was named after him, a fact that makes us both quite proud. Mom told me all about his life before I came along. As a young man, C married a beautiful young woman who left him after a year to pursue a career as a movie actress. Somewhat successful, she had small roles in many pictures. 'Uncle C' as I called him as a youngster, never tried marriage again. The several long term relationships he experienced eventually soured. He never got over one long relationship with a lady named Carla. She was something special because whenever C talked about her he would be misty eyed.

"I remember once asking him why he hadn't married her if he cared so much. He stared off almost like he was in a trance and said quietly. 'I was young, foolish and with a bad case of low self esteem. I didn't realize what a wonderful person she was or what a beautiful relationship we had. Letting her go and ending their relationship was one of the stupidest things I ever did. By the time I came to my senses and realized the gross mistake I made, it was too late.'

"Most of the time he was light hearted and easy going. He seemed never to take life seriously and was always upbeat. Nothing ever seemed to get to him except thoughts about Carla. These were the only times I ever saw my uncle get melancholy. Everyone in the family suspected he never got over her. Afterward he embarked on a nomadic life of searching. He did so many offbeat things in his life he's hard to describe in a few words. He made a lot of money on one business venture, only to lose it all on another, ill-fated one.

Afterwards he worked hard to pay his debts and managed to build himself a small fortune of some two hundred thousand dollars. He gave a portion of this to my folks so they could acquire some additional land adjoining their farm. In his late forties he embarked on a six-year trip through the Far East which exhausted his remaining fortune. When he found himself stranded and out of money in the Philippines, my folks scraped up enough money for his ticket home. With no place to live, he stayed for several months on our farm. I was starting school when he moved in.

"On the farm is a thirty-acre wooded area with a small pond. The woods and the pond remained undisturbed since loggers cut all the useable timber back in the late eighteen hundreds. On a small rise near the pond, Uncle C built a neat little cabin and moved in 'to be out of everyone's way,' he said it was summer, 1979 and I was an eager eight-year-old, who became a fascinated helper as he built his cabin. During the next few summers I spent many hours listening to stories of Uncle C's adventures around the world while we worked on the farm, fished on the nearby lake, or walked through the woods. During inclement weather we worked on projects in his workshop. I also read from the thousands of books C collected and which filled the shelves on two walls of the main room of the cabin. His collection held texts on a wide variety of subjects from Astronomy to Zoology, several sets of encyclopedias and quite a bit of fiction from the classics to Jules Verne and several modern authors. Stacks of National Geographic and several scientific magazines filled the lower shelves on one wall of the room. I did a lot of growing up in his cabin."

"Sounds like a wonderful place for a young person to learn."

"It was. In his workshop, the largest of the three rooms in the cabin, C kept an assortment of tools fitting many trades. One corner of his workbench was devoted to the assembly of one of the new 'computers' that were beginning to hit the electronic hobbyist market. I was fascinated by this new gadget and worked on it with C every chance I got. By the time I was nine, C helped turn me into a bonafide computer whiz.

"For income, C did odd jobs, construction work, auto repair, and even spent a year as a preacher for a nearby evangelical, nondenominational Christian church. This led to a short career as a DJ and talk show host on a local radio station. His offbeat views covered the whole spectrum including politics and religion. Those views soon gained the animosity of many listeners. He was fired in spite of the fact his audience soon grew to huge proportions for the local area. His short-lived, local-celebrity status was a mixed blessing as it earned him a reputation as 'the crazy who lives in a cabin in the woods.'"

"People can be so cruel to those who are a bit different. Probably because of their own weakness or low self esteem."

"It didn't seem to bother C. He let it slide without reacting. His lack of reaction seemed to aggravate those who were trying to agitate him even more. He even told one of his antagonists he was sorry for him because he was so narrow minded. C was not above antagonizing those who taunted him. Most of them were too dense to understand when he tastefully insulted them."

"I'm beginning to like your uncle C."

"He's quite a decent person. Helped out around the farm at every opportunity. His meager odd job income barely covered his living expenses and fuel for the old pickup he drove. When he qualified for Social Security, it took a load off my folks including the financial worries about his health care. He was fortunate to be healthy as a mule with few health problems or medical expenses.

"One day, after I graduated from high school and before leaving for college, I was visiting Uncle C at his cabin and helping him repair a TV set. I will never forget our conversation as we worked on the TV. I can tell it best by relating our conversation. It all started when I asked him a question.

"'How did you learn so much Uncle C? You know more about almost everything than anyone.'

"'It's probably my insatiable appetite for information about everything. You show the same hunger young man. I can tell by all the questions you ask me. Graduating from high school at thirteen is an unbelievable feat. I am amazed you can be so smart yet still remain a nice, normal, young man. Your mother and dad are justifiably proud of you, and you know how proud I am. I'll miss our talks about everything under the sun when you go off to college.'

"'Don't worry! I'll be back to visit often, and we'll discuss all the new things I'll be learning at college.'

"'I look forward to those discussions, Charlie. Just remember, I'll be proudest of you as you find your niche in life and make your own mark on the world. In the meantime, enjoy being a kid as long as you can. You're being thrown into a competitive, adult world at an early age, so stay a kid as long as you can. I still enjoy being a kid at times, even at my age. Try for the best of both worlds and remember what I told you about being your own person.'

"'I'm kinda scared about going to college. It will be a lot different from military school and I'll be without any friends my age.'

"'Now that's one problem you can handle for yourself. Find a place where you can meet and interact with other young people. Try to find for a youth club or a church group where you can be with those your own age. Your educational level doesn't seem to create any problems with your friends here. You'll do fine.'

"'I hope so! Thanks for the encouragement. You always seem to say the right thing to help me out.'

"'It seems some folks around here don't think I ever say the right things. The **local nut** they call me. I guess I've earned it by opening my mouth about the wrong subjects at the wrong time, but it still hurts. I never get the chance to explain. Other than a few good friends, you and your folks are the only ones who respect me or what I say.'

"'They don't know you the way I do!' With emphasis I said, 'You're the wisest person I've ever met, and about the kindest.'

"'That's the nicest thing anyone has ever said to me. As long as you think that, I can stand all the criticism in the world,' Uncle C said as his eyes filled with tears. I knew he loved me and I adored him as well.

"'Remember, you were going to tell me something secret before I went off to college? Well, I'll be leaving in a few days so how about it? Will you share your big secret now?'

"Uncle C leaned back on his stool and looked me in the eyes. 'I did promise you didn't I? I tell you what, let's finish this TV and go sit on the sofa. This story needs a private place with no distractions because I want you to think hard about what I will tell you.'

"After I agreed, we finished and tested the TV. In about fifteen minutes we left the workshop and went into the main room. C headed to the fridge for a pair of cool drinks to accompany the tale. When we sat down on the sofa, C leaned back and stared off into space for a few minutes. I sat and watched him in rapt expectation. He told me an incredible story of an event that changed his life and has dogged him ever since. He made me promise never to repeat it to anyone."

Charlie gulped as he realized what he almost said. "Someday, I hope to tell it to you, but now is neither the time nor the place."

"You mean you're going to leave me hanging?"

Charlie felt terrible. For an instant his enthusiasm made him forget about his promise to C. "I'm sorry Jenny. I almost forgot my promise to C not to repeat his story to a soul. As a result of his experience, C knows things of science he has not learned in the usual way."

"I can understand a promise. I wish you hadn't told me as much as you did. Now, it will drive me crazy."

"I promise you I will ask C to release me from my promise made so long ago. Remember, I was thirteen at the time. If he'll release me, and I'm sure he will, I'll write it down and send it to you. I didn't mean to whet your appetite and then quit. I hope you'll forgive me."

"Nothing to forgive. You didn't mean to do it. I can wait for his story. I can see why you care so much for him. He taught you a sense of honor. That's rare in this day and age."

"Yeah. Between him and my folks I got a strong dose of what's right and what's wrong. They gave me strength to do things I otherwise might not do."

"Last night, on the beach was an important magical moment for me. I've changed in a way I don't quite understand, but I've changed. If we never meet again I will still treasure that moment."

"Don't ever say, 'If we never meet again.' That's not an acceptable possibility in my book."

"Charlie Botkin, we never said it in words last night, but I tell you now, I am falling in love with you and I've never said so to another man."

"Pull over. Right now."

Jenny pulled over on the shoulder as soon as she could. "What now?"

"I've already proposed to you. And, as I remember, you didn't turn me down."

Jenny laughed. "Yes, but that was during our first conversation over the phone. You weren't serious."

"Well, miss Corso, I am now."

"It's way too soon."

"Why?"

"We only spent some twenty hours together. Don't you think we should know each other better first?"

"My dad told me he knew he was going to marry my mom within an hour of when they first met."

"And how long was it before he proposed?"

"Okay, so he took a few years. What's that got to do with us?"

"I'll make you a bargain."

"Am I going to like this?"

"You will."

"Shoot."

"You've already proposed and I did not turn you down, right?"

"No, I can't remember a refusal."

"Let's leave it as such for now, an open proposal. When I can answer you, I'll let you know."

"Nothing like leaving a man hanging."

"Just like you and your uncle C story."

"Ouch! I guess I deserved that."

"Now, let's go. As much as I want you to stay, I'd rather you caught your plane."

"Before we leave here I must tell you, I thought about you every moment since dinner on Friday. If I'm not in love with you big time then I won't kiss you before we leave."

Saying those words, Charlie took her in his arms. After a long, lingering kiss they drew back and gazed softly at each other. Jenny spoke first. "We are falling in love, aren't we?"

"Yes, it's a wonderful, senseless, and hopeless happening, falling in love. Feels good doesn't it?"

"Yes, yes."

"Now that's settled I suppose we'd better go to the airport."

The rest of the trip was spent in the happy, nonsensical conversation of new lovers. The parting at the gate was long and teary as neither was aware of anything but their separation. Jenny followed the plane until the tiny speck disappeared. She continued watching, tears streamed down her face for a long time. At last she walked back to her car for the long, lonely ride home. *I don't think I've ever been this lonely*, she said to herself more than once during the trip home. As soon as she was home she phoned her sister.

✳   ✳   ✳

Charlie stared out the window for about an hour. Tears came and went unashamedly. He never felt anything like this before in his life. He never was the least bit serious with any of the women he dated. Jokes and laughs were his style. Those who expressed any kinds of feelings to him were dropped. No woman friend was ever important in his life. He avoided love like a plague. Now everything has changed. Waiting for his flight from LA to Chicago, he phoned Jenny several times. Each time her phone was busy. Jenny connected with her sister after trying many times. When Susan arrived home, she returned the last of dozens of messages from Jenny. They talked for longer than four hours. Charlie was on the plane halfway to Chicago before he managed to get through from the in-flight phone.

"I can't believe you and your sister talked four hours. What did you tell her?"

"Everything."

"Everything?"

"Everything."

"That we're going to be married?"

"Of course not. Just about your proposal."

"Did you tell her when?"

"I tell my sister everything. We're close."

"You mean she's going to know everything about us, always?"

"Everything she has a right to."

"That's a pretty broad statement."

"She will learn only what **we** decide is all right to tell her."

"Do I have veto power?"

"You will."

"When?"

"When do you suppose, silly?"

"Oh."

"Where are you?"

"Somewhere over - Nebraska, I think."

"Nebraska seems so far from Hilo."

"It is. Hey! I'm glad you made it home all right."

"I made it home, but I wasn't all right."

"No?"

"I've never been so lonely in my life. The drive was terrible. I don't remember ever feeling so alone."

"I thought about you the entire flight."

"Even when those cute flight attendants walked by?"

"One is a man and the other is old enough to be your mother."

"Some consolation. I already miss you more than I can bear. I can't imagine what it will be like after several months."

They talked on and on until Charlie joked, "This air phone bill from the air-phone company may bankrupt me. We'd better say good-bye. I promise I'll call you from home Monday evening."

For the rest of the flight he recalled his conversation with C those many years ago. He took out a yellow pad from his briefcase as he decided to write down what he remembered so he could send it to Jenny if C said it was okay. In a strong hand he started writing.

✳   ✳   ✳

Dear Jenny,

I just finished talking to you from the plane. I decided to write what I promised to tell you about C. It's the story I promised him I would not tell. I'm sure when I ask him, he'll tell me it's OK. Then I'll send it to you. You remember we went and sat on the sofa when C said he wanted to tell me something important.

I can picture sitting on the sofa with C. He leaned back and stared off into space for a few minutes before beginning his story.

"I'm going to tell you about something that happened to me a long time ago, something I never told your mother or anyone else still alive. This is for your ears only and I hope it will remain between us. You are the one person on this earth who will hear this story without prejudice. After you hear it, you can ask anything you want. You won't hear many answers from me, but it may explain how and why so many of our little talks went the way they did."

As C paused to gather his thoughts, I looked at him in wonder and amazement. We talked about so many things, I couldn't imagine what new marvel was about to be revealed. I was enthralled, almost enchanted. I sat, expectant.

Then C began, "I was walking the few blocks home from grade school for lunch one cold, crisp, blue-skied, January day in 1935. I was walking past the Buhers' house, about half way home, when I happened to look up and see a shiny object through the naked branches of a wintering tree. At first I though it to be a new kind of balloon caught in the branches, but as I took a few more steps I realized it was above the tree and almost overhead, far from the winter sun hanging low in the southern sky. I was fascinated for this was an exciting new wonder for an inquisitive second grader still in the intoxicating time of life when new things were being discovered on an almost daily basis. I leaned against the concrete wall separating the Buhers' yard from the alley, right where Mrs. Buher would place food for wandering depression beggars.

"The object seemed to be round and about the same apparent size as the full moon in the sky. It was shiny, almost like a mirror yet I saw no reflection. Transfixed, I watched it for a long time for a small boy, almost a minute, at which point it began to move toward the west. The object accelerated and disappeared over the western horizon a short time after it started moving. As soon as it was gone, I was so excited I ran home to tell my mother and find out from her what I saw. This was at a time when people ran outside to watch when an airplane flew over and my favorite was the new Douglas DC3. This object was not like any airplane I knew of before.

"When I arrived home for lunch my mother asked angrily, 'Where have you been? I've been worried sick!' I was astonished and didn't even ask her about the marvelous shiny object when she scolded, 'You'll go without lunch young man. Now hurry back or you'll be late for school.' I found the time lapse hard to explain as I took a full hour for lunch and school was five minutes away. At most I was held up three minutes by the strange object. What happened to the missing time?

"I remember nothing of the rest of the day until I came home and my mother again questioned me about why I was so late. I described the strange object and asked her about it. She thought it was another of the 'stories' I used to invent to liven up my life and amaze others. I discovered the price you pay and the pain of what happens when you become a 'story' teller and people learn not to believe you. Every single person who heard my story laughed at me and ridiculed my tale except one, my grandfather. A story teller himself, he listened attentively to my tale and wondered with me what the object was and what happened to the missing hour.

"I was so humiliated at every attempt made to find out about the object I gave up. For the next fifty or sixty years I told no one else about my experience. My grandfather and I discussed it a number of times over a number of years, often when we were fishing together on the lake. I was about fifteen the last time we talked about it. It was our little secret.

"When I was in junior high school, I began to experience a strange phenomenon which has continued unabated to this day. In Mr. Armstrong's science class I understood a lot about things not in my experience, reading, education, or communication from anyone. For me, this started a fascination for things of science which would last my entire life. I also found I knew the answers to many questions I should not know. My classmate and buddy, Fred Hunziker who sat next to me, was utterly amazed at my knowledge. Even Mr. Armstrong was flabbergasted to the point where he quit letting me answer questions in class. Another classmate, a bright girl, told me she thought I knew more about science than our teacher. They began calling me **the brain** and not always in a complimentary fashion.

"Your aunt Matty, my sister, who was six years older and ahead of me in school, brought home her chemistry book and gave it to me. In my mind, I can still remember the diagrams of atoms with electrons in circular orbits about a solid, compact nucleus in her book. I knew those diagrams were wrong, but my sister thought I was crazy when I asked her about it. I was crushed when she ridiculed my ideas, but what could I say? She was a high school senior and far wiser than I about everything. Her book piqued my interest in chemistry which then led to my selection of chemistry for my college studies. Many years later I read an almost exact description of the indefinite **cloud** structure of electrons about a tighter cloud of protons and neutrons, the nucleus, I tried to explain to my sister so many years before. This was the latest concept of atomic structure, developed many years after I tried to explain the same concept to my sister as a boy of twelve.

"Many other concepts of our physical world I 'know' without any idea from where the knowledge came. I keep searching and reading to gain confirmation of many of these things. For example, one important concept I can describe and conceptualize, is an understanding of our universe yet to be discovered or explained by anyone. I've written this all out and will give you a copy. I'd like your comments about it.

"Many years later when I first heard a **flying saucer** or **UFO** story, I remembered and thought of my childhood experience. The experience was so clearly described by so many of these tales. The ridicule heaped on those who said they saw a UFO caused me to rethink my experience and continue not to talk about it to anyone. The first time I heard an **abduction** story, I thought about the missing hour so long ago. In the same way, I also considered my knowledge with no logical reason for me to possess such knowledge.

"I make no conclusions or claims other than those I just described. The mystery to me is now greater than ever and I surely will not find an answer in my lifetime. I search and ask in every way I can yet the mystery only continues to deepen. If others experienced similar happenings, I would like to meet them. Yet I hesitate even admitting what I experienced. I fear the resulting ridicule might destroy even my own knowledge. I tell you this now only because I am nearing the end of my life and fear so much less than when I was younger. You can decide for yourself, if the story is for real or the ravings of a crackpot. A discovery confirming the view of the universe I described would change the acceptance of my story now wouldn't it?

"Would it ever!" I replied, then asked, "What do you think it was?" I was utterly amazed, barely grasping the implications of the story, but never doubting a single word uncle C spoke.

"I gave up such speculation years ago," C replied. "I only know what I told you, no more but no less either. Many years later, when the first UFO stories began appearing, I thought I might find an answer, but soon realized all I would do would be to make a fool of myself if I came forward with my story. If a conspiracy to discredit all UFO stories exists, as many people claim, it must be international and I can think of only one reason for it."

"What's that? I mean what could the reason be?"

"There is one circumstance which would explain a conspiracy of silence about any extraterrestrial or far advanced technology. If I were the possessor of this technology, all I would have to do would be to threaten the complete destruction of any nation acknowledging the technology existed. This would cause that nation to deny the existence of even the most obvious UFO sightings since an acknowledgment would bring swift and certain destruction to the nation doing so. That's my best guess at present and I admit it's not a strong argument."

"Could it be the alien technology accomplished a similar result without governments knowing they were being manipulated?" I asked. "Wouldn't such a situation result in the same effect? "

"That is one of many similar scenarios that would accomplish the same results of discrediting anyone who announced a sighting of any kind."

"Why wouldn't they annihilate everyone who saw them, or who speculated about them?"

"Such action might not fit in with their purpose, whatever it is. It's plain to me that whatever or whomever they are, they must have a purpose to their activities. I've wondered for years what their purpose might be without ever coming up with anything logical. I can't even determine if it bodes good or bad for humanity. It's a real mystery. Why would they imbue a small child with advanced knowledge? I'm convinced that is what happened to me so long ago. Others may have received similar treatment. Though I've searched my whole life, I've never found another person who shared my experience. I've met and spoken with people who reported sightings and abductions, but none were anything like mine. In fact, I find myself doubting the truth of their stories like everyone else."

"Maybe that's part of their plans," I commented. "Couldn't the method they used to give you this advanced knowledge be used to make you distrustful of these people?"

"I've speculated many times why I come up with so much unusual knowledge. I've concluded the suspicions are mine and mine alone. Those people must have embellished what happened to them, adding things they read or learned about in the media. It's all such a hodgepodge of information in conflict with known facts and other so-called contacts the truth of it has become impossible to discern."

"The truth is like the proverbial needle in the haystack isn't it?"

"That's almost an understatement. Over the years many incidents where the announcement of a new discovery was something I already *knew* happened. Did I *know* it, or was it a trick of the mind — a fortunate deja vu experience? I've pondered the same question many times. Once, while talking with a group of engineers about a particular metallurgical problem, I posed a solution to them I didn't think about, I just *knew*. Several months later, the specific problem was solved by the precise method I proposed. One of the engineers from the group contacted me and asked how I came up with the exact solution. He knew I was not a metallurgist and wondered how I knew the particular answer to a problem no one else could solve. I was at a complete loss to explain. Did my lack of knowledge in the field let me think outside the limits imposed by an expert understanding? Was my solution one of those serendipitous **aha** moments we all experience on occasion, or did I **know** the answer? It puzzles me and I would not claim to even understand where the answer came from.

"There are only two concepts I feel certain were placed in my mind by an extraordinary process. The understanding of the true nature of the particles in the atom is one, and the general makeup of the universe with the gravitational effect on light and other electromagnetic waves or particles, is the other. The first was only postulated by particle physicists many years after I knew and described it. The second seems only to be a theory in my mind. No theory I learned of is similar in any major respect. I wonder if it's correct and can't prove it—not yet."

At this moment I decided to set as one of my goals, to prove or disprove C's theory about the universe. That's why I became a specialist in particle physics. It proved to be a daunting task.

✳   ✳   ✳

Charlie finished writing, looked out the window at city lights punctuating the darkness, and placed the pad back in his briefcase. As he did so, the announcement came over the PA, "Fasten your seatbelts, replace your tray tables and raise your seat backs to the upright positions please. We are on our decent into Chicago's O'hare field and will be arriving in a few minutes."

Charlie was finishing the reliving of his unusual conversation with Uncle C as the plane touched down at O'Hare field. He wondered what C's reaction would be to the information about the "Ghost" star he was about to share with him. Charlie changed planes to the small commuter craft for the flight to South Bend. After the short flight, his parents picked him up and headed for the farm less than an hour's drive away. Sunday had been a long day. In spite of this, he was wide awake and animated. He recalled how much of his life changed in five days. Add his new knowledge of the real menace of the "Ghost" star is only two weeks old. It is mind boggling.

3

Crazy Charlie Comes Home
✳ Sunday Aug 19, 2001 ✳

Charlie's mom and dad were delighted with this unexpected visit. They saw their son far too seldom. His busy schedule at the university and their own ties to the requirements of the farm didn't leave time for many gatherings. Charlie didn't want to divulge the real purpose for the visit because of the secrecy director John Carrol and the Gemini group requested. Uncle C would be the only one to learn about the "Ghost" and he knew how to keep a secret. The rest could enjoy a few more months not knowing about the menace. They would learn soon enough. He knew he would want to be with his folks when the news was released.

As they turned into the driveway at the farm, C was stepping out of his pickup into a warm, afternoon breeze which whipped his fine, rather long, white hair around his head. Several days' growth of white stubble showed on his face and he wore a tattered T-shirt, jeans and sandals. His little back and white dog, "Ralph" bounced happily around his feet. C was Charlie plus forty-five years. C walked over and wrapped Charlie in a bear hug as soon as he stepped out of the car. The two held each other with obvious affection.

"It's been too long since we had one of those knockdown, drag-out discussions," C commented, a wide, happy smile splitting his face.

"I'm sure we'll have several while I'm here this time," Charlie replied, his smile mirroring his uncle's.

"Now let's take your things inside," his mother said. "Look at those dark clouds to the west. This breeze is going to blow us up a storm. We don't want to be caught out here with your things when it hits."

Her words were greeted with the distant rumble of thunder and soon after they were inside, big drops started pelting the western side of the house. A sudden summer thunderstorm indeed overtook them. They all helped close the many open windows before taking Charlie's thing up to his room. As he placed his suitcase on the stand at the bottom of the bed he glanced around his room little changed through the twelve years since he first went away to college. His old room even smelled the same. For a moment he regretted having left home at such an early age, depriving his two wonderful parents of their only child. Then he thought of the many times he returned to visit and help on the farm and he didn't feel so bad. He enjoyed the change from the academic life and his parents treasured those annual visits. He knew they were not lonely having many close friends and some family nearby. Aunt Matty Beck, his mom's sister, was twelve years older than his mom and a widow for fifteen years. Three of Matty's six children and many of her grandchildren live within a few miles and often visit. Her family treat his parents as a second set of their own parents, so there is plenty of family around.

Charlie's mom, Edith, was a typical member of the Miller family. Outgoing and talkative, she, Matty and C could go on for hours talking and laughing about practically everything. His father, Ray, was the opposite. Quiet, reserved and almost stoic, he rarely spoke more than a few words unless it was important. A kind and caring man, he loved his family, but had a hard time expressing his feelings. A hard worker with strong, rough, farmers' hands, Ray Botkin was respected in the community. After years of trying stiffly and uncomfortably returned hugs, Charlie now shook his dad's hand in greeting. Still, he knew his dad loved him and was proud of this son, so different from himself.

After they all sat down in the living room to relax and visit, his mom told them Matty, her two oldest granddaughters and C would be joining them for dinner. Charlie was anxious to sit down with his uncle, but their confab could wait for tomorrow. Charlie could not discuss any of this with his folks. His job was alien to their knowledge and his rock music was almost as strange. He did relate some of his experiences from the talks he gave to troubled youths. His parents were proud of his efforts in this area, although this too was a bit alien since he worked with inner city youths. His detailed description of his trip to Hawaii and his time with Jenny brought a strong response, from his mom in particular.

"You mean after just two days you were smitten? I hope you're not about to rush into something foolish."

"Don't worry. Even if I wanted to, Jenny would put on the brakes. She's a sensible gal."

Even his dad spoke up. "Sounds to me like she's got her hooks into you pretty deep."

"C'mon dad, we're kindred souls. No one's using any hooks. I'll say one thing. She's smart as a tack and as pretty as a young movie starlet. Sorry I didn't take a picture of her."

C laughed. "Go for it Charlie. She might break your heart, but then again, she might not."

Edith turned to her brother. "Of all things. I would think you would be urging caution."

C shook his head. "Now Edith, your son's got a good head on his shoulders. I say throw caution to the wind and follow your heart, Charlie. Young love is a thing to savor and treasure. Even if you are burned you'll still remember those magical times and smile. The pain will go, but memories of those wondrous joys will be with you always."

A long silence followed. Everyone knew C was speaking from his own experience.

Charlie spoke up. "Thanks C. I kinda thought likewise."

Another long, almost painful silence ensued. Edith smiled, stood up and gave Charlie a hug. "C may be right. Jenny is the first girl you ever talked with us about. I guess the protective mother's instinct took control. You must tell us more about your young lady at dinner. Matty will want to hear."

The family dinner was lively with a barrage of questions from everyone including Matty and the two girls. It was *old home week* and Charlie enjoyed the exchanges. Even his dad got into the act with several questions about the people at Gemini and Jenny in particular. They soon accepted Jenny as an important part of Charlie's life. Things quieted down before nine when Matty and the two girls left. When his mom went out in the kitchen to finish cleaning up, his father went to help. Before Charlie said a word, C stood up and motioned him over.

"Your mom and dad will head for bed in a few minutes. Why don't you come with me back to my cabin and we can have one of our old talkathons? You don't seem the least bit tired and I'm good for three more hours myself. Besides, I've something to show you."

Charlie was delighted. It was still only about seven his time and he didn't want to go to bed. "Good idea! Let's head out right now."

They walked through the kitchen and told his folks where they were going. Edith became a concerned mother.

"Don't you keep my boy up too late, C. You two start talking and you can go on all night. You both need some rest. C, you're not as young as you used to be. Try not to stay up all night."

C grinned as the two headed out the door. "I promise."

The storm passed long ago and the night was clear with a hint of light marking the last of the day on the northwestern horizon. Instead of driving the pickup, they chose to walk the ten minutes it took to reach the cabin. The lane and path were clearly visible in the moonlight so they didn't need the flashlight C grabbed as they went out the door. Ralph ran on ahead of them down the path. The little dog went everywhere C went for the last ten years. As soon as they entered the cabin, C led Charlie to his workshop. "Take a gander at this." He pulled what appea5red to be a small suitcase out from a shelf and placed it on the bench. "I've been working for a computer repair shop in town when they need help. I built this from parts they gave me for cost. I've got about fifteen hundred in this baby and it will outperform any portable you could buy today."

C laid the case flat and opened the top which displayed a full nineteen inch LCD display screen mounted inside. He lifted a keyboard and mouse from a space in the bottom where the guts of the computer were hidden by a removable tray. He plugged in the power cable to an outlet and booted the PC. Soon the screen came to life and the music of startup announced the system was ready to use.

"With the latest technology including lots of memory and storage, this baby's about as up-to-date as any system you could find today, a state-of-the-art and then some. Of course, it will be obsolete in a few months, but that's true for any computer you buy today. What do you think?"

Charlie was wide eyed. "Wow! I think it's great. It's more powerful than any PC we use at Cal Tech. Of course, we do all our high powered computing on a Cray supercomputer, but you built a phenomenal PC, considering the cost. I'm impressed."

The two worked the computer for about twenty minutes, loading and trying program after program, shutting down after trying an auto racing game. As they walked back into the living room, Charlie thought about the best way to pose the question he needed answered. He had no idea how, but felt quite sure the way he posed the question would affect the response. He considered this almost since the first moment he thought about asking C for help. As C relaxed in his lounge chair, Charlie sat on the couch in front of him.

"I've a serious scientific question to ask you, a question concerning mass, relativistic speed, gravitational waves and even time warping. Are you up to it now?"

Sensing his serious mood, C sat up in his chair. "You're serious, aren't you?"

"Yes, quite serious."

"I'll bet you will be posing questions hoping my mysterious knowledge can answer."

"Do you think you can help?"

"I hope I can. I've always been certain this would happen some day. Your probing at the frontiers of science would eventually lead you to a place where some extraordinary knowledge would be needed. Even if the answers are in my head, I might not be able to find them and bring them forward. Always in the past these bits of knowledge seemed to appear out of the blue in matter-of-fact answers to seemingly casual questions. My only suggestion is we talk about the subject in a normal fashion. Interject the question in a rather casual manner during the conversation. The harder I try for an answer, the less likely I am to find one. You do understand what I'm saying?"

"I understand the general idea. It makes sense to me. Let's give it a try. Here's the scenario. A star half the mass of the sun is found to be moving at 90% of the speed of light. We'll call it 'speedy.' We don't understand how it attained such a speed, but it makes for an unusual object doesn't it?"

"It is unusual for certain."

They continued discussing the possible origin of the star for some time.

C came up with a possible answer. "Could be it passed between the two huge black holes astronomers suspect are orbiting each other at the center of our galaxy? If a star moved into the areas between the event horizons of those two black holes, intense gravity could cause the star to be 'whipped' away from the binary black holes by a type of 'slingshot' effect?"

"Excellent idea. At the present time we are trying computer simulations to reverse engineer such scenarios to find out what's possible. All we need is one scenario where we decelerate such a star to normal speeds without it being gobbled up by one of the black holes. Reversing a successful scenario of this type would give us the answer."

"I may be on the right track," C said, smiling.

"You are, like always. Now let's suppose speedy passes another star, say twice the mass of speedy and at close range. Make the distance one tenth of a light year. What would happen to either star then?"

C thought for a minute. "A cone of gravitational waves set in motion by the fast star would ring the bell of any object it passed. The effect would depend on the speed of propagation of the gravitational waves and the distribution of inertia in the second star. My guess is any non fluid object, or part of an object close enough to the path of speedy might be broken apart. It would need to be close for any substantial effect. The star might 'burp' or resonate like a big bell, but a solid object like an asteroid or even the solid parts of planets including the earth would likely be fractured and even shattered. Another possibility is that any gravitational waves generated by an object moving that fast would be very weak and have little or no effect on a stationary mass. Do we know the force or speed of gravitational waves, how fast they move?"

"We are just beginning to try to detect gravitational waves at Laser Interferometer Gravitational-Wave Observatories (LIGO) in Hanford Washington and Livingston, Louisiana. Knowledge about their speed of propagation is either inferred by relativity theory or flat guessed. I'm not knowledgeable about that since those factors are in the field of cosmology and not quantum physics. We are dealing with questions in areas where the surface has only been scratched, and where scientists are just beginning to work."

"That's heady stuff for an old amateur scientist. One thing though, those gravitational waves are subject to the same gravitational effects on a universe sized scale as light and all other EMF waves. Isn't that part of the unified theory? Of course, those waves will pass unimpeded through materials that absorb or reflect EMF waves and may give different results."

"C, you never cease to amaze me. You may not get all the terms correct, or even the math, but you understand more of what's going on than anyone. You've already given me several new slants on setting up simulations."

"Tell me more about this 'speedy' star. Does it exist, or is it an exercise?"

"I was certain you would come around to that question sooner or later so I've planned an answer with strings attached."

C scratched his head and looked Charlie straight in the eye. "It's for real, isn't it? And I'll bet the damned thing's headed in our direction."

"You're right as usual. I'll tell you all about it, but you must keep this confidential. Don't tell anyone until the information is made public. I can trust you. You're no blabbermouth!"

With those comments, Charlie launched a full-blown history of how Angus Thomas discovered the star, it's projected path and arrival time, and how John Carroll involved him in the project.

When Charlie finished, C asked the big question. "It sure scares me, but what's the world going to do when the news comes out? It scares the bejabbers outa me."

"I couldn't agree more. I can't imagine what's going to happen when the general public all over the world learns about this star and what it could do. I only hope all the crazies don't create chaos around the world. They could turn this into a real mess."

They continued to talk about the situation until Charlie headed for bed after two in the morning.

Charlie stayed at the farm for a week before returning to California. During this time he and C spent many hours going over possibilities and rehashing their earlier conversations. They even spent time working on C's universe theory to see if it might be a factor. They ultimately decided the human species is resilient and would not be as likely to go off the deep end as they feared in the beginning. When his folks took Charlie back to the South Bend Airport for his return trip, C went along with Ralph sitting happily in his lap.

4

Cal Tech Computer Provides a Nasty Surprise
✳ Thursday, August 30, 2001 ✳

As soon as Charlie was back at Cal Tech he set up several new simulations using the information developed from C's input. He wanted to run the results of the simulations past C as soon as he could. It was several days before the Cray super computer was available and laid-back Charlie was up tight by the time he viewed the results. Again, the uncertainty of the path and date of passage made for a number of simulations with several sets of selected hypothetical data. Charlie hoped to pin down a best case—worst case scenario, but could only do so for a few sets of data in the time allotted. He needed more precise data from Dr. Thomas' Gemini observations and this data would come in every six months for the foreseeable future. With the newest data from Gemini almost three months old, and the next readings not due until December, Charlie took the time to work on his other projects. He realized he could not set up and run any new simulations before his annual trip home. It would be a long, three-month wait for the next updated data.

After receiving a monstrous phone bill, he and Jenny decided to communicate by email. They discovered voice communications via the Internet and were soon back talking to each other daily.

One of his grad students, Dale Yu Lin, a slight, bright eyed young man of Korean ancestry, brought him the first data set of the new simulation. "You're going to like this, Dr. Botkin. That wild star's gonna wipe out the earth for sure." Dale, of course, did not know this was a real star.

"What makes you think I'd like the idea? Wiping out all life here is not a pleasant scenario."

"I didn't meant to sound as though I liked it. The results are so interesting. It would be terrible if true."

Charlie reached for the folder Dale held. "Let's see what you've got."

Dale was excited about being part of this project. "Let me tell you what we found."

Charlie indicated the chair by his desk. "Sit down and give me your slant on all this. You ran six simulations, right? How about a brief rundown on each?"

"Sure! First run, we brought the path close to the earth's orbit and set the time of passage so the "Ghost" would pass about five million miles from the earth. In this case, destruction of all life was certain. Even thought the energy output would be only about 10% of the sun's, at such a distance it would still send a flash of heat and other radiation that would bathe the earth with deadly force for the ten minutes it would be closest as it passed. The side of earth away from the star might not be damaged, but there would be other effects. When the gravitational waves struck and distorted the earth, it would ring like a bell. Huge tides would pass over the entire surface as the oceans would be dragged from their beds and slung round the earth. The hard crust of the earth would be shattered like a clay pot and the molten interior would burst through and mix with the water of the oceans. The resultant massive amounts of water vapor would overpower the atmosphere creating sea level pressures of several hundred to thousands of pounds per square inch. All life would be extinguished within a few hours. In addition, the earth's orbit would be stretched into an ellipse taking it from as close to the Sun as Mercury at one point, and beyond Saturn at it's farthest. The orbit would be inclined at 12 degrees from the ecliptic as well."

"Interesting. Frightening but interesting. What about the relativistic effect on gravity? Did you take that into consideration in your simulations? After I go through this I'll tell you if I agree or not. What about the other simulations?"

"Next we ran identical data except the Ghost was to pass six months later with a similar path. It would be 190,000,000 miles distant at its closest point and would cause no problems, save a tiny change of the orbit inflicting little or no damage to life on earth. The danger then would be from disruption of the asteroids, Kuiper belt, and Oort cloud objects. These could wreak havoc on earth by bringing in all sizes of objects in unprecedented numbers for many years. If one hit like the one that caused the extinction of the dinosaurs, we'd be in big trouble for sure. This scenario would bring about a thousandfold increase in the likelihood of the collision of many different sizes of objects."

"What about the other four at more distance from the sun?"

"Those were hardest to pin down. Too many unknown variables. For instance, the one in which the star passed at one light year from the sun still caused disruption of the Oort cloud and an increased danger from large objects striking the earth. All the other simulations projecting paths within even two light years posed some danger to life on earth ranging from complete annihilation to possible disruption. The most likely path as projected by Dr. Thomas' last data set would destroy most multi celled life on earth leaving only bacteria, viruses and a few simple multi celled creatures. Should this be the case, evolution would start all over again. We need a more clearly defined set of data about the path. Otherwise, the possibilities are almost infinite."

"Thanks Dale. After I've looked this over, we'll talk about it. I'll provide some new parameters for more simulations in the next few weeks.

*   *   *

Charlie was expecting some updated numbers from Angus in the next day or so. When it didn't arrive as expected, he tried to contact John Carroll at Gemini to find out why and discovered communications were down. He even tried contacting Jenny at home with the same result. All communications with the big island were shut down, even Internet access. This worried him. The only mention of it on the news was about both radio and satellite links to the islands being shut down, someone suggested by a possible solar flare. A check with a nearby observatory added to his concern when they said the sun was in a rather quiet period with no solar flares. Something strange was happening and he could find nothing out about it. It bothered him as now he would be unable to make simulations with the new data until after he returned from his annual fall trip to Indiana. What troubled him far more was Jenny could be in the middle of an unknown, harmful situation.

Charlie met with Dale and the rest of the grad students working on the simulations. "I read through your results and came up with several questions and suggestions. The extent and variety of damaging effects predicted by the simulations surprises me. I looked through the available data used for the simulations and checked through the simulation setup again to see if we were using a true representation of the conditions. Everything seemed to be in order except for the relativistic effect. I did not see where you used that in your simulation so I want you to run those again using that effect. Note where it is used and continue with similar basic data. I'll be away the first three weeks in September and I'd like you to pick four more paths and run simulations while I'm gone. It's all outlined in the instructions provided in the envelopes on the table. Diedra can call me should you have any questions or problems after I leave. Since I'm up to my ears in preparing my work here for a three-week hiatus, please save your questions till after you've gone through my instructions. We'll be together once more this Friday before I go. Meet here at ten in the morning." After making the comment he dismissed the group. He worked the entire weekend preparing for his absence.

✳   Monday September 3, 2001   ✳

Even though he went home in August, Charlie still took the usual three weeks in September to help his dad on the farm. Those treasured times he valued now more than ever before. This trip he could also go through his data and simulations with C who might be able to see something he missed. At least he hoped so.

Monday morning, September 3, 2001 Charlie boarded the plane for Chicago. He walked down the steps from the small plane in South Bend trying to find the faces of his folks in the waiting crowd. They were not there. *That's unusual*, he thought. *I hope nothing's wrong.* He became more apprehensive as he walked to the baggage carousel, waited for and picked up his luggage and still no one appeared. Now he began to worry. He walked outside and waited for about ten minutes. *I'd better call to find out what's happened*, he thought as he started to go inside. As he turned to go in, he saw his mother's car coming around the bend. When she pulled up to the curb, she was the only one in the car.

"Where's everyone?" he asked as he placed his bags on the rear seat. Even when he sat down in the front seat, his mother stared straight ahead and said not a thing. Charlie sensed something was wrong indeed. "What's the matter, Mom?"

"It's your uncle C," she said through tears. "He's disappeared. We went to his cabin to see if he wanted to come with us to pick you up and he was nowhere to be found. His door was standing open and last night's supper was still sitting on the table, uneaten. Ralph was sitting on the porch, whining. I'm afraid something terrible has happened."

"Did you check the pond?"

"That's the first place we looked. It's been bright and sunny all day. The pond's crystal clear and only a few feet deep. If he were in the pond, we would see him since he always wears a white T-shirt. No! He just disappeared. His pickup's still here and with Ralph on the porch it's obvious something strange happened. Your dad stayed to search for him while I came to pick you up. Maybe he'll be found by the time we return."

On the way home, Edith drove much faster than usual until Charlie became alarmed. "Slow down Mom! You're in a hurry, but let's not add an accident to today's problems."

"I'm sorry! I didn't realize I was driving so fast. I'm worried to death about C."

"I'm concerned myself. Does he ever go off without telling you where he's going?"

"Never! Even when we're away he'll leave a note on the door telling us where he's going and about when he'll be back. He's good about letting us know. Besides, he always takes Ralph with him wherever he goes. If he walked away, Ralph would be with him. He wouldn't be sitting by the door."

"I'm sure it's something simple. Perhaps a friend of his came over and picked him up."

"Not a chance. Anyone driving would go right past the house. We'd hear them no matter when they went by. Besides, how do you explain the uneaten meal on the table? C would never leave the place like that under ordinary circumstances. He eats at about dark this time of year, so he left between six-thirty and seven."

"Did anything unusual happen right about then? What were you doing about then? Think hard Mom. Try to remember anything unusual."

"I hadn't tried to remember before. We were eating at the time ourselves. One strange thing did occur, a bright flash of lightning, a brilliant, sustained flash of light. Remember how sometimes, when it's dark out, a lightning flash lights up the whole sky and the area nearby for almost a second and you can see everything, even in the pitch black?"

"Yes, I know what you mean. A thunderstorm came in from the west last evening, right?"

"We thought so at first, but after that flash, your dad went outside to close the windows on the car and saw the sky was crystal clear. That's when he heard Ralph barking. Your dad commented on how he almost never barks unless another dog comes around the cabin. Also, we heard no thunder. We decided it was a bright flash of lightning from so far in the distance, we couldn't hear the thunder. Most folks call it heat lightning. What else could we think."

"It sounds strange to me. As soon as I am home, I'm going to check the neighbors to see if anyone else saw that flash," Charlie commented. The car was quiet during the rest of the trip home. Charlie was hoping C would be waiting when they arrived.

As they crested the rise in the road north of the farm, they could see two Sheriff cars parked in the driveway. Ray and two deputies were standing in the back yard. They were all looking back toward the woods where C's cabin was hidden. The deputies were friends of the Botkins and long time members of the local Sheriff's department.

As soon as the car rolled to a stop, they stepped out and walked quickly over to where the men were standing. "What did you find?" Charlie asked as soon as he joined them.

His dad turned to his son in distress. "Nothing! We found nothing at all. I called Pete and John here to see if they could find anything I missed."

Pete Lucas, the junior of the two deputies, replied, "we looked over everything and couldn't find anything suspicious. Wherever he went, C didn't leave a trace. We don't make missing person reports until the individual has been missing for twenty-four hours, but this seems far too unusual. We hightailed it out here as soon as Ray called. John and I combed the area for more than an hour and found nothing, nothing at all."

"We called for some dogs to come out to track him in case he walked off somewhere and can't make it back," John added. "They'll be here in less than an hour. Pete is going to stay and work with the dogs. I've got to go back right away, but I leave you in good hands. If he's here, those dogs will find him."

After John drove away, Charlie got his bags out of the car and took them up to his room. When he came down, the three of them were sitting in the living room talking, wondering about C's whereabouts. After a while a truck drove up in the driveway. It was the dogs and their handler, Tara Bailey. Tara was a well-known dog trainer and breeder who trained two hounds that were often used by law enforcement all over the northern part of the state. Ken Bailey, her husband was a veterinarian and together they owned an animal hospital, training center, and boarding kennel in the next county about thirty miles away. All four of them went outside to greet her.

After talking to Tara for a few minutes, Pete said. "She asks that none of you go with us to the cabin. The less people around, the better the dogs work. We'll drive the truck back to the cabin and release the dogs there. I need an article of his clothing. Some you can remember him wearing recently to give the dogs his scent."

Edith thought for a moment and then said, "He puts his dirty clothing in a hamper in the bathroom closet. He hasn't brought them up to wash for a while, so look in his closet."

"That's perfect. I'm sure the hounds can find a good scent in those clothes," Pete answered.

"Where did you leave Ralph?" Edith asked her husband.

"We left him inside the cabin," Ray answered, then added, "You'd best leave the little guy inside. His name is Ralph and he'll be friendly enough to you folks, but he wouldn't take kindly to a couple of hounds poking around his property."

"We'll make sure he's okay and kept out of the way," Pete remarked as he stepped into the truck with Tara.

-- THE DOGS ARE BUFFALOED --

Tara guided the truck down the bumpy lane toward the cabin."How about some details, Pete? John only said someone disappeared when he called and asked for me to bring the hounds here as soon as I could."

"The missing man is Charles Miller. Everyone around here calls him C. He's an eccentric old man about seventy-five, the brother of the woman at the house. I've heard some strange stories about him, but I've talked to him a number of times and other than his appearance, he seems normal to me. In fact, I found him to be sharp as a tack. He's got a keen clear mind. He had a radio DJ show locally for a while and angered a lot of people with some of his comments to callers. That's when the stories started. I think those stories are a lot of bunk. The ones who spread them are jealous of his intelligence. I only heard a few of his broadcasts, but I thought he was brilliant. He stepped on a lot of sensitive toes with comments I found to be accurate, if a bit harsh at times. They had what I call a career lynching and got him fired from the radio station. I'll say one thing. The man can build or repair about anything. You'll see what I mean when we go in his cabin. He built it all by himself about sixteen years ago. It's a neat little place. Perfect for a man living alone."

Tara was struggling with the rough drive. "Sounds like an interesting man." They reached the end of the lane where the path crossed a tiny, dry streambed. "Do we turn here?"

"Follow the streambed right into the woods. You can see where he's driven his truck over the years. It's a bit bumpy, but high enough above the streambed to be out of the water in the spring and early summer when the stream runs."

Soon after they entered the woods, the trail made an abrupt right turn and led about fifty feet to a cleared area by the cabin. As they stepped out of the truck, they heard Ralph inside barking. He knows strangers are outside and is giving them what for.

As they walked up to the door, Tara asked. "He's not a biter is he?"

"He was friendly when we were out here an hour or so ago. I'm sure he'll be okay."

Tara crouched down as she entered, extending her hand along the floor palm up in a friendly gesture. The little dog stopped barking, came over and sniffed her hand, wagging his tail. He was happy to see them. He did not like to be left alone. "Good boy," Tara said sweetly as she patted him lovingly. Her pats were soon rewarded with several doggie kisses. Ralph was friendly. After putting Ralph at ease, she retrieved several shirts from the hamper to use for the scent. "Pete. Why don't you stay inside and keep the little guy company while I work the dogs? If he can be kept from barking, he won't distract the hounds and my job will be easier."

"Okay! Only give me a call if you find anything. Use your two-way and set the frequency to our standard channel."

"Good idea. I hope I don't find anything gruesome. You'll remember the last tracking we did for your department was unpleasant."

"You can say that again. He was the most brutally beaten murder victim I've seen or hope ever to see again." Pete scrunched his face in repugnance.

Tara headed for the rear of the truck. She opened the small door and released the two hounds who proceeded to bound around for a few moments, glad to be out of their confinement. Soon they were back at her side knowing full well what their job was. They sniffed the shirt Tara held out, then sat down to announce they were ready. Her hounds were well trained. She didn't need to run them on leashes as they knew not to outrun their handler, waiting patiently at times so she could catch up. She directed them to the porch where she wanted to start the search. Hand signals were her method of directing the dogs who worked in relative silence.

As soon as she gave them the signal to begin, they headed off the porch and trailed about fifty feet to the center of the clearing where they began circling. Several times they started off on a track only to stop and return after twenty or thirty feet. These were old, cold tracks. After returning to the porch several times and sniffing for other tracks, the dogs returned to the center of the clearing and sat down. Their message held no ambiguity. The track ended in the center of the clearing and was the only fresh track the dogs could find. She had them try several more times with the same result. It could indicate several things. She had no way of determining which direction the short track was laid down. It could be from the house to the clearing or the reverse. The track indicated C either walked from a vehicle parked in the clearing to the cabin, or walked the other way, from the cabin to a vehicle. No other possibility existed. Tara examined the ground for tire tracks or other markings around where the track ended. Other than what looked like a single, very faint set of footprints in the soft ground, she found nothing. She took a marker flag from the truck which she stuck in the earth to mark the spot. Knowing they would stay nearby, she let the dogs roam as she headed for the cabin to tell Pete what she found.

"Did you forget something?" Pete asked as she entered the cabin so soon after leaving.

"No, but the dogs did find the end of a short trail in the middle of the clearing."

"What do we do now?"

"I marked the spot where the track ends. I let the dogs roam to see if they could find something else. When we drive back to the house, I'll let them search the way back and around the house. We should take this little guy with us. He's not very happy being left alone, I can tell."

She called Ralph over to her. When she picked him up, he gave a low growl to tell her he didn't like it. "Easy little fella. I'm not gonna hurt you." Ralph endured the indignity without complaint after her soft words and gentle touch reassured him. Tara knew how to handle dogs.

As soon as she walked outside, the two hounds romped over to investigate this little pooch their master held. A few words and a hand command and the two hounds sat while Tara took Ralph and placed him in an empty kennel in the back of the truck. Signaling them to begin tracking again, Tara got in the truck with Pete and they headed back, following the dogs as they searched back and forth across the stream side driveway and then the lane. When they reached the house, the dogs cris-crossed the entire yard, pausing several times by C's pickup where they found an obvious but weak scent. It had been several days since C drove the pickup and he had last walked to the house on Friday, so all the tracks were old and weak. The dogs followed tracks up to the house and the truck, but these, too, were old tracks. Tara retrieved Ralph from his cage in the truck and carried him into the house. He never made a sound, resting in her arms.

"I didn't think this little guy should be left alone in the cabin. Is it okay to bring him in?" she asked Edith who stood in the doorway.

Edith smiled at Ralph as she opened the door for them. "Of course! C brought him here often. He knows his way around. We even keep a bed for him and food and water bowls. He can stay with us till we find C." They all walked into the living room where Ray and Charlie waited. "What did your dogs find?"

"Not much I'm afraid. They found just one, fresh but short trail. When they couldn't find any others, I marked the end of the one scent trail with a little flag. Just in case anyone else wants to search for signs of what happened. I couldn't see any indication of tire tracks or anything other than the single set of very faint footprints. Tire tracks showed near the cabin where cars were parked and to the drive but nowhere else in the clearing. If your brother walked anywhere other than the one scent trail, the dogs would have found it. We've had no rain to wash the scent away and the one scent track we did find was fresh and definite. He walked the track one direction or the other within the last twenty-four hours. The dogs told me so in no uncertain terms."

Ray looked puzzled. "That's strange. It seems like he disappeared into thin air, right at that spot. Since that is impossible, we must try to come up with something else, something that makes sense."

"I can't think of anything," Pete commented. "If it isn't a wheeled vehicle, it must be a helicopter. Could a chopper set down in the clearing? It doesn't seem big enough to me."

Charlie shook his head no. He was familiar with the clearing."The clearing is big enough, but those big trees hanging over the clearing would keep a chopper from landing. A chopper could only pick him up on the end of a cable lift, dropped down while hovering above the trees."

"We would hear any chopper hovering over the trees at that time of night," Ray commented.

Pete, an ex-ranger familiar with helicopters, commented, "The military fly birds that can hover almost silent. They make some noise when they fly fast, but at slow speeds and while hovering, they are very quiet. You wouldn't hear them from here. The cabin is about half a mile away isn't it?"

"Yes," Charlie answered. "Besides, what would the military want with C? He's never even been in any of the service. He traveled all over the Pacific rim for a number of years, and he's done some contract work with the Navy, but that was twenty years ago. I can't imagine what the military would want with him. They could drive up in a car and pick him up. Why would they lift him out with a chopper?"

Pete's expression was one of incredulity."A good point. What a mystery. A chopper still looks like the only way possible for him to be spirited away. No sign of a scuffle appeared anywhere. I looked for those signs where the scent trail and footprints ended in particular. Those footprints were very hard to see. Tara noticed them while watching the dogs sniffing at several of them. They were slight indentations spaced as normal walking prints would be. We couldn't even be sure which direction they headed, but one complete print in some softer ground toward the porch showed they were headed away from the cabin. We examined the ground and found no other prints of any kind within ten or twelve feet of the end of the marker Tara placed."

"What about your own footprints?" Ray asked. "Couldn't they cover or obliterate other footprints?"

"One of the most important aspects about inspecting a crime scene is how to do so without destroying evidence. We receive extensive training on how to walk slow and careful to avoid areas we believe may contain clues. I can assure you, no other footprints were around the marker. We can't consider it a crime scene, but we did treat it in a similar careful manner."

"My dogs were the only ones who left prints in the area, and the ground is quite hard, so I doubt they left much of a mark. It would take a person more than a hundred pounds to leave any mark on that ground. I'm a hundred and forty and I left a light print where I walked."

"So that leaves us without a clue," Charlie said. "Your dogs found significant information, but that only added to the mystery. C couldn't just evaporate into thin air, but that's what the evidence points to so far. Where do we go from here?"

Pete stood up to leave. "Well, I must go write a report. I don't look forward to that, seeing as we came to no conclusions with any merit to write down. I hate to leave things so unresolved, but we all need to move on with things. I'll do some checking in a couple of areas including the nearest military bases, but I am at a loss as to how to proceed from here. So far we generated a lot of questions and no answers. I'm sorry folks, but that's the reality. If you think of anything else, please call me."

Tara stood up as well. "I'm sorry we didn't find more, but I must gather up my wondering hounds and head for the barn. I hope you find him and soon. I'd like the answer, so please call me when you learn anything new. I'll leave my card for you."

After Pete and Tara left, Charlie and his folks sat in the living room and talked about the last twenty-four hours. "The last time either of us saw C was on Friday evening when he was here for dinner. He walked up to the house two or three times a week and stopped in whenever he went off in his pickup."

Charlie wondered, "Could the meal left on C's table be from Saturday?"

Ray shook his head. "No, or the meat would smell rotten. In this warm weather it was all right after about eighteen hours, but another 24 and it would smell bad. That was the first thing I checked. There is no doubt he fixed his dinner Sunday evening and never ate."

"Did he seem worried or preoccupied Friday during dinner?" Charlie asked. "Was anything bothering him, anything at all?"

"No, nothing. He was his usual happy self. He talked about your coming visit and was looking forward to it. He thinks you are the greatest scientist in the world." His mother said affectionately.

Charlie looked and sounded worried. "And he's about the greatest uncle and friend a young man could have. I hope and pray nothing's happened to him. Run through Sunday evening again, will you? Try to remember even the slightest thing that happened out of the ordinary, no matter how insignificant."

They talked about the strange lightning flash and Ralph barking, but all they could remember that was unusual were those two. Then his mother recalled something. "We missed our favorite Sunday evening TV show. The satellite signal got messed up. Remember Ray? You tried adjusting the dish? No matter where you searched you found no signal. You shut it off to silence an awful hiss so we could eat our meal in peace. Right afterwards we saw that unusual lightning flash with no thunder. Half an hour later we tried the TV again and everything was okay."

"That's significant," Charlie said softly. "Did anything else strange occur during the evening? Think hard. It's important. Dad, did you find anything at all unusual when you went outside?"

"It was quiet as a tomb outside, an unusual silence. The only sound I heard was Ralph's incessant barking. He never barks like that unless another dog or some critter is outside. I thought it unusual since C quiets him down after he barks for a few moments. Sunday he kept barking and barking. I remember thinking C should silence him and wondering why he didn't. The cabin is far enough from the house you can barely hear Ralph when he barks. If I hadn't gone outside I wouldn't have heard him. I didn't see anything unusual, nothing I remember. Afterwards I went in to eat and nothing unusual happened. We watched TV for a while and went to bed. We discovered C was missing when we stopped out to see if he wanted to go with us to meet your plane. You know the rest."

Edith suppressed a tear. "I've got to talk to Matty and tell her about C. I can't wait any longer. She'll be worried sick. I'll ask her to come over so I can tell her in person. Her whole family will take the news hard. What will we do when this hits the news? I hate to think of how some of the local news people will treat it."

"Maybe they'll ignore it," Charlie replied. "He's not a celebrity so the news may not even mention him."

Charlie would prove to be right but not for the reason he thought. On Tuesday, September 4, 2001, news of the "Ghost" star was announced. This obliterated all other news for the foreseeable future.

-- HOOSIERS HEAR THE NEWS ABOUT THE GHOST --

Charlie drove C's pickup as he spent all day Tuesday checking with the neighbors about the strange flash of light his folks saw on Sunday evening. No one else saw it including the Swenson family on the farm the other side of the woods. He didn't ask about C since he didn't want to tell anyone he was missing. He ended up spending considerable time at each family he visited. They all knew him and asked to be brought up-to-date on what he was doing. A universal question at each place was, "Aren't you married yet?" He answered truthfully that he had proposed but hadn't received an answer. It seemed to answer the question, but he felt a bit guilty about using a proposal made in jest as the real thing. By dinnertime he still had several places to go but quit and headed for home. He decided to concentrate on helping with the farm work the next morning. He had talked with everyone close by with no results, so the ones farther away could wait. The sun was setting as he drove the pickup in the driveway and parked in C's spot.

As he got out of the pickup, his mother was so excited she came running out the back door calling, "Did you hear the news? Something terrible! A star might destroy the earth! It's on the news right now. Hurry!"

Charlie rushed to meet his mom who, by now, was all out of breath. "My gosh, Mom, relax!" He took her arm and helped her into the house and to the TV. *So the news is out*, he thought to himself as they sat down in front of the TV with his dad. The national news was about over, but they were in time to see a rerun of the clip from the LA sports program with ex-NFL star, Cy Dooley reading the complete release Dr. Thomas had sent him. Cy was now an evangelical minister in South LA.

After reading the release entirely, Cy passed copies to the host and several others on the set. "There's a note included here that says the Pope received this same information today. Since we're sort of in the same line of work I hope the Pope will confirm this message and read it to his people. I guarantee this release confirms what my old friend told me over the phone. This is no hoax! If necessary, I will go to Hawaii for Dr. Angus Thomas and his latest info on the star and bring them before the public so the truth will be known! Let's see if those keep-it-from-us boys in Washington can stop this old lineman. Here's one for the people!"

A stunned sports announcer looked at Cy incredulously and said, "This is for real, right? I remember Angus Thomas, friends. He was as honest and straight as they come. I never knew he became an astronomer though. Thanks, Cy, for being here with us and sharing this startling news. I am confused as to how to respond. We . . . we'll wait for more news about this."

There were no details, just the almost cryptic release about the star and the possibility of the threat. As soon as the news was finished and the local news came on his mom asked, "Didn't you go out to Hawaii and visit Gemini, the place they're talking about? Didn't you say something about meeting a Dr. Thomas as well? Do you know anything about this?"

"Yes, Mom, I do. I've been running computer simulations on the star they call the ghost for months. I've been doing this in complete secrecy. It's been confidential until now, and I couldn't talk about it to anyone, not even you two. I realized the news would be out sooner or later, but I had no idea when. Now that the news is out, I can share what I know. Don't tell anyone else or we'll be deluged with reporters."

Charlie had just begun to explain his involvement with Gemini and the group dealing with the discovery and knowledge of the Ghost star when a special news program came on. Charlie was animated as he explained what they were seeing as the news played the entire camera interview with Drs. Thomas and Carroll at the entrance to the Gemini Operations canter. "That's my friend, Dr. John Carroll. He's the director of the Gemini telescope project. The burly guy is Dr. Angus Thomas. He's the one who first discovered the star and where it might be going. The blonde reporter asking questions? Her name is Ginger Cari. She's also involved in the group handling the information about the star. Several other members of their group I have yet to meet. I did meet Dr. Thomas's wife, Lani, who's a native Hawaiian. The two of them met when she worked as his assistant at Gemini. If she's as smart as she is beautiful she's a genius. I don't see her at all. That's not surprising since she prefers to stay out of the media spotlight. I met Dr. Carroll at a seminar at Berkeley and he's the one who got me involved with this 'Ghost' star."

Eventually, two popular news analysts went through the interview and the Cy Dooley one in detail, trying to explain what had transpired. Charlie was frustrated at the inaccuracies in their handling of the facts and explained the errors in more correct detail.

"I'll say one thing good about that report," Charlie commented during a commercial break. "They did a good job of being positive in their approach. They emphasized the probability nothing bad would happen and minimized the threat. I was afraid they might do the opposite."

"I wonder how many people will go off the deep end over this?" his mom questioned. "A whole lot of people are crazy. I can imagine what some of those looneys might say or do. I'm glad we live out in the country. I can imagine the mobs of crazies that might erupt in the cities. No telling how far they might go."

After the analysts returned they were interrupted by an announcer who explained the Pope was about to make an announcement and the program would be switched to the Vatican. Soon a Vatican spokesman came on and said the Pope would say something important in a few minutes. He gave a little background on the Pope and explained how he had received a very unusual message he wanted to read and comment about. He assured those watching that the message would carry world wide interest.

The Pope appeared and after explaining he had talked with Dr. Thomas and been assured the news release was factual, he read the release slowly and in total. He followed the release by repeating the quote he had obtained from Dr. Thomas when he was asked, "Does the earth face possible destruction by this new star you found?"

Dr. Thomas' answer, "Possible? . . . Yes! . . . Probable? . . . Maybe! . . . Certain? . . . No!" would be quoted many times, becoming a byword referring to the danger from the star.

The Pope went into detail about the meanings of possible, probable, and certain. He left no doubt it would be a long time before the outcome would be determined. He thanked those responsible for providing him with the information with the following words:

"I thank Reverend Cy Dooley of Los Angeles for having the courage to make the earlier announcement and for asking me to talk about it. I thank Dr. Thomas and his dedicated group for the way they handled this potentially damaging information. I thank a young lady who prefers to remain anonymous for the clever courage to send the message to Reverend Dooley and the Vatican. This is all a demonstration of the power of God to direct us to the best conclusions. Consider what has happened. A minister of a small church in America makes the first announcements of one of the most momentous things to face the human race and while on a sports program no less. The second announcement, the one just made, came from another servant of God here in the Vatican. With God's grace, this terrible menace will pass without harm to our precious earth."

"That should put a lot of people at ease," Ray commented. "I hope that message is heard by everyone."

Edith rose and turned off the TV. She wanted to talk without competition. "It was positive and uplifting. Knowing what you do, Charlie, was he right or is the situation worse than he said. What do you think?"

"He was about on track with what we currently think will happen. It's unfortunate, but it will be years before we are sure, not until the star arrives here. We've run several simulations, but they are based entirely on data we picked out of the blue. We need far more accurate data before we can hope to make any kind of practical prediction. There's a good chance the star could pass by with almost no effect on the earth. It will be ten or even more years before our data is accurate enough for any kind of predictions."

"What I hear you saying is we should hope and pray for the star to pass by without harm, and that's about all we can do?"

"You're right mom. Even if we knew when and where the star would pass, we would be uncertain what would happen to the earth and the other planets. We couldn't change anything if we did. Because of its speed, we are dealing in areas scientists never studied or even thought about. It's a whole new ball game. My work is with the tiniest objects known to man. When I consider an object as massive as a star moving at the speeds of those tiny objects, I am at a complete loss as to what might happen. It's inconceivable an object that massive could be accelerated to that speed by any known circumstance. Just thinking about it is mind boggling!"

Edith sat solemnly. A sadness pulled down and aged her face. "C's mysterious disappearance and now this. In a sudden blow our world, our sanity almost, is turned upside down and we are put to the test. With all our knowledge, all man's technology, we are still helpless. We are left in God's hands. I hope the Pope was right and we come through this."

"Sometimes praying is all you can do," Ray said. "I'll bet a lot of people will be in church Sunday! We'll see folks who are only at church on Easter, maybe even some new folks who never go to church."

Edith began breaking into sobs. "I'd like to hear C's slant on this. I hope nothing bad has happened to him."

When his mother mentioned C, Charlie remembered the new portable PC his uncle showed him during their last visit. He wondered if C had entered anything that might throw some light on what happened. He explained to his folks he was going to fetch the computer from C's cabin and see if he could find anything that might help.

Charlie grabbed a flashlight to light his way as he walked out to the cabin. As he headed for the door, he called Ralph to join him for the trek. Ralph bounded out the door and trotted along in front of Charlie as he made his way to the cabin. As they entered the clearing, Ralph put his nose to the ground, found the end of the old scent trail and sat down next to the yellow marker Tara had placed in the ground. As soon as he sat down he began to howl. Charlie flashed the light all around the clearing and nearby woods but could see nothing. He called Ralph who stopped howling but stayed firmly where he sat. "Okay, little guy, you stay. I'm going inside," he said to the dog as he turned and headed into the cabin.

Once inside he went straight to the workshop for the PC. When he turned on the lights, he found it was not on the desk where C and he tried out programs. The printer and scanner sat on the workbench with their cables, but the PC was gone. Maybe C had taken it with him. He continued searching back in the main room. The PC was nowhere to be seen. He next went into the tiny bedroom where he opened the closet covering an entire wall. Many things were in the closet but no computer. As he started to leave the bedroom, he discovered C's briefcase on the floor behind the open door. Next to the briefcase was a shipping box all sealed and ready for shipment. The box was about twice the size of the briefcase and had a label with Charlie Botkin written in C's printing. He picked up and examined the box. Nothing else was written on the box, no address, just his name. He placed it on the bed, took out the pocket knife C had given him many years before, and opened the box. Inside he found the computer and a note in C's handwriting dated Sunday, September 2, 2001. He sat down on the bed with the note which read as follows:

Dear Charlie, it is early Sunday morning as I write this note. Since you are reading it, I am either gone or dead as I plan to destroy it if I'm still okay when you arrive. Some strange things happened the last few days. I've been having dreams about the past like I never had before. They've been almost like TV shows where I am reliving that experience when I was seven and saw that strange object. I've had the same dream four times in the last few days. I never dreamed about that before in my entire life. I wonder why now? During this time I often felt weird. I've felt dizzy and light headed and my heart seemed to beat erratically for a few minutes. I keep seeing strange flickering purple and orange auras. Sometimes they blind me. I experienced those same auras once or twice a year for my entire life, but now they come more and more often. After about ten minutes things go back to normal. A couple of times I thought I might be having a heart attack, but it would go away and I would feel fine again. I made an appointment with Doc Markley for a physical next week, but until then I plan on relaxing. Ralph must be noticing something as well. He follows me around and stays right by me when we're outside. That's unusual as he always heads off for a jaunt in the woods when we go out. This morning I had one of those *spells* and when I sat down on the couch, Ralph sat down on the floor facing me and let out a howl. He has never done so before! He must sense something. I can't even surmise what is happening, but it is strange indeed.

I logged those spells once I realized they came more and more often. The results startled me as the time between spells has been decreasing steadily by about one third each cycle. Projecting this forward, the time between spells will disappear at about seven this evening. Whatever this means it deeply puzzles me, but there must be some significance. I'm not in fear, but I am strangely sad about this. Each time a spell comes, I experience an overpowering feeling of sadness which makes no sense at all. I look at Ralph and almost burst into tears as he looks back at me. Maybe it's an unusual hormone imbalance that will pass and things will return to normal.

I thought a lot about the star you told me about and came up with a few new ideas I've recorded in a word processing file called **NEWSTAR** in the Charlie directory of the computer. I also created a spreadsheet with the same name where I set up a series of calculations which may interest you. Take the computer. Consider it a gift. Take the briefcase as well. Tell your mother and dad and your aunt Matty I love them dearly and thank them for being such a wonderful part of my life. Share with them whatever of this note you feel is appropriate. I love you very much. You are to me the son I never had. I am so proud of you, what you've done and of the man you are now. Keep that spirit of adventure and hunger for knowledge alive all through your life. We may be lucky and the star will pass without incident. Then you will live a full life.

In the briefcase and also in the Charlie directory of the computer you will find a collection of sayings, poetry, essays, letters and miscellaneous quotes and writings I saved over the years. These are ideas, happenings, experiences and concepts that are of value to me and tell about the man I tried to be. I hate to give advice, so consider this collection of words as a sharing for you to use as you see fit. I finish this note with a quote from Alfred Adler that I applied liberally to my life. His words may partly explain my unusual outlook on life. "There is only one danger I find in life. One may take too many precautions."

The note was signed, "With love and respect, C," After finishing the note, he sat on the bed, tears streaming down his face. Charlie was sure he would never again see his uncle. He sat on C's bed for a long time, staring into space and recalling memories of happy times with his uncle. He missed C and now the big empty place in his heart would hurt for a very long time. This was his first loss of someone close Charlie had ever experienced and he knew he wasn't handling it well. He dreaded sharing the note with his folks and Matty, but he knew he must. He also knew he must convince them C was not coming back. The only troubling thing was, what happened? Not knowing the answer would be maddening, but he was now convinced they would never learn.

A few minutes after ten Charlie heard the cabin door open and his father walked in. "Are you all right son? We were beginning to worry when you didn't come back. When Ralph showed up at our door we thought something else happened so I came out to find out."

Charlie handed the letter to his dad. "I found this note from C. I don't think we'll ever find him. He's gone, and not under his own power."

Ray read and reread the note without saying a word. A tear crept down his cheek. Charlie stood up and turned toward the door. "Right now I feel tired. Let's go back to the house. It's late, I feel dejected and exhausted so let's hold off examining and talking about the note until tomorrow."

They left the computer and briefcase where they sat and headed out the door. Charlie put his arm around his dad and the two of them headed home in silence. For once his dad didn't stiffen at his touch, but responded by placing his arm around Charlie. It was a powerful, loving message that warmed Charlie's heart.

When they reached the house, his mom opened the door. "Is everything all right? We were worried."

Charlie looked at his mom with a sad face, tears in his eyes. "No mom, everything's not all right. Dad and I are okay, but we think C's gone for good and that's not okay." They stood together, arms around each other, tears streaming down all their faces as Edith prayed. They broke apart and headed somberly to bed. Neither of the men mentioned the note to Edith. They would talk about that tomorrow after a fitful night's sleep.

The next morning, Charlie sat his mother down in the living room and read her C's note. She was soon in tears. Ray and Charlie did what they could to comfort her.

"What does all this mean? I don't understand," Edith said through her tears

"Mom, We know no more than you. It's a complete mystery."

"I must call Matty and tell her. . . . No, I'll call and ask her to come over. She'll do better if she's with us when she learns."

Matty came over at Edith's mysterious request, made without divulging why in spite of Matty's protests.

While they all sat in the living room, Charlie read C's note once more. It brought on a repeat of Edith's earlier reaction. The three of them did what they could to provide comfort and share feelings. Matty used Edith's exact words.

"What does all this mean? I don't understand."

Charlie was reassuring. "We're quite sure he's still alive, just gone somewhere that he can't contact us. Don't give up. He may be coming back. I feel certain about this." Charlie did not share that he thought C would never return.

Matty looked at Edith and said, "It's all so mysterious, so unknown. It's frightening."

"All we can do, Matty, is to pray and hope for the best." Edith said. "That's what I'm going to do."

They sat, shared thoughts and feelings for more than an hour before Matty headed home.

-- SOMBER VACATION GETS SHORTENED --

Ray was right about church. The sanctuary overflowed with worried faces including a number of new ones. Even Charlie, who was lukewarm about church, prayed with them for deliverance from the menace of the star. The next week they worked almost in silence at farm chores. Ray was even more quiet than usual.

✳ **Thursday, September 6, 2001** ✳

Thursday evening Charlie received a call on his cell phone from the university. Diedra, the department secretary, had some special instructions for him.

"Dr. Botkin?"

"It's me, Diedra."

"As you can imagine, things are quite hectic around here since the announcement about the star. Your computer simulations received a lot of attention. Because of the news about the star, they wanted you to meet with a Dr. Simms at MIT as soon as possible."

"Osgoode Simms? He's an old blow hard, stuck in the past. Why him?"

"He has scheduled access to their supercomputer and is willing to work around current commitments to run some more simulations. You are to share your data and simulations with Dr. Simms and help him to set up more simulations. Since we link with MIT, you'll be able to access all your data right from one of their terminals."

"He's an opportunist wanting some publicity. Did he mention security?"

"I can't comment on that, Dr. Botkin. I'm just reading to you from what they gave me."

"I assume that means standard security protocols. I don't like it, but I guess I can live with it. When do they want me?"

"My instructions say ASAP. Can you get to Ft Wayne?"

"Sure."

"By eight tomorrow morning? Your flight to Toledo leaves at nine-fifteen."

"I can handle that. Don't like it though. How long am I to stay in Boston?"

"They want you back here as soon as you've worked out the simulation details with Dr. Simms. You are scheduled for an early morning flight to LA on Tuesday. They say Dr. Simms is planning to work through the weekend and Monday to accommodate your schedule."

"I'll bet! It will mean working long hours with that jerk. He'll make a long weekend into a miserable one."

"Try to keep things as pleasant as you can, please."

"Oh, I'll be pleasant enough. If he can just keep things on a professional level. He's got the credentials. Simms is a stuffy old man with an unpleasant nature who tends to get personal. He'll surely find a way to muck things up. I'll only be with him for a few days, thank God."

Charlie spent a few minutes writing down his flights and hotel confirmation. Diedre was cooly efficient as always.

"Okay Deed. All the info I need is written down in my notebook."

"Safe travels and we'll see you Wednesday."

Charlie's parents were not happy hearing the news. Edith in particular was upset.

"Why do they want to tear you away from your family at a time like this? That's cruel."

Charlie put his arm around his mom. "I don't want to leave after all that's happened in the last few days. I'll phone you often until we discover what's happened to C."

She burst into tears, then stifled them. "I'll be okay. Your people at the university don't know about C. I'm sure they're considering what's best in the big picture. Sometimes it's hard for me to realize my son is such an important person—too bad as well."

"Mom, you're all so important to me. I don't want to leave either, but it's my job and lots of other people depend on my work. If we discovered the star will pass without harming the earth, it would put the fears of billions of people to rest. That's why my work is so important."

"We know, son. We're so proud of you. Sometimes we'd just like to visit with you a bit more."

"Don't worry. I'm hoping to come back for a week around Christmas. Maybe I can persuade a little lady from Hawaii to come with me. You'll like her."

"My goodness. Are you that serious? She must really be special."

"Never been more serious and she is special, very special."

"I'm sure she's a lovely person. We'll be so pleased to meet her."

"I'm not sure I can manage, but I'll try."

"You'd best put your things together. Your dad and I will take you to meet your plane. If we start early we can stop for breakfast in Columbia City."

✳   **Friday, September 7, 2001**   ✳

At 6:30 in the morning we stopped for breakfast at Richard's Restaurant in Columbia City. While we were waiting for our food to be served, Mom suddenly burst into tears. It was several moments before she could speak.

"Why has all this come down on us? I hope I can cope. C disappears, and now we learn about this terrible star and you off to Boston when we were looking forward to your stay. Your aunt Matty is in an even worse state of mind. What's happening to us?"

Dad reached over and took her hand. "Now Edith, don't take the weight of the world on your shoulders. Charlie says the star will most likely pass by without doing any harm. Isn't that right Charlie?"

"That's right." I said. "For several reasons including its speed, it could even pass by rather closely without causing any damage. Besides, we can't predict where it is headed with any degree of accuracy for twenty-six years, or even more."

"You're sure?"

"Mom, I'm dealing in scientific probabilities, most likely events to make it plain. I'm not saying so to make you feel better. If things were any different, I would tell you. If that ever changes, you'll be among the first people I tell. I promise."

Dad said, "Remember, Edith, our son knows as much about this star as anyone in the entire world. We can be proud."

Edith regained her composure. "You are still torn away from us at this trying time. Thank God you two helped me over these rough spots. I'm OK now, and here comes our breakfast."

We had a quiet breakfast, got into the car and headed for the airport. Mom shed the usual goodbye tears as I went up to the gate. I choked back a few of my own since I had no idea when I would see them again.

✳   ✳   ✳

I took a cab to the MIT super computer access room where Simms was waiting. I downloaded my data and completed simulations from the Cray at Cal Tech into available memory for the MIT Cray. It took us several hours to set up the first simulation, mostly because Simms wanted to change so many data points in the simulation. He became quite upset when I insisted on organizing and recording every change in the data points. I refused to back down.

"Damn it, Simms. There's no point in making these simulations if we do not keep an accurate record of every change made from the originals." I told him. "I did not come all this way to waste my time and effort running simulations impossible to duplicate."

"I'm the astronomer here. You should offer me some flexibility."

"How many simulations have you generated on objects moving at 90% of the speed of light?"

The question seemed to shut him up for the rest of the time. It set the tone for the rest of my time working with him. He was almost tolerable. For dinner he had Chinese food sent in so we could keep right on working. We managed to run two simulations before calling it quits. I crashed when I reached my hotel room about midnight.

✳   ✳   ✳

By Monday afternoon we completed running two dozen simulations using data different from any we used before. I complimented him on his selection of data and constants for the simulations.

About seven, after we finished our last simulation, Simms calmly says, "I would like to run three more simulations. Could you go to your hotel, pack, check out, and bring your stuff back here? We can work through the night, finish those three simulations, and take you to your flight by eight."

"I must leave by six thirty."

"The airport is only fifteen minutes away. We can take you to the gate on time. A cab will be ready."

I agreed, reluctantly. We started in on the simulations about nine, after I returned. Four o'clock we started on the third simulation.

"We're cutting it pretty close aren't we? My plane leaves at eight. I must be at the terminal by seven thirty at the latest."

"Never fear. We will finish by seven at the latest and the airport is only fifteen minutes away."

✳ Tuesday, September 11, 2001 ✳

I did not put much stock in his assurances. I left in the cab at seven-fifteen in the morning.

"Can we make my eight o'clock flight?" I asked the cabby.

"You've got to be kidding. It's morning rush hour and we must go through downtown. I could try the Mass Pike, but it will be jammed with traffic. Your only hope is right through town. I can use some alleyways and side streets once we cross the Charles River. If we're lucky and make the tunnel without a jam we might be in time. Hang on."

"Go for it!" I yelled.

We turned into the airport parkway with fifteen minutes to spare. Then my luck ran out. We came to a screeching halt at the boulevard bottleneck to the outgoing gates, too many cars. At eight the cabby dropped me off at the gate.

"Thanks for trying." I told the cabby.

"Sorry we didn't make it. If not for all the traffic on the boulevard to the gates we were okay."

"I'm sure I can catch another flight. I'm going to LA, a busy route."

I paid him and headed into the terminal to find out what later flights were available. I caught a nine o'clock flight on Delta through Detroit.

✳   ✳   ✳

Tuesday morning Matty called and told them to turn on the TV. Edith and Ray Botkin were shocked and horrified like so many Americans as they watched the towers collapse. When the report of the planes was aired, Edith shrieked.

"Oh God, no! Where's the paper Charlie left us with his flights?" She rummaged through some notes in the kitchen and found the information.

"My God, Ray. That flight, American flight 11 out of Boston. Look here, That's the one Charlie's on."

They stood holding each other, sobbing, for a long time. Ray looked his wife in the eyes. "Let's make sure as soon as we can. Isn't there some way we can check? Couldn't we call the airline to make sure?"

Edith grabbed the phone. Her hands were shaking so badly she couldn't dial the number from Charlie's list. Ray took the phone and dialed, then handed her the phone.

"All I hear is a recorded message saying all flights are grounded until further notice. - wait - now they're saying information about specific flights will not be available for several hours. Apparently they want to make sure they give out the correct information. Now, what can we do?"

"About all we can do is wait and pray.

✳   ✳   ✳

For the next few hours they sat in front of the TV watching the terror unfold over and over. They both jumped when the phone rang. Edith looked at Ray in apprehension as their eyes expressed their fears without words. She answered the phone and promptly fainted into the chair, dropping the phone in the process. Ray went over to help her as she slowly came to.

"Pick up the phone," she whispered amidst her tears of joy. "It's Charlie."

Ray grabbed the phone. "Hello?"

"Hi dad. I guess you didn't expect to hear from me, did you?"

"Thank the Lord. You're all right? Your mother passed out when you spoke to her."

"I realized that when the phone banged after I said Hi Mom. How is she?"

"She's coming around. Here Edith. Talk to our son. I'll use the other phone."

Tears of joy poured out as they spoke. Even Ray bawled like a baby. They settled down and asked what happened, where he was and what was he going to do.

"I'm in Cleveland trying to rent a car so I can drive to the farm. They wouldn't let me use my cell phone while the plane was in the air so I dialed as soon as we were on the ground."

"When your dad and I learned the flight number, I checked and saw it was the flight you were to be on. We were horrified. Thank God you weren't on that plane. I feel so much pain for the families of all those who died. They won't be getting a call like this."

"In spite of all my bad mouthing of Dr. Simms, I'll be forever grateful he was the reason I wasn't on the plane. Because of his insistence that I conduct one more run through of my program early this morning, I missed flight 11. Ironic, isn't it?"

Edith remarked, "The Lord wanted you alive. He must have a plan for you."

"Mom, you may be right. I would never consider that until this moment, but I must admit, what happened was a very unlikely series of events. I'm happy to be alive."

"No happier than we are."

"Anyway, I picked up another flight, half an hour later. We were on our way to Detroit when the news of the attacks came. They diverted us here when all flights were grounded. We waited a long time on the ground before a gate was open. I hope I can find a rental car available. Must be lots of people trying to rent one. They may all be taken."

"We can come up for you son. Might stay overnight, but that's no problem."

"Let me see what I can do here first. Now, I need to call several people. I'll call you back as soon as I find out what I am able to do."

Charlie snapped his cell phone shut, then opened it and called Diedre. She burst into tears at the sound of his voice. It was several moments before she regained control so she could try to speak. "Is it really you? - - - We all thought you - - - we were horrified - - - When I heard your flight hit the towers and realized I was responsible for putting you on that plane, I . . ." Diedre broke up again. "I'm sorry. I felt so terrible, so responsible. Now I'm elated you missed it. The whole department heard." Her voice left the phone and Charlie could hear her talking to the people in the office. "It's Dr. Botkin and he's okay." This was followed by sounds of clapping and shouts of joy in the background.

"I'm in Cleveland and don't know how or when I'll be back. You'll need to hold down the fort for a while." He provided the details of his situation and explained he was going to try to go to his folks in Indiana.

"Keep in touch. I'm sure it will be some time before the planes are flying again so you can come back."

As he was dialing Jenny's number, Charlie was thankful he hadn't even told her he was going to Boston.

"Hi Jenny," was his response to her cheery hello. "I'm stuck in Cleveland and have no idea when I'll be able to go anywhere yet."

"What are you doing in Cleveland? I thought you were in Indiana."

"It's a long story. I was on my way back to California when the towers were hit. My flight landed in Cleveland. I'm going to go to my folks if I can find a rental car."

"Wasn't that a terrible thing? All those people killed. Those sick, evil monsters who did that. What a mindless bunch of slaves they were. How did you end up in Cleveland? Don't you fly out of Chicago on your way back? Cleveland's east of Chicago."

Charlie explained why and what happened.

"That scares me even thinking about what could have happened to you." Jenny said. "Thank God for the guy making you miss the flight."

They talked for about half an hour before Charlie said, "I've got to try to find a rental car ASAP, hon. I hate to say goodbye, but I'd best hurry."

"I understand," Jenny said. "You be sure to call me when you know what you are doing."

"OK, Jen. Bye for now."

"Bye Charlie."

After four frustrating hours, and with help from a friend at NASA's Lewis research center, Charlie was able to wrangle a rental car. As he headed south on I-71 toward the toll road, he called his folks and told them he would be at the farm in about four hours. Once more his mom burst into tears. The day was filled with emotion yet, in the end, it became one of thanks for a missed flight. Again, Edith expressed concern for those who were not so fortunate. As soon as he hung up, he called Jenny to tell her what he was doing.

Right on the dot at seven he drove up the familiar driveway at the farm. His mom gave him a big hug with tears flowing. Even his dad was teary eyed. The shock and then relief took a toll on both of them.

"Did you eat anything? I fixed dinner for you."

"My gosh, Mom, because of all the excitement and trying to find a rental car, I forgot all about eating. I'm starved."

5

The CDC Pays the Botkins a Visit

✳ Thursday, September 13, 2001 ✳

Ray and Edith watched out the window as Charlie headed for town in C's pickup. They hadn't turned away from the window when a dark sedan pulled in and parked in their driveway. A woman and two men in business suits were in the car. When one of the men got out and walked up to the house, Ray went to meet him at the door. "Can I help you?"

I'm Dr. Gerald Reimer of the Center for Disease control in Atlanta. We'd like to speak with a Charles Miller. Is he here?"

Ray turned and looked at Edith who burst into tears when C's name was mentioned. "I'm sorry, but he's not here."

"I'm sorry. It seems I upset - is it your wife?"

"Yes, and Charles Miller is her brother. He simply vanished about a week ago under mysterious circumstances and we don't think he's ever coming back. She's upset about his disappearance. I'm sure you understand."

"Disappeared! You mean he just left?"

"We only know that he's gone. How and why he left is a mystery. We don't think he left under his own power and we fear he'll never be back."

"I'm sorry to hear that. Did you contact the authorities?"

"Of course." Ray started out through the door. "Can we talk outside, please? This is all upsetting to my wife."

Dr. Reimer stepped away from the door. "Of course. Why don't we sit in our car. My colleagues will want to learn about this."

Ray got into the back of the car with Dr. Reimer who then introduced the others. "This is Dr. Amos Chalberg and Cerrita Gottenborg of the CDC. I forgot to ask your name."

"Ray, Ray Botkin. Pleased to meet you - I think."

"Mr. Botkin is Mr. Miller's brother-in-law. He tells me Mr. Miller has disappeared, mysteriously."

Dr. Chalberg was alarmed. "You mean he's gone? Vanished?"

"And not of his own choosing according to Mr. Botkin."

Dr. Chalberg seemed almost in shock. "This is terrible. You mean you don't think he's coming back, ever?"

Ray shook his head. "We're sure. He told my son, Charlie . . . It's a long and complicated story. He won't be back is all."

The two men kept asking Ray to repeat what he knew and to tell them more. After a long series of questions Ray was exasperated. "I said that was all we know, dang it, and that's all. Why are you so interested anyway? You never met him, have you?"

Amidst his distress, Ray realized he had no idea why the CDC would want to see C. "What's this all about anyway? Why do you want C? That's what the family calls him, C."

The two men's eyes met. One of those what-do-we-do-now? looks painted their faces reddish as they tried to decide what to say without success. Before they could say anything, Ms Gottenborg, who was silent while sitting in the car, suddenly came to life and turned toward Dr. Reimer.

A slight sneer distorted her otherwise expressionless face. "It is obvious someone beat us here and spirited our man off somewhere. Our project may become an accidental victim of those terrorists. Whoever did this frightened these people into denying what happened."

Ray bristled, opened the car door, and stepped out. "If that's what you think, I'm done talking and I suggest you leave our property. You can find all you will be able to find at the sheriff's office. I won't put up with any more abuse."

Before they could reply, Ray headed inside. Charlie returned, drove C's pickup past the sedan and parked. He stepped out of the pickup and headed for the door.

"Hey, kid!" Ms. Gottenborg called out. "Come here a minute."

Charlie stopped, turned and slowly ambled over to the car. He did not feel comfortable about the car's occupants. "Whatcha want?"

"Do you live here?"

"Sometimes."

"Don't be a wiseacre, what do you mean, sometimes."

"Who are you people , and what are you doing here?"

Figuring Charlie as Ray's teen-age son, Ms. Gottenborg replied, "Listen kid, if you don't want to get into a lot of trouble you'd better loosen up and answer a few questions for us."

Charlie knew they grossly misjudged him. He decided to play along and find out what would happen. "Yea? Trouble from whom?"

"Your parents for beginners."

Charlie howled and almost doubled over laughing.

"What's so funny, kid?"

"What makes you think my parents would ever give me any trouble?"

"How about the police?"

"Call them. Call the sheriff. I could care less. Besides, you have not answered my questions yet."

"What questions?"

"Who are you and what are you doing here? I should call the sheriff and he will check you out."

"We're from the Federal Government and you'd better cooperate with us."

Charlie was enjoying his little game. He pulled his cell phone out and began dialing. "I'm a US citizen which means you work for me. Since you seem unwilling or unable to prove who you are, let's find out if the local sheriff's department might be interested in you."

"What are you doing? Who are you calling." Ms. Gottenborg was quite distressed and at a loss as to what to do next. She was even more upset when she heard what Charlie said over the phone.

"Tell Pete there's a car full of people out here who say they are US Government agents of some sort. Ask him how quickly he can send someone out here. - I'll wait."

Dr. Reimer stepped out of the car, walked to the side where Charlie stood and looked daggers at Ms. Gottenborg. "I didn't think we needed security on this trip. I will handle this Ms. Gottenborg."

Charlie was finishing his call. "Okay, Pete. Eight or ten minutes will be fine. Thanks a lot."

Dr. Reimer was incredulous. "Young man, am I to understand you called the sheriff and he's coming here?"

"You got it, Pops. The sheriff will be here in a few minutes."

"That wasn't necessary."

"If not. Pete will go on his way, but I'll still find out who you are and what you're doing here. Won't I?"

"Let me introduce myself, I'm Dr. Gerald Reimer from the Center for Disease Control in Atlanta. The other gentleman is Dr. Amos Chalberg, also from the CDC and Cerrita Gottenborg is a security officer assigned to us for our trip here. We came by car for obvious reasons."

"That's a start. I assume you carry credentials to prove who you are?"

"Of course we do." Dr. Reimer started to reach for his pocket.

"No need to do that now. Pete will check you out when he arrives. You still did not answer my question. Why did two research doctors from the CDC drive a thousand miles and end up on a small farm in the middle of northern Indiana, and with a security officer?"

"It's quite important that we see . . . If you're the Botkin boy . . . your uncle, Charles Miller."

"Well, I am, as you say, the Botkin boy. What do you want with my uncle?"

"It doesn't concern you."

"Au contraire Herr doktor. My uncle and I are close. What you want with him concerns me a lot. Let's wait till Pete is here. I'll feel a whole lot more comfortable with local authorities in control. While we're waiting, I'll step inside with my folks"

About ten minutes later Pete drove in, hoped out of his car and joined them. "What's going on here? Where's Charlie? Who are you people?"

Before they could answer, Charlie stuck his head out the door. "Thanks for getting here so quickly, Pete. They claim to be from the CDC. Check their credentials and anything else you can check out about them. I'll be out in a few minutes."

Pete set about checking credentials and drivers' licenses. Dr. Reimer smiled as he handed his CDC ID card to Pete. "The young man has quite a way with words. He needn't bother you. I hope this doesn't cause him trouble."

Pete suddenly realized what they thought. "You don't know who he is, do you?"

"The Botkin's son, I believe. He's also the nephew of the man we came to see."

"True, but let me enlighten you. You are scientists, right?"

"Yes we are, two of us anyway." Dr. Reimer replied, again looking daggers at Ms Gottenburg.

"Are you familiar with the high energy physics research department at Cal Tech in Pasadena?"

"I only know Cal Tech by reputation and that they excel in that area, but it's a bit far from my own field."

"Well then, would you say an intelligent and experienced person would head that department?"

"Of course, but what has that to do with us, here and now?"

Right then Charlie walked outside and came over to where Pete was talking to Dr. Reimer.

"I thought you might like to meet the head of that department. Gentlemen and lady, I would like to present to you, Dr. Charles Botkin, professor of high energy physics at Cal Tech and head of the HEP research department."

Three jaws dropped in amazement, but not a word was spoken.

Without missing a beat, Charlie asked. "Now what did you want to see my uncle about?"

Ms. Gottenborg spoke up. "This is confidential government information and cannot be divulged."

"What kind of security clearance do you hold, Ms. Gottenborg?"

"Why is that of concern to you?"

"Because I hold top secret, the highest level of security clearance with both the DOD and DOE and therefore may not be able to respond to your questions unless you hold an equal level of clearance."

Ms. Gottenborg seemed almost to shrink as she replied, "Secret."

Charlie smiled, "Now that we all know where we stand I will repeat my question. Why are you looking for my uncle?"

Dr. Reimer grinned and seemed almost relieved. It was obvious he didn't care for Ms. Gottenborg and her high handed security measures. "It's quite simple. Your uncle recently had a blood test with amazing results. The tests results were forwarded to us because of this. His blood carried some unusual genetic abnormalities. Good abnormalities that could be of assistance in some of our efforts at fighting cancer and several other diseases. We wanted to ask him if he would care to donate some of his blood for our research. That's all."

Charlie didn't believe them. "C'mon now! I can't believe the CDC would send such a group without a lot stronger reason. There's 's a lot more to it than you are telling me."

Dr. Reimer took a quick glance at the other two who stood like apprehensive stone statues. "There is something else beyond what I said, that is true, by the way."

"And what is that?"

"He has several unusual genes, a totally unknown grouping that is vastly different from anything in any known human genome. That's why we came here and what we would like to research."

"Could those genes be evidence of alien genetic manipulation?" Charlie asked.

The two doctors exchanged uneasy glances at each other. Then Dr. Chalberg responded nervously, "Why would you say such a thing?"

"To be honest, it was the first thing to come into my mind. No real reason."

"We considered many things, but that was not one of them. Dr. Reimer did you ever consider such a possibility or know of anyone else who has?"

"No! Certainly not. It is an interesting idea though. None of the other avenues of thought we pursued brought us anywhere near to a reasonable answer."

Dr. Chalberg looked at Dr. Reimer, "If we even hinted at such a thing back at CDC they would tell us we were out of our minds—crazy. Tell me, Dr. Botkin, what would you do if you were in our position?"

"Well, since I am not in your position that would be hard to do. Since my colleagues at Cal Tech referred to me as Crazy Charlie for years, I could make such a proposal and they would take me seriously."

"And what would you suggest?"

"I would search out all C's blood relatives I could find and ask if they would be willing to provide samples of their blood, then go on from there."

Dr. Reimer smiled. "Can I assume you would be willing?"

"Yes! And if you asked them politely and explained the basic reason, I feel certain C's other blood relations would agree as well."

"Dr. Botkin, I must thank you for your considerable help. After our original high handedness, you are most gracious."

"You now seem almost human." Charlie said with his broad grin. "I suggest you make one quite important consideration. Give serious thought to an extraterrestrial origin for his genetic abnormality. Think outside the box."

"You act as though you have knowledge about that."

Charlie smiled once more. "Let's say any such knowledge, if it existed, would be beyond your level of security clearance."

The three responded to Charlie's smile and comment with total defeat.

Reimer changed the subject. "You said you would be willing to give us a blood sample. Could we do that now, please?"

"Sure! Just as soon as your vampire is ready."

"I beg your pardon?"

Charlie laughed. He was enjoying their discomfort. "Vampire! Blood sucker! You know—someone who draws blood. Lighten up, Doc, it's a joke."

"Oh, I understand." The doctor could not be so casual. "Could you give me the names of your uncle's blood relations?"

"We'll do better then that. I'm sure my mom would call them for you. Only a few are here about and they would be much less resistant to my mom than complete strangers. By the way, I would like a complete report of your findings sent to my office at Cal Tech. You'll find that all security measures will be met, but don't hesitate to check to be sure."

"Thank you so much. We appreciate you being so helpful, especially since we were so callous earlier. You will receive copies of all our findings."

Acquiring blood samples from all seven of C's blood relatives took two days. Everyone received a letter of thanks from the CDC and an invitation to a VIP tour of the facility should they ever be in the vicinity. Some time later Charlie received a complete run down and analysis of the results of the blood tests. C was the only one who's blood contained the strange and different gene grouping. No conclusions were expressed about that fact.

6

Dr. Osgoode Simms Creates a Major Problem
✳ Friday, September 14, 2001 ✳

Friday Charlie took back any kind thoughts he held for Dr. Simms as he watched the morning news on TV. Being interviewed by Les Willig, the NBC host, was Dr. Simms announcing, "My computer simulations indicate the future path of the Ghost star will cross the solar system close to the Earth's orbit and near enough to the earth to annihilate all life on the planet." He stated, "The simulation shows this close approach with a 90% probability." No mention was made of Dr. Botkin.

Charlie, who rarely vented his anger, exploded, "That bastard! I'll kill him!"

"My goodness, son. What's the matter?" called out his mother as she rushed into the living room from the kitchen at Charlie's outbreak.

Pointing at the TV and trying to hold his anger Charlie said through clenched teeth, "I'm sorry, Mom but that . . . That idiot, that miserable, self-serving, egotistical idiot, has done terrible damage to the public just to gain some momentary fame and publicity. He lied and did so on top of the terrible terrorist attack."

"What on earth did he do to make you so angry?"

"He lied through his teeth to be on TV."

After Charlie explained the situation to his mom she asked, "You may dislike him, but could he possess some new information gained since your meeting with him?"

"To prove what he said? Not a chance. He's faked it by back tracking the data in a simulation after fixing the intersect, and then using those results to replace unknowns in a new simulation."

"I don't quite understand what your saying, but that sounds like cheating to me."

"You're dead right. He is cheating, and this is no game of solitaire."

"What can you do?"

"One thing is to contact Max and the group at Cal Tech. They are sure to still be asleep and do not realize this has happened. I'll call Max at home."

The sleepy voice of his friend and fellow Cal Tech professor, Max Groenburg, answered the phone and responded to the information. "That imbecile should be hung!"

"Those are my exact sentiments. Will you tell the others?"

"I'll call Diedre. She will arrange a meeting as soon as everyone can be present. I'll call with the details as soon as they are available."

Charlie refused to watch TV for a while, but then decided he should do so to help decide a course of action. Less than an hour later the phone rang. It was Diedre Gonzales, the department secretary who knew everybody, their whereabouts and their duties. She was more in charge than any one else in a department with lots of chiefs with big egos and few Indians. Her organizational skills were impressive. Everyone depended on her.

Her first words when she knew Charlie was on the phone were, "They're all here and heard the interview. You were right. Simms is an ego maniac and an idiot—a bad situation."

"Got any ideas how we can repair the damage? I mean after I take my Glock 17 and blow his head off."

"Are you really that angry?"

"I'm a lot angrier than that, but I still retain enough sanity to prevent me from carrying out my instincts."

"The consensus here is that censure, serious censure should originate from the President of MIT. Frankly, most of the faculty doubt he'd alienate one of his own benefactors. Simms is the one who helped bring Mutchler to MIT."

"I didn't know."

"What does Max think?"

"Max would go along with shooting him."

"Let me think about this for a while longer and contact some of the Gemini people to see if they can help. I hope the airlines start flying again soon. I need to be present to confer with Max and the group."

"We are all gathered in the conference room watching a New York TV news program. Max asked me to call you to tell you they are trying to set up an Internet conference so you could join in. They called in a sleepy tech crew to set up the meeting. We'll call you back as soon as it's ready."

"In the mean time I'll try to contact the Gemini group on the phone, but they're four hours earlier than you. Incidently, isn't the ET room already set up for an e-conference?"

"You may be right. I'll check it out. In the meantime, keep your Glock oiled and ready."

"You got it!"

✳ Wednesday, September 19 ✳

Five days later, when the ban on flying was lifted, Charlie headed for New York and a TV interview with Les Willig, the science talking head who interviewed Osgood Simms a week earlier. He was armed with the decision made by the group including the Gemini people who were also infuriated by the actions of Professor Simms.

Because he couldn't find an open flight from Ft Wayne, Charlie drove his rental car back to Cleveland and boarded an almost empty flight to New York. The devil was about to get his due. Dr. Angus Thomas, of the Gemini group, the one who first discovered the Ghost Star, suggested Charlie do an end run around Simms and cut him down quietly in the process. Angus and Charlie conferred over the Internet for more than an hour, planning how to handle the interview. They decided a low key explanation of the realities of computer simulations as applied to the Ghost would be the best way to go about it. Diedra performed some fancy footwork to arrange the interview so soon. Everyone at Cal Tech and at Gemini would be watching this interview along with Charlie's family and Jenny.

✱   ✱   ✱

After behind the scene preliminaries were set up and Charlie was instructed on how the interview would be conducted, he sat down with Les Willig in front of the cameras.

"My guest this morning is Dr. Charlie Botkin. Dr. Botkin is the head of the high energy physics department at Cal Tech in Pasadena. You are the one who provided the computer simulations Dr. Osgoode Simms used to make his startling predictions on my show a week ago, correct?"

"You are quite correct."

"I understand you do not agree with Dr. Simms predictions. Could you explain why?"

"Of course. First I'd like to explain, computer simulations are only as good as the degree to which the simulation mimics the actual events, combined with the accuracy of the data fed into the simulation. It's a nebulous situation with numerous mathematical answers ranging widely because of the extremes of accuracy of both the simulation and the data. We ran hundreds of simulations based on rather sketchy data we gathered on the star and its path."

"You mean your measurements of the star are faulty - inaccurate? I thought astronomy was an accurate science."

"The observations and measurements made with the Gemini telescope and confirmed by a number of others, are not faulty. The accuracy of any measurement is subject to probabilities and the limits of the system of measurements being used. Astronomical measurements are subject to equivalent laws. The Ghost is a small star that is about 30 light years away at this precise moment. To add to the difficulty of making accurate measurements, we now see it as it looked about 280 years ago because light takes that long to reach us. That's far too great a distance for accurate predictions of its future path."

"So you're saying Dr. Simms was wrong in his prediction."

"Out of the hundreds of simulations we ran, the one he described is a worse case scenario. I'm sure that's how he meant it. Another equally probable path would take the star no closer than four or five light years. In any case, the chances are the star will cause little if any damage on Earth. We won't begin to be able to predict the star's path with any degree of certainty for twenty to twenty-five years, or even more. It's difficult to say at this time."

"Dr. Simms is an astronomer and you are a particle physicist. Why would a particle physicist be involved in this? Don't you deal with the tiniest particles, and not objects as large as a star? I would think this situation to be more in the purview of an astronomer."

Charlie laughed. "The laws of physics determine the motions of all objects including stars and particles. The astronomers at Gemini called on me to help with simulations because this is the first object larger than an atomic particle known to be moving at relativistic speeds. That is in an area quite similar to the field of particle physics. Over the past year, we ran a hundred simulations on the Cal Tech Cray supercomputer using the data from the Gemini telescopes. Recently I worked with Dr. Simms running more simulations on the MIT Cray supercomputer, a virtual duplicate of the one at Cal Tech. The data used in those simulations originated mostly from the Gemini twin telescopes. With identical telescopes on Hawaii and at Cerra Pachon in Chile linked, Gemini is uniquely equipped to make measurements at very large distances. Still, these measurements and the resulting simulations are subject to equal limits of accuracy as are all measurements."

"I'm sure our listeners are having difficulty grasping this concept. I certainly am. Can you explain this in terms a laymen can understand?"

"I'll try. Mount an accurate rifle in a rigid device holding the barrel in one precise position. Fire several shots with the rifle at a target. At close range, the grouping of bullet holes in the target might be a single hole. Move the target out to a mile and the grouping of several holes will be around six inches across. The farther away the target, the larger the grouping indicating diverging paths for each bullet. The paths vary because of numerous factors. These include variations in wind, and the effects of gravity, the rotation of the earth, and even tiny differences in the weight and shape of the bullets. The science of ballistics developed by artillery experts is old and clearly demonstrates the limits of accuracy even when the barrel of the gun is rigidly held. Do you follow?"

"Yes, that's clear enough. I'm sure many listeners are familiar with the windage correction, one of the adjustments made in aiming a gun over long distances. How does that bear on the movement of the Ghost star?"

"In the case of the Ghost, the movement of the star for the two years since we first started plotting its course could be considered as the fixed barrel of the rifle. Our measurements of that path, the *barrel*, are not yet precise, only probable. The star will then pass through 280 light years of space within the gravitational effects of several known stars and possible unknown dark matter. Our best estimate of the spread of these paths over that distance, is eight light years. The solar system lies somewhere within that eight light year diameter circle, the *grouping*, so to speak."

"That's quite clear to this hunter. I've fired at a few targets and know what is meant by a grouping. I never thought to apply that concept to this star. Interesting. So why did Dr. Simms make such a definite and terrifying statement? He must understand the situation as you explained it."

"I can't speak for Dr. Simms, but I am quite certain he meant the simulation was a worse case scenario which he neglected to mention. Even men of his stature in the scientific community are known to misspeak on occasion. He is human."

"So, when will we understand enough about the path the Ghost will take to be able to predict any danger to Earth and its life?"

"The spread of possible paths will slowly shrink over the years. The certainty of any path of danger will likely not be known until three or four years before the star arrives. Even then, we may not know what will happen ahead of time. No scientist I know of has ever considered the realities of an object as large as a star moving at 90% of the speed of light. It is even possible the star could pass by rather closely with no ill effects. We don't know."

"That's a bit unnerving."

"As we speak, numerous scientists are working on the new situation. We will propose a number of good theories, but won't be able to confirm any of them for certain until the star passes by in about twenty-eight years. That's the reality."

"Thank you so much, Dr. Botkin, for coming on my program and explaining all this to us. I'm sure your words eased the minds of a lot of people. They have mine. Now Charlotte, our weather lady will bring you up to date on today's weather."

As they walked off the set Les said, "You treated Dr. Simms kindly. From what I heard from several people, a number of scientists are angry at him for making such a statement, on national TV to boot. I was shocked when he said it."

"No one was any angrier than I was. I'll leave it at that. In this instance, my purpose, our purpose, that of the entire group at Gemini and at Cal Tech, is damage control. That's why we contacted you."

"I'm glad you did, for all of us. It will be interesting to see how the various news services deal with your interview. I fear some will crucify Dr. Simms."

"I hope not, but his reputation will suffer. I trust he will make a public apology for not saying his comments described a worse case scenario. That should ease things a bit."

"Can we call on you for further interviews as the situation progresses?"

"Certainly. Just call Diedra at Cal Tech. She handles all these things. Sometimes I think she's the one who runs things. She keeps about a dozen of us in line and on time. She's fantastic."

"We have a dynamo like her in our office as well. Nice meeting you, Dr. Botkin. I hope to see you again."

"Likewise, Les. Just call me Charlie. Everyone else does."

"Ok, Charlie. Evan here will show you out. I must be back to the studio."

"Bye." Charlie said as he started down the hall with Evan.

That evening Charlie returned to Pasadena.

✳   ✳   ✳

Before long Charlie's cell phone was carrying the furious response of Dr. Osgood Simms. Charlie tried several times to interrupt his diatribe, but had to wait until he stopped yelling.

"Dr. Simms, I suggest you listen to and heed my words. I gave you a positive and face saving out for your making a truly stupid mistake. I suggest you thank me and publicly confirm that you forgot to state your prediction was a worse case scenario. If you do not, the media will crucify you and I will help them. In addition, our department at Cal Tech will press for public censure and your dismissal and loss of tenure by MIT. Your professional future is now in your hands. I will not speak with you of this again and will not accept any of your calls until you make your public statement Goodbye!"

I clicked off the call and called Diedra. "That jackass called me screaming. When I got him to shut up, I laid down the law in no uncertain terms."

"Good for you. Did he listen at all?"

"I hung up and never gave him a chance to respond. Will you arrange for monitoring any response or comments by Dr. Simms and tell me what he says in detail?"

"You bet. We'll record anything we can including video of any televised comments. Our communications department will do so, and they'll provide copies to you. I hope he will realize his untenable position and do the right thing."

"He should be smart enough to follow the out we provided if his ego isn't in the way. If he does what I suggested, almost all of the damage he caused will be reversed. No matter what, I will never deal with that man again under any circumstances."

✳   ✳   ✳

Three days later Dr. Simms again appeared on Les Willig's TV program. After Dr. Simms made a profuse apology and admission of his error, Les diplomatically said, "That's what Dr. Botkin said you did, made a simple error of omission. I'm glad you cleared that up for everyone."

After watching this on TV, Charlie called Deidra. "Well, our plan worked. The SOB did what we told him to do and saved his own ass. Now, I don't ever want to be put into the same room or even the vicinity of that sleazebag, no matter what."

Diedra commented, "All of us here feel like you do. Incidently, Les Willig's program director asked if we could put the two of you on together. I told him under no circumstances would that be possible. I didn't think it necessary to check with you."

"Bravo! Of course, you responded rather mildly compared to my likely response. You are indeed a kind soul."

"No! I just wouldn't lower myself to his level."

"Well said. Now we both have more important things to do than concern ourselves about an egotistical fruitcake. The next data from Gemini is not due until mid December and our simulations are all set up from the last time so we're at a standstill. I will go back to work on some of those projects we set aside before all the excitement.

7

December Readings Come with a Few Surprises
✳ Monday, December 10, 2001 ✳

The first few computer simulations Charlie ran with the December data from Angus provided a clearer definition of the path of the Ghost, but also threw them a curved ball. Charlie immediately called Angus.

"Remember how you and Pat first discovered those strange images, before you knew about the star? Pat told me about it. Haven't you put that together with the star's path?"

"No, I never gave that a thought. What are you getting at?"

"I didn't either until I studied the path defined by the data we discovered from the latest simulations. The Ghost is going to pass extremely close to Barnard's star, less than a light year. One light year is near to the limit of our ability to resolve distances as far away as Barnard's star, but the projected path meets Barnard's Star dead center."

"Oh oh! I see we'll need to make a few more observations of Barnard's star. We'll also check to see if Barnard's proper motion or the different position of the Earth in its orbit caused that faint image to move behind Barnard's. I can't believe I missed that possibility."

"Don't beat up on yourself for that. We all missed it. I only caught the fact when I set up the simulations to indicate other objects that might affect the path. Barnard's jumped right out in the simulation."

At first, Angus was not happy. "That creates problems for our calculation of the path. We may not be able to calculate or define the path until the Ghost passes Barnard's. That will not be until it's about six light years away, six years and eight months before it will pass the solar system. I hoped we could define the path ten or twelve years before then."

"One thing it might do for us is provide real data on the close passage to a star. That should help us predict what will happen when it passes the sun, a big help."

"It will also make us wait years longer to learn what might happen to us. The public won't like that one little bit. That brings up another big question."

"Yeah? What?"

"We're right back smack up against our first big problem. It was the problem that first brought our group together. When and how do we tell the public?"

"We should tell the simple truth, the path of the Ghost will be unknown until after it passes Barnard's star in twenty-six years. It's quite possible that encounter could send it off in a different direction, far away from the solar system. That's the real truth."

Angus laughed. "Just think, if we make this announcement saying the encounter could send the Ghost off on a direction far from Earth and leave it at that, a lot of people would be relieved, and relieved is not strong enough language."

"Why don't you make that as a proposal for the group when we meet in two weeks at your mom's Mohawk Inn in St Regis? We will be discussing the latest simulations and that would make a good lead-in for our news release."

"Good idea. Those news people are always looking for sensation. They'll come up with a headline like, 'Ghost Star may be thrown off course for Earth,' or even, 'Ghost could head for outer space after the encounter with Barnard's Star.' Readers and viewers would eat that up."

"Angus, changing the subject, the next time we meet in December, couldn't you arrange the meeting at a less frigid location? The June meeting would be terrific in St. Regis. It's a beautiful place in the summer but in December? Flights into Watertown are a bit iffy what with all the snow."

"What's the matter, a little snow and cold gonna bother the Indiana farm boy? You lived in California too long." Angus kidded. "Seven of use were going to be here anyway, so St Regis worked out as the most logical place."

"I understand. That was just a suggestion. I'm not complaining. I am planning some personal activities for Christmas and New Years including a trip home to Indiana to introduce a special lady to my folks."

"Yes. Rumor around Gemini says you have more than a passing interest in our receptionist, Jenny. Is that true?"

"Well, I did ask her to marry me."

"Everyone at Gemini knows about that, but it was a joke, right?"

"Yes, back then, but during my last visit to Gemini when I spent several days with her, that proposal became dead earnest. I've never been more serious about anything in my life."

"She's quite a decent young lady, and pretty as a picture. Everyone at Gemini adores her. She brightens up the place."

"Spectacular is my word for her. She's the first female I ever became even the least bit serious about. The wonderful thing is, she seems to feel the same way about me. She plans to stop and meet my folks in Indiana after she goes home to Long Island for Christmas. I'm going to try to go and meet her family then."

"You **are** serious. You two make an interesting couple. I'll wager life for you will be active and exciting—never a dull moment." Angus chuckled as he said it.

"For a long time I thought I was destined to remain a bachelor. Oh, I met some quite nice ladies, but never met a single one that held my interest, my romantic interest that is. My mom frequently asked if I had a girl friend. She was disappointed at my answers. Jenny sure changed everything, in spades."

The two of them talked for some time about Jenny, marriage, and other personal things until Angus said, "I'll see you in a few weeks in St Regis. Then we'll tackle this new situation with the rest of the group. If the path doesn't change, six years and eight months after passing Barnard's star, the Ghost will pass the solar system. If the path does change, everything else will change, drastically."

"I hate having a new and major factor injected into this problem, but the result might end up much better for Earth and her people."

"Let's hope so. Bye Charlie."

"So long, Angus."

✳ Thursday, December 20, 2001 ✳

The December 2001 meeting added little new information. In the end, the group determined two more years of readings of the positions of both the Ghost and Barnard's star would be required to learn how close their encounter would be. The path of the Ghost after interacting with Barnard's has a wide range of possibilities making any projection almost pure guess work.

8

The Gemini Group Meeting at the U of Arizona
✳ Sunday, December 14, 2003 ✳

Sunday afternoon the Gemini group met at their hotel near the astronomy department of the University of Arizona in Tucson. The only one missing was John who was not able to be there until Tuesday. Serena brought Kat's withdrawn son, Michael, with her. She was always hopeful contact with Angus, his idol, might help him recover from the emotional trauma of the tragic death of his wife, Soleia. Angus's close friend and fellow astronomer, Pat Yamaguchi also joined the group for this meeting.

The first get together at the hotel on Sunday afternoon was more of a social gathering and cocktail party than a serious scientific one. Two members of the astronomy department spoke to the group and welcomed them to the university. Angus's friend and colleague from his university days, Pat was one of them. He managed to poke some good humored fun at Angus which brought roars of laughter from the group. Angus outlined the purpose of the meeting, explaining it was to analyze the results of the most recent readings on the position and path of the Ghost star, and decide what their next priorities would be.

"John will not be here until Tuesday afternoon," Angus said. "He sends his regrets and urges us to delve into the newest data with speed and care. He hopes we obtain a good fix on the new path past Barnard's Star and what would happen to the path past our sun. Here are packets with the latest readings, the projected probable paths, and the range of most likely paths past the sun. all of this is in both printed and electronic records to suit all tastes and requirements. Please pickup your packet before you leave. I hope you will all read this information, digest it, and be ready to participate in our first serious meeting tomorrow morning at nine sharp, right here. For now I suggest we all get reacquainted with each other, share our latest stories, and finish our socializing so we can go to work tomorrow."

✳   ✳   ✳

At nine o'clock Angus convened the meeting. More than twenty graduate students of astronomy were present as guest observers. They would be given the opportunity to ask questions on the last day of the meeting. Angus announced, "I hate to be the bearer of bad news, but according to our latest data, the projected path the Ghost will take past Barnard's Star takes it so close we have no chance to make a reliable prediction as to its path past the sun. We are faced with unknown variables so large and daunting as to defy rational conclusions. Charlie, will you elaborate using the example you gave me last night?"

Crazy Charlie Botkin stepped to the podium. "Angus sent me the newest data on the path of the Ghost a day before I was to leave for this meeting. I had but a short time to run preset simulations using our Cray. I ran a few probabilities of the possible path of the Ghost past Barnard's Star to present at this meeting. The results were indefinite. Even tiny variations in the path past Barnard's resulted in huge variations in the resulting path past the solar system. Because of the huge distances we are dealing with, the incoming variations were far larger then the limits of accuracy of our data. Here's the example I gave Angus. How many of you are golfers?"

All but three hands went up.

"Let me ask the question in a different way. How many of you do not understand the basic physics of one object striking another?"

Not a single hand was raised.

"Good. Consider a golf ball being struck by a normal golf club. How can any of you predict where that ball will go?"

"I'm a golfer, and a consistent one." Ali said. "Even my best shots would vary quite a bit. Is that what you're getting at?"

"Yes, but with a different club," Charlie said. "Imagine if the club head were not flat but of a similar size and shape as the ball, perfectly round. How easy would it be to predict its path?"

"Impossible!" Ali exclaimed. "Is that what we're dealing with here?"

"No, but close to it. Another example would be two billiard balls on a huge table. Shooting at a ball a hundred or even a thousand feet away, how easy would it be to predict the path of the ball even if you could hit it?"

Angus broke in. "Of course, those examples are not mathematically correct, but they do illustrate the type or order of the problem of predicting not just the path of the Ghost after its gravitational interaction with Barnard's Star, but before as well. There exists no data on the gravitational effects of one star-sized body passing another one at relativistic speed. All we can do is make intelligent guesses. After all, that's what a computer simulation is, an intelligent guess. Its accuracy is dependent on the accuracy and lack of variability of the data used, and the relationship of the simulation to reality."

Serena, the practical and realistic business woman, stood up to address the group. "I don't see as this changes the purpose of this group in the least. From the beginning, the purpose of this group has been to see that any information about the Ghost star is released to the general public in the most accurate and least threatening way. I see the present situation as an opportunity to relieve the minds of literally billions of anxious people and do so honestly. The examples Charlie gave are powerful to that end. What I heard you say was that now there could be an almost infinite number of possible paths for the Ghost. All but a tiny fraction of these would take it far away from our solar system and into open space. Is that not truly what you are saying? Do not your commonplace examples say that? I understood so from your examples."

Chelton spoke up. "Makes perfectly logical sense to me. What do the rest of you think?"

A general nodding of heads and spoken words of agreement followed.

Lani spoke. "From my understanding, and from an astronomer's point of view, the final path of the Ghost is still most likely to pass through or near our solar system, in spite of the travels of golf and billiard balls. Still, I like the story it would tell the public, an honest if somewhat skewed story. After all, we truly won't know what will happen or even the likely path of the star until it arrives here. That's still twenty-seven years away, a long time. The path doesn't need to vary much to miss us entirely."

For the next few hours a lively discussion took place among the group. Then someone shouted, "Lunch time."

During lunch, Charlie said, "I cannot believe how far afield we drifted this morning. The sobering fact is nothing humans could do would alter the outcome of the passage of the star near or through the solar system. Everything physical involved will conform to the laws of physics. That makes one realize how helpless we are in the large scale."

Serena summed up everyone's thoughts. "After lunch let's concentrate on what we should say in the news release the media will expect, and how we should say it."

✳   ✳   ✳

Through the afternoon they finalized several drafts of the news release. When they were finished, Angus said, "I'll ask John to go through these tomorrow when he gets here. After we decide the exact wording of the final release, we can do some planning of future meetings. I don't anticipate any new developments for quite a few years so we should consider scheduling meetings only when we really need to. I enjoy these gatherings with all of you, but until and unless a significant new development appears, these meetings are rather irrelevant."

"I'm certain any new news releases can be handled over the Internet," Chelton added as they were about to adjourn.

✳   ✳   ✳

That night the entire group ate dinner together. Michael ended up sitting between Angus and Chelton and right across from Charlie. He couldn't help being drawn onto the spirited conversation among the three of them. When the discussion moved to the physics of a star moving at 90% of the speed of light, Michael talked a lot. It was obvious he understood the subject.

"I didn't realize you knew so much about physics, Michael," Charlie said to him. " I thought you were an iron worker with a law degree."

"I started in physics at Penn, one subject that fascinated me," Michael said. "Then at the end of my sophomore year I decided to go into law. I don't remember why, but it was a definite decision. I'm still fascinated by physics and read a lot about particle physics, your field. That's why I'm so fascinated by this Ghost star of yours."

"It's an amazing thing. I wish we knew more about it."

"What do you think will happen when it passes? You must have some inkling."

"Michael, an object as large as even a small star like the Ghost is very different from atomic particles and their pieces. It's an area where no thought has been given before. Big things don't move that fast. It's a real aberration, but one thing is for certain."

"Oh! What's that?"

"We will learn a whole lot between now and when the Ghost passes us thirty some years from now."

The four men discussed the Ghost and what might happen for hours. Serena was thrilled to see Michael so involved in the discussion. At midnight they broke up and went to bed.

9

A Flight for Jenny and Her Dad
✳ Thursday, December 11, 2003 ✳

Jenny beamed with excitement when her dad called and told her he would be in Hilo for a few days and was bringing a surprise for her. He would be arriving Thursday, December 11.

Jenny met his plane. "What's this surprise, dad?" she asked when they got into her car.

"I'd like to wait until we are at your place where we can sit down and I can show you."

"I'll be a nervous wreck by then. Can't you give me a hint?"

"Not even a hint. Why don't you bring me up to date on this new man in your life, Charlie? Tell me all about him. You only hit the highlights when we talked on the phone."

Jenny burst into an animated, nonstop description of her meeting and beginning involvement with Crazy Charlie that lasted until they arrived at her apartment. Once inside and after stowing his suitcase, Martin followed his determined daughter into her kitchen where she plopped down on a chair at the table.

"OK, dad, I can't wait any longer. Tell me."

"Here's the first surprise," he said, handing her an envelope which she opened immediately. Inside were airline tickets to Fort Wayne and New York.

"Dad, you're an angel, but how can I be away from work?"

"I talked to your boss and he told me you accumulated three weeks vacation time. I talked him into giving you another week so you will be home with us for Christmas and can visit your Charlie after. The entire family will be together. You can even bring Charlie with you if he can make it."

"Oh, Dad. That's the best Christmas present I ever received."

"Actually, it's a present for the whole family, myself included. That's not all."

"Oh? What else?"

"I seem to remember you wishing we could fly around Hawaii, visit all the islands. Well, I rented a small plane for the weekend. We'll be flying over each of the islands and making several stops. We will arrive back in Hilo on Sunday evening. I have not taken you flying with me for several years and I decided this would be a good time to grant you your wish. Then, Monday we head for Long Island. We'll be home a full week before Christmas."

"That's fantastic. Dad, you're the greatest."

"Here's a map with our tentative route," he said as he spread a map of the islands out on the table. "You can change them if you wish, as long as the changes fit into our three days."

After a quick look at the flight plans Jenny said, "I don't think I'll need to make any changes. You've done a lot of planning. It's a wonderful trip."

"Friday, after you are off of work, we'll fly over here to Maui and take an aerial tour including Haleakala crater where I hope it won't be too cloudy. We'll stop for an early dinner in Kahalui before we head back to Hilo for the night. Saturday we'll tour the big island, then fly over Molokai and Lanai. After lunch at an airport on one of those islands, we'll head for Oahu. We should be able to make Kaneohe in time for dinner. We'll spend the night in Kaneohe as well. Sunday we'll take a spin around the southern end of Oahu before heading to Kauai. I want to fly over Waimea Canyon and then the length of the Na'Pali coast. After lunch in Lihue, we'll fly to the north coast of Oahu and stop in Hale Ewa. After dinner at either Pizza Bob's or Kau Aina we'll head for Hilo. We should land shortly after dark. How does that sound?"

"I don't know what to say except it's a dream come true. It's terrific. You're absolutely the best dad in the world."

"And you, dear, are a special daughter who makes me proud to be your dad."

"Wow. How about I come down to earth and fix you some dinner? You must be starved. Those airlines are quite stingy about food."

"I thought I would take you out for dinner."

"Not on your life. I have some lamb chops, your favorite, and you can help fix the veggies and salad. We'll enjoy a sumptuous feast right here."

"I'd like that. I miss your mom's cooking when I'm on a job. I am so tired of eating in restaurants. Besides, you always were a good cook. Your mom taught you well."

✳ Sunday, December 14, 2003 ✳

The entire flight went smoothly. The weather was perfect. They enjoyed the scenery and the stops. About fifty miles away from Hilo on the last leg of their flight, the last light from the sun was disappearing behind Mouna Loa. The lights from Hilo were clearly visible beneath the dark form of the volcano. Suddenly things went terribly wrong. A loud bang preceded a clanging rattle as the engine quickly stopped. A valve broke in the engine. This led to a broken piston and a seized engine.

The tower in Hilo received Martin's calm mayday call. They immediately contacted the Coast Guard who instituted a search and rescue operation. While the crippled plane was still airborne, they managed to get a fix on the GPS. Fifteen minutes after the Mayday call the GPS signal indicated the plane was stationary. Not long after it was received, the GPS signal quit. The Coast Guard knew they hit the water, but were puzzled about the GPS which would not quit if the plane was intact.

The Coast Guard chopper took nearly an hour to reach the location of the last GPS signal. They saw no lights and received no signal on the emergency frequency. Finding anything without lights on the wide expanse of ocean at night is virtually impossible. They dropped two life rafts with lights and radio signal devices near the last GPS location. The chopper searched as long as their fuel supply allowed them to fly back to their base. In the mean time, a cutter was dispatched to the scene. Two hours would be required for the cutter to cover the distance, even in the relatively calm seas at the time.

When the cutter arrived on the scene, they swept the area with their searchlights in a defined search pattern. They saw nothing but the two life rafts and no sign of any wreckage either. The skipper of the cutter reported the plane probably hit the water at a steep angle, broke up, and sank taking the occupants down with it. The cutter continued searching all through the night.

Two search and rescue planes were dispatched at first light, a chopper and a light fixed wing craft. They both homed in on the life rafts dropped at the scene. One raft used a sea anchor which helped it stay near its drop point in the water and not be blown by the wind. The other one was designed to move in the wind at the same rate as a life raft with occupants. The search would first be concentrated in the area between the two rafts, then widened.

The chopper returned to base to take on more fuel. The small plane would be able to search for about six hours before refueling. Neither one found anything on the surface other than the two rafts the first chopper dropped. Both were empty.

The plane that went down carried a life raft designed to deploy when the plane hits the water. The raft holds a GPS, a radio beacon, and a smoke signal, all of which should activate when the raft is deployed. The rescuers concluded it caught in the plane when it hit the water and went down with it.

The details of the tragedy were immediately reported by the media. No names would be released until the customary notification of next of kin was confirmed. By evening of the next day, Monday, the news reports held little hope the occupants of the plane would ever be found.

✳ Monday, December 15, 2003 ✳

Monday morning, John Carroll was watching the news over breakfast. The instant he heard the news report about the plane he had a bad feeling and called Jenny's phone. No answer. He then called a reporter he knew, Pete Radcliff of the Honolulu News Service and got him on the phone.

"Can you give me any info on the plane that went down last night? I'm worried that our receptionist may have been on that plane."

"John, I have no direct knowledge about that, but I can check and call you back."

"Thanks, Pete. Call me at home. I'll stay here until I hear."

About ten minutes later the phone rang once before John grabbed it. "Yes?"

"John, I can trust you so I'll tell you this, the plane was rented by a Martin Corso of New York."

"Damn! Damn! Damn! That's Jenny's father. Is there any chance they will find them?"

"Because of the lack of any signals or lights from the plane's life raft, the Coast Guard thinks chances are slim, but will continue searching all day if necessary. The guy our people talked with thinks the plane hit the water at a steep angle, too hard for the life raft on board to deploy. Says it most likely caught in the wreckage and went down with the plane. He thinks they were both killed instantly in the crash. They should have found something by now, wreckage, cushions, gas tanks, something. They told our people that it was extremely unusual for rescuers not to find a whole lot of stuff on the surface from such a crash, especially since the winds were so light and the waves so small. They were curious about that, said it did not make any sense."

"The Gemini folks will take this hard. Everyone loved Jenny."

"Yeah, I seem to remember talking to her more than once when I called for information. She was sharp as a tack. One more thing that is odd. In the Mayday call, Martin reported seeing some lights on the surface and that he was going to head for those lights and try to set down gently on the water near them. No known ships of any size were in the area so it was a small ship, a private one without an electronic ID. I understand he's an experienced pilot and with the calm seas and the landing lights on the plane, he should have been able to set down gently on the water. The Coast Guard also said that particular plane should float for several days if it was set down carefully, particularly in the light seas. That's why they think he hit hard and broke up the plane."

"Yeah, but that doesn't explain the lack of wreckage, does it?"

"We'll wait until the Coast Guard finishes their search and investigation."

"That will be hard with no specific clues about anything,"

"I've gotta go, John. I'll call you if anything else turns up."

"Thanks, Pete. I'd appreciate that. And thanks for the info. Oh, I won't mention this to anyone until I hear confirmation of notification of their next of kin."

After hanging up the phone he started thinking about Jenny and wept. He would calm himself before talking to the folks at Gemini. He knew it would be difficult facing Siri, the Indian girl who was taking Jenny's place while she was on vacation. He decided to hurry and go in early so he wouldn't meet or talk to anyone right away. He also knew the final meeting with the director of the Gemini installation in Cerra Pachon, Chile would take place tomorrow. But for that important meeting he would be in Tucson.

✳   Monday, December 15, 2003, 6:58 am   ✳

John entered the Gemini building with a heavy heart and went straight to his office. He decided to write a formal statement to read to the press when the time came. The first thing he saw on his desk was the itinerary, list of contacts, and phone numbers Jenny gave him before she left on Friday. One name stuck out, Charlie Botkin. He would be seeing Charlie Tuesday at the meeting in Tucson. Knowing of their relationship, what could he say to him. Right next to that were his plane reservations and the stack of things Ani'i put together for today's meeting. He almost forgot he was leaving early Monday evening for Tucson. Fortunately he packed for the trip before hearing the news.

He agonized over the formal statement when he realized that right at this moment he couldn't ask anyone for help. Gemini people would soon start arriving so he hurried to finish the statement. His meeting would start at eleven and take the rest of the day. He printed the formal statement, then folded the paper and sealed it in an envelope.

When Ani'i arrived, he called her into his office. "I have an important request for you," he said, handing her the envelope. "Please open and read this to the entire Gemini staff when the news media releases the names of those lost in yesterday's plane crash in the ocean near Hilo. I would prefer to do so myself, but the news may not be released before I leave."

Ani'i was disturbed. "Why? Who was lost? Can't you tell me?"

"Of necessity I promised my source to tell no one until the next of kin were notified. It's important that I keep my promise. You'll understand when the names are released."

"I will not even ask."

"Thank you. I knew I could trust you and I hate to lay this on you. Should the news break before I leave today, I will read the statement in that envelope."

John's flight on Delta left at quarter to seven Monday evening.

✳ Tuesday, December 16, 2003 ✳

Tuesday morning the news services had not as yet released the names. They did report that the Coast Guard cutter found several small pieces of wreckage from the crash. They were brought to Hilo and examined by the authorities. The people who examined these small pieces concluded that the plane hit the water so hard it was demolished and that the occupants most likely died instantly and went down with the main part of the plane. The ocean is so deep where the plane went down, retrieving the wreck would be impractical, impossible for divers.

Among the pieces found were parts of a seat and two pieces of the wing tips containing the landing lights. The light fixtures held enough air that they floated. The examiners thought that was strange because those lights should have been demolished by the force of the crash. They finally concluded the wings folded back in the crash slowing down the wingtips before they hit the water. The other pieces were plastic from the interior of the plane. The thing that bothered the examiners was the complete absence of any pieces of clothing. Any crash that so badly tore up the interior of the plane and produced so many small pieces, particularly of fabric, would tear up the luggage and clothing of the occupants. Some of this would be present on the surface. They finally decided that light weight Hawaiian clothing would not float.

✳   ✳   ✳

Dr. Carroll was about to land in Tucson at noon on Tuesday when the names were released. Ani'i called right after he landed to tell him. She was obviously in tears.

"Everyone here is upset. Your nice statement I read over the PA system couldn't stem the tide of tears. Everyone here loved Jenny."

"I'll be meeting Charlie Botkin in half an hour. I doubt he knows as yet. I don't relish telling him."

"Oh my God - - - I don't envy you, Dr. Carroll. My heart aches for both of you."

"Thanks. It's one of those things that must be done. It's not a pleasant chore. I hope I can handle it well."

"You'll do fine. You're a caring man."

With that John said good bye, picked up his luggage, and took a cab to the hotel.

10

Revelations of Tragedy to Family and Friends
✳ Tuesday, December 16, 2003 ✳

Notifications of the tragedy hit the Corso family hard. Susan left school Tuesday morning and went to be with her mother and brother. Eileen and her family arrived late Tuesday evening. They shared tears and stories well into both nights, trying to adapt to the loss of two beloved members of the family. Questions about the last may day message and unusual lack of any significant wreckage left them with an extremely faint ray of hope which dimmed as the days passed.

✳   ✳   ✳

By Thursday the grief-stricken family gave up hope after days of fruitless, wider and wider searching of the ocean where the plane went down. At her minister's suggestion, Ellen Corso decided to go ahead with memorial services. Her minister also suggested they hold the service as part of the Christmas eve service on Monday evening.

The church would be overflowing with family and friends for the service. The entire Gemini group would be coming from their meeting in Tucson to be at the service. With Eileen's help, the local police agreed to check on everyone coming for the service, admitting only church members and those identified as family and friends. With the tragedy covered by the news, the publicity would bring out hundreds of onlookers most of whom would not be admitted to the church for lack of room.

The minister agonized over what to say and how to conduct the service. This would be the saddest event he ever presided over. Eileen would be the only member of the family composed enough to speak and she shed many tears preparing her words. It would be a moving tribute to loved ones.

✳   ✳   ✳

John arrived at the hotel a bit after one and headed directly for the meeting room. The joviality that greeted him as he entered informed him the news had yet to reach them. He held his hands up as he entered the room.

"I bring you some tragic news so prepare yourselves for a shock. There is no good way to say this, but Sunday night while returning on a flight from Oahu in a small plane, Jenny Corso and her father crashed into the sea about fifty miles west of Hilo. Their bodies were not found. The Coast Guard thinks they went to the bottom with the plane"

The room was dead silent for a minute, followed by sobbing and exclamations of "No, it can't be." and "Not Jenny."

Everyone was crying. No one knew what to say.

Michael rushed over and threw his arms around Charlie. Both of them began to cry and hold on to each other. Others were soon holding others and crying. A surreal scene of shared grief, shared tears, and shared comments about Jenny and what a huge loss it was for them all gripped the group. Soon everyone was watching Michael and Charlie. They stood clinging to each other in the center of the room.

Michael held Charlie's face gently in his hands and stared straight into his eyes. "Let it go, Charlie. Let the pain go where it will. Don't fight it. The worst is not over so hold on to me. Let me share your pain. I know it well. This is your worst day ever. I'm here to help. We are all here to help and try to comfort you. We are all hurting as well. Share what you feel. Let us share the burden."

Charlie exploded. "Damn! Damn! Damn!" he shouted struggling against Michael's hold.

"Let loose. Shout! Scream! Let it out!" Michael yelled. "Whatever you do, don't hold it in. We are here to share your grief."

Soon the entire group surrounded Charlie and Michael, giving encouragement and expressing shared concerns. For quite some time no one but Michael knew what to do. He became Charlie's physical, emotional, and spiritual support.

After sitting for a few moments, Charlie hopped up. "Oh my God, her family. They lost two precious loved ones. I must go to them. What happened? Tell me please."

Michael gently took Charlie's hand and led him back to a chair and placed him in it. "Calm yourself dear friend. You'll have plenty of time to decide what to do and when. Right now you must try to be calm and not plan or do anything without thinking. This entire group of people will support and comfort you if you let them. Dr. Carroll can tell you what happened. Would you like that?"

Charlie slowly nodded his head, then began holding it in his hands, elbows on his knees.

Michael looked toward John. "Dr. Carroll, can you tell us what happened and why? At least tell us what you can."

"I'm so sorry, Charlie," John said tearfully. "I hardly know how to start."

John related all he knew, his initial suspicions and his contact with Pete Radcliff. Quiet sobs and sounds of grief accompanied his tale.

✳   ✳   ✳

Saturday afternoon a subdued Gemini group arrived at the Corso home after checking in at a nearby hotel. Many tears and hugs were shared by people who never met that were bound together by the tragedy. Then Charlie saw Susan.

"My God, Susan, my eyes see Jenny," was all he could say before they rushed together and held each other crying for a long time.

For quite a while everyone was red-eyed and nearly silent. The shared grief was a powerful force. Each time one of them attempted to speak, tears interrupted. Ellen finally brought them out of it as she passed around a box of tissues.

"I hope we can all regain the power of speech before we run out of tissues. A number of you are not known to us so why don't we all introduce ourselves."

Gradually, quiet conversation replaced the sobbing as introductions were made and people began to gain control of their grief.

Ellen finally took control and explained to all, "This is all extremely sad, but our family would prefer to make this a celebration of two wonderful lives. That was Martin's exact request about such an eventuality. I'm sure Jenny felt the same." She paused, used a tissue, and glanced around at all the somber faces. "Some wonderful friends and neighbors brought us food and other refreshments. It's all in the dining room so please help yourselves. You must be starving after your long flight."

Eileen held up her hand and headed for the dining room. "Follow me everyone. I'm sure a bit of refreshment will help us all."

With that the sad chill was broken. They relaxed, broke up into small groups and began talking as they walked into the dining room and kitchen.

11

Crash Landing in the Ocean
✳ Sunday, December 14, 2003 ✳

Before the Mayday call Sunday evening.

"Oh my God, Jenny, we're going down. We'll be OK if I can land gently enough on the water. This bird has an automatic life raft with all kinds of survival gear and we're no more than fifty miles away from Hilo. Don't be afraid."

"What can I do, Dad?"

"There's a release lever on the side of the cabin behind the door. See the red handle?"

"Yes, I see it."

"Remove it from its holder and hook it on the fastener in the door. Don't pull it until we hit the water and stop. Don't worry if you can't pull it as an automatic system will do that if you can't. It will be a lot less hectic if done by hand."

"I understand. How far can this plane glide?"

"Not long enough to keep us out of the water, about fifteen minutes from this altitude. Look! See those lights over toward Hilo? Must be a ship. I'll head that way and try to set down near them. I'd better report that to the tower."

After calling the tower and telling them he was going to set down near the lights, he instructed Jenny, "remember our crash drill? Well now's the time to follow those instructions. Put on the life jacket from under your seat.

Then check to make sure your seat belt is fastened tightly. When I say **now**, double up, place your face on your knees and fold your hands on top of your head and hold on tight. Got that?"

"Yes, got it."

"I'll be doing likewise. Then, as soon as we stop, pull the red handle to release the life raft. Then pull the breakaway lock on the door, unfasten your safety belt and jump into the water. I'll be doing the same thing on my side. Paddle to the raft and climb into it. I'll do likewise and take care of releasing it from the plane. We should float free. This particular plane will float for several days if I can land gently enough so it doesn't break up on hitting the water."

"What happened to those lights? I don't see them anymore."

"Yep, they're gone. Well, no matter. We will still do what I described. I'll turn on the landing lights so I can see the water. Any boat will be able to see us and come to our rescue. We're getting close. I'll dive a bit to gain speed, level off above the water, and stall. We will be slammed hard when we hit so be prepared. Now, fold forward and grab your head."

The plane clipped two wave tops before settling in with a sudden jolt. Jenny yanked on the red handle and the life raft deployed. Soon they were both in the water paddling toward the raft which was still tethered to the plane. As soon as they climbed into the raft, Martin released the tether and they floated free.

Suddenly a bright light lit up the plane that was slowly settling. This was followed by a flurry of gunfire from the direction of the spotlight. They were shooting at the plane which soon sank beneath the waves. The spotlight edged closer. This was followed by shouted words in a strange language. The light came closer still and more strange language was being shouted at them.

Two shots punctured the raft which began to sink.

Her dad shouted "Jump Jenny, jump in the water. Swim away from the raft."

As soon as they were in the water, a volley of shots destroyed the raft which soon joined the plane beneath the waves. The men continued shouting in the unknown language as the light drew closer. They were roughly hauled aboard, their life jackets removed, and all their signaling devices were taken and destroyed. All of their possessions were removed from their pockets.

The boat seemed to be a small commercial fishing boat that smelled strongly of fish. A short oriental man led them down and without a word, locked them in a tiny room behind a steel door. A narrow cot hung on one side wall. They both sat down on the cot.

"I don't know what we've gotten into, but my guess is this boat has to be part of an illegal operation of some kind. These are US territorial waters and if they are fishing, they're most likely not here fishing legally."

More gunfire came from up on deck.

"They're shooting up everything of ours that floated. They don't want any part of the plane or raft to be found. We're lucky they didn't shoot us as well."

"Dad, I'm frightened, but I'm more angry than frightened. How can they do this and what will they do to us?"

"Your guess would be as good as mine, but nothing looks good. I overheard two of them talking in Portuguese. I don't plan on letting them know I can understand Portuguese unless I must communicate with them."

"What were they talking about? Did you hear?"

"They were wondering what the captain planned to do with us. So do I. I'm afraid we may be in for a rough time."

Suddenly the engines roared into full speed.

"Well, we're off for somewhere in a hurry. My guess is they fish illegally in American waters at night and move out beyond the two hundred mile limit by daybreak. This ship is quite small so they must offload their catch to a bigger processing ship that stays out of our waters."

"If that's so, what were they doing where they were? They couldn't reach their present position from the two hundred mile line since dark. They must have been here in the daylight, for hours."

"That sure shoots down my theory. They may be masquerading as another type of vessel and don't need to hide."

Two small oriental men burst through the door and reached for Jenny. Martin, about twice his size, struck the first man who went down. He then pushed Jenny behind him and faced the one still standing. Shouts came from the companionway outside the door. The one standing helped his companion up and pulled him out the door, closed and locked it. A lot of angry words were shouted from the other side of the door, then silence.

"Jenny, now I know why we're still alive and what they are planning to do with us. Those men outside were speaking Portuguese. Thank God I understood them."

"What did they say?"

"First of all, I think they told the two who came after you, that they would be thrown overboard if they tried that again. They are going to ask a ransom for our safe return so they don't want anything to happen to us. That is encouraging, as far as our health is concerned. That's about all I could gather from what they said."

"I wonder how long they are going to keep us in here. Sooner or later nature is going to call. What will we do then?"

"Let's find out."

That said, Martin started banging on the door. He banged the door until one of the men who spoke Portuguese opened it a crack. Martin repeated, "Bathroom, Toilet, loo," over several times. Apparently the man outside understood and left to get his partner.

"I'll go first, just in case." Martin said. "Look! At the top of the door, a bar lock. Pull it down and they can't open the door. I didn't notice that before. They probably forgot it as well. Try to do it quietly so they don't hear."

"How will I know it's you when you return?"

"I'll call to you from outside the door. Any problem and I'll knock twice and then three times. Again, try to be silent when you move the lock."

About fifteen minutes later the man reappeared and opened the door.

"I Yahkub. You come. I keep safe," he said haltingly and with a wide grin. He knew a few words of English. That would be helpful.

"I don't have any idea how this will go so keep your fingers crossed and the door locked."

"OK. Don't try anything dangerous."

"Don't worry. We should be as friendly as we can until we learn what's going on. Here goes nothing."

He left with Jacob who closed and locked the door from the outside. Jenny pulled down on the lock moving it slow and silent. She began to worry when about half an hour passed and her dad hadn't returned. She heard her dad's voice outside the door, reached for the lock, and slid it open. Her dad's knocks reassured her and the door opened.

"You're next, hon. I'm sure you'll be safe, but be careful. I learned quite a bit I'll tell you about when you return."

Jenny left the room with Jacob and was taken to a tiny toilet that was not clean and smelled horrible. Jacob waited outside.

As they walked back to her prison, Jacob said, "You nice. Yahkob keep safe."

"Thank you Jacob." Jenny said as he ushered her into the small room, then closed and locked the door.

"OK, Dad. What did you learn?"

"The two Portuguese and the captain are running the ship. They spoke quite a bit while I was in the can. Thank God they don't know I understand their language. When I stepped out of the toilet, I tried communicating with them in a kind of Pigeon English. I learned more from their talking to each other than from my questions. They are taking us to another ship and turning us over to a man named Chekhov. Must be a Russian and the head man of this entire operation. They think Chekhov will ransom us and split the money with them. They are not sure they can trust him though and will ask for half their money before handing us over."

"Anything we can do, other than wait I mean?"

"We can try to figure out something so we are prepared for the unknown. We should arrive at their mother ship by one o'clock tomorrow, fifteen hours from now. Now we should take turns trying to sleep. You first, sweety."

"Oh, Dad. I don't think I could sleep now."

"Lie down and try anyway. I'll sit on the edge of the bunk and rub your back. That might help."

"I wonder what my friends at Gemini will think when we aren't found, probably the worst. And Mom, what will she hear? She'll be frantic, both of us lost. I worry about that."

"Please try to relax and quit worrying. We can do nothing at the present but rest up for any trials we may have before this is over. Hope for the best and prepare for problems. That's about all we can do under the circumstances. We have about fifteen hours to prepare for what comes next. Let's rest."

12

A Change of Ships in the Pacific
✳ Monday December 15, 2003 ✳

The sudden slowing of the ship's engine woke Martin who managed a few hours of fitful sleep after Jenny awoke.

"We may be arriving at their mother ship. We ran at high speed for half a day, maybe longer."Half an hour later a knock on their door was followed by one of the Portuguese men opening it.

"You come up on deck."

When they did, they saw a much larger ship alongside. A crane on the deck of the larger ship was several stories above the deck of their ship. Being lowered to the deck was a cage. Two crew members guided the cage down to the deck and opened the side. It was made of heavy-gauge screen with steel angle frame and corners.

"You go in," a man said. "Go aboard big ship."

"OK, Jenny. We'd better do as requested. I'll go first."

"Can both of us fit in together?"

"I'll squeeze into the corner and you can squeeze in against me. It will be tight, but I'm sure we'll be all right."

As soon as they were inside, the crewman closed the door and threw the bolt to latch it. Suddenly they were lifted up, swaying from side to side. It took about fifteen minutes for them to be lifted aboard and set down. They were dropped on the deck of the big ship with a jolt, and bumped up and down a few times before crewmen grabbed and steadied the cage.

As soon as the lift cable was slackened, a crewman unlocked and opened the door. Jenny extracted herself from her father's arms and stepped out. Her father soon followed. They were greeted by a burly man of about Martin's height. He wore a neat, clean uniform with insignia and gold stripes.

"I am Uri Chekhov, captain of this ship, the Star of Murmansk. Mr. Martin Corso and daughter, Jenny, you will be my guests for some time until we make port. You will find our hospitality pleasant and our services efficient. You will be treated much better than you were on the small ship. Those are rough men on that ship and I must apologize for any discomfort you may have experienced. Please follow me."

He turned abruptly and led them up several companionways to a room near the bridge.

"This is my dining room. Usually my officers join me for dinner, but now we will use it to become acquainted in comfort. Please sit down."

Martin spoke up. "First I would like our family and friends to be notified we are all right."

"All in good time, Mr. Corso. Before that we will need some rather complicated issues decided. Those decisions will take quite a bit of time. Would you like something to eat or drink? How would you like to freshen up? Your ordeal included being in the ocean so you might need a change of clothing."

"The first priority would be notification of family and friends. By now they must think we are dead and at the bottom of the ocean."

"Please try to understand, no messages will be sent until we are in port and that will not be for about two weeks."

"Why not? I insist the American authorities be notified, right now."

"My dear Mr. Corso, I am the supreme authority on this ship and will make all those decisions. When everything has been arranged, and we arrive at our destination, all necessary parties will be notified. Then, when all of our business has been taken care of, you and your lovely daughter will be free to go where you wish and do as you wish. Until that time, you will remain as my guests."

"In other words we are your prisoners."

Uri chuckled. "Except for some secure and dangerous areas, you have complete freedom of my ship. You must realize there is no way off until we make port. I suggest you relax and enjoy our hospitality."

Martin understood escape from the ship would be impossible so he shifted mental gears. "We need something to eat. All we were given to eat since our crash was a little bread, fish, and coffee. The crew of the small boat did give us those things. Also, could our clothes be cleaned and dried? They are quite uncomfortable wet."

"You will be taken to a pair of cabins down that passageway." Uri said pointing to the entrance. "One of my crew will supply you with robes and slippers. Remove all of your clothing and place them in the laundry bags provided. Your clothes will be cleaned and returned to your cabin in no more than two hours. My galley will prepare you a proper meal and whatever you would like to drink. The larger of the two cabins has a small table where you can eat in comfort."

"What must be arranged or decided as you said?"

"All in good time, Mr. Corso, " Uri said. " After you eat and sleep, we will meet in my dining room. Then I will explain the arrangements and what decisions must be made, and not before. Until then, rest, relax, and enjoy our hospitality."

"Not until morning?"

"I think I made myself clear. Now, go with Keeto. He will show you to your cabins and be at your call for anything you may need."

Keeto, a small oriental man in crisp white uniform entered, bowed and directed his hand toward the exit and passageway. Two white robes and a laundry bag were draped over his arm. Two pairs of grey slippers hung from his hand. He did not speak, but lead them a short distance down the passageway.

He opened the first door to a cabin with a bunk, two chairs and a small table. He opened another door on the left to a small cabin with but a single bunk. Both cabins were cramped spaces, just large enough to serve their basic purpose. Keeto placed the smaller robe and slippers on the bunk, indicating it was for Jenny with a wide sweep of his hand. He placed the other robe and slippers together with the laundry bag on the bunk in the larger cabin. He opened a door between the two cabins to show them a room with a head and shower.

"How do we call you?" Jenny asked.

Keeto turned and pointed to a gray push button near the entrance. He pushed sharply twice ringing a bell somewhere outside the cabin. Without a sound he swiftly exited and closed the door as if he was in a hurry to leave. He did not lock the door.

Jenny turned to her dad. "What do you make of that? He can hear and understand English but never spoke."

"He may have been instructed not to talk to us, or it could be he can't speak. We may never find out. Now, take those wet clothes off and step into the shower. I'm sticky and uncomfortable and you must be as well. I'll put our clothes in the laundry bag and ring for Keeto. Those robes look comfortable enough and they smell clean. Let's make the best of what we can, while we can."

"OK, dad."

13

Aboard the Star of Murmansk
✳ Monday December 15, 2003 ✳

Martin sat calmly sipping a glass of sherry. "Well, so far the captain has been a man of his word. They gave us a good meal, wine and everything. Our clothes came back clean, dry and pressed neatly. I feel almost human."

"I find it hard to believe. He even provided us with some books to read, in English."

"Yes, and most all of our possessions so unceremoniously taken from us, were returned. Without our electronics and signaling devices of course. You seem to be holding up well."

"I had a good teacher. My biggest concern is our family and Charlie. By now they must be certain we are at the bottom of the ocean. That worries me a lot, and I'm no worrier."

"That's true and I share your thoughts, but your mom, in fact, our whole family, are strong and smart. They'll manage, and think of the joy when we show up hale and hearty."

"That can't be too soon for me. Can you think what might be in store for us? What plans the captain has?"

"Well, one thing we know that he doesn't know we know, is that he is planning on ransoming us for a whole lot of money. That gives us an edge, not a big edge but nevertheless, an edge. If we play things right, it could work in our favor. He'll want us to write or record some sort of message begging for someone to come up with the ransom money. We may receive threats of harm, even murder. That may all be part of the game he'll be playing. They could also play the role of having saved us from the jaws of death and asking for just compensation for all they did for us, maybe even diverting his ship from its normal route. That's all guesswork. Still, it's good for these things to be kept in mind. Oh, another thing, You are a strong young lady, but could you please try to appear a bit fearful—the frightened little girl clinging to her father for protection? That might help our cause."

"Sure, Daddy, protect me, please." She responded with a fearful cry.

"Now that's a bit of overdoing, don't you think?"

"Don't worry, Dad. I can play it without overdoing."

They discussed possibilities for several hours. Martin leaned back and smiled. "We've about talked ourselves out. We should try to get some sleep."

✳   ✳   ✳

A loud pounding on the door jarred Martin awake. He wondered about the time when the pounding was followed by a gruff voice. "The captain wants you to meet him for breakfast at seven o'clock in his dining room. It's now five-thirty ship time. Please acknowledge."

"OK, we will." Martin hollered at the voice. "It would be nice if we had a timepiece in here."He received no response.

At what they guessed was the right time, they walked down the passageway to the officers dining room. Captain Chekhov was seated at the table with another man in officer's uniform. The man was much younger then the captain and of a slight build. His head was covered with a mop of curly red hair and he wore thick eyeglasses.

"Martin and Jenny Corso, This is my first mate, Gregori Tomkin. He will be with us during our discussion."

"Mr. Tomkin, under the circumstances, I'm not sure whether I am pleased to meet you or not. You understand, of course."

"I am pleased to meet you and your daughter," Tomkin said in a big gruff voice with a slight British accent, quite unexpected from such a slight man on a Russian ship

"You don't sound Russian to me, Mr. Tomkin. Why is your name Russian and you are on a Russian ship?"

"I am very much Russian. I grew up in England and didn't return to Russia until I was almost thirty."

The captain did not care for this conversation and showed it. "Gentlemen, We can dispense with the social and ethnic explanations and start on the main business. That is deciding how best to return the two we rescued to their homeland."

Martin bristled. "Rescued! You mean abducted after shooting up our airplane and our life raft. We were lucky we weren't killed. You sure as hell didn't rescue us."

"Relax Mr. Corso, and try to see things our way. I was merely using the narrative we will use in our negotiations with your government. You will learn to use that narrative or you and your daughter may not leave this ship in good health."

"Thank you Captain. Now I understand our situation. Since we are totally under your power and control, and must do as you order. Will you shoot us if we don't, or chuck us overboard?"

Captain Chekhov retained his composure and replied softly, "We have no intention of harming you. You are far too valuable to us alive and well. If that were not the case, you would be down on the bottom with your plane. Right this moment my first mate has some papers we would like you to go through. You will notice we listed your assets and those of your immediate family. They add up to a considerable sum. I am sure your family would pay handsomely for your safe return. We also noted your connections with government officials and corporations you dealt with in the past. They too may be financially interested in your safe return. Your lovely daughter has a few contacts with access to considerable wealth as well. Do you understand?"

"I understand we were deliberately kidnaped for ransom. I'm wondering, did you also shoot down or disable our plane? At this point, it would not surprise me."

"I can honestly say that we had nothing to do with the demise of your aircraft until it was in the ocean. The fortuitous occasion came to our attention when we heard your may day call. One of our small fishing vessels was near to where you came down and—you know the rest."

"You think you can get away with this?"

"Mr. Tomkin, will you explain to Mr. Corso and his daughter what will happen in the next few weeks?"

"Of course, Captain. Mr. Corso, during the week before we arrive in port, our ship's doctor will inject you with increasing quantities of a drug that is used in chemotherapy on cancer patients. You will become increasingly nauseous and unable to keep food down. In fact, you will not be able to eat for the last two or three days. You will become weak and quite confused. You will not know who or where you are, but you will be alive and will recover. We will notify a hospital in the port we have an ill patient who will be taken off the ship and sent to the hospital.

"That will be the situation when we take you off the ship on a Gurney and turn you over to the doctors. Our story, we found you floating in the ocean almost dead. Our ship's doctor did his best to restore your health and that of the young woman found with you in a deflated life raft. Neither of you carried any form of identification and naturally, neither could speak. We decided our doctor will do his best to keep you alive until we reach port. We headed to our port at great cost since we had to abandon our commercial operations. We would then ask to be compensated for our losses of about two million dollars US."

"What will happen when I come to, become lucid, and tell the authorities what really happened?"

"When you come to, Mr. Corso, you will tell them the story you just heard. You will do so since your daughter will still be aboard the ship, far more ill than you and unable to be moved to the hospital. Our medical staff will be attending to her night and day, doing their best to keep her alive and help her gain enough strength so she can be moved ashore and to the hospital."

"What are you going to do to my daughter?" Martin shouted.

"Calm down. Your daughter will be perfectly healthy but kept locked away from any who would seek to find and talk to her. As soon as just compensation of two million dollars is in our bank, she will experience a remarkable recovery and be escorted off the ship. The two of you can then go and do as you wish. Before you will be able to convince authorities of anything, the Star of Murmansk will cast off and head back out to the open sea. We'll again be fishing the Pacific."

Martin was grasping at straws. "What if something goes wrong and things don't work out the way you plan?'

Captain Chekhov laughed. "We will still sell and deliver our frozen shark fins destined for Asian soup pots. That happens to be even more than our *just compensation for your rescue.* Our reward for rescuing you is a bonus, most of which will end up in the pockets of Mr. Tomkin and myself, after a few payoffs to helpers of course."

Martin cursed and said, "You, Captain Chekhov, are a sick and evil man."

"Come now, Mr. Corso, I'm merely an opportunist taking advantage of an opportunity. Now, I will offer you the opportunity to avoid all the coming nastiness. If you can come up with a way of paying the just compensation, a way we can be certain will hide no traps or bad consequences for us, the injections will not be made and you and your daughter can walk off the ship free as birds."

"And how would I be able to do that?"

"Come now, you are a clever and successful entrepreneur. If anyone could figure out something, you could. You have about a week to come up with an acceptable alternative before we start the injections. Think about it but don't wait too long. In the meantime, take advantage of the freedom to wander about the ship, except for those few forbidden areas. Enjoy yourself. There are deck chairs on the upper deck, the weather is warm and sunny, and the bar is open. And for you two, the drinks are on the house. Should you want for anything, anything at all within the necessary limits, see me, Mr. Tomkin, or Keeto. We now leave you to your own devices. Good day."

The captain and first mate left the room and went about their duties.

Martin looked at Jenny. "Well, it's all spelled out for us. No surprises except for some of the details."

"Daddy, what they are going to do to you sounds awful. Can you think of anything you could do to, as he said, avoid all the coming nastiness?"

"Jenny, something is not copaesthetic. Two million dollars is a small amount to ask in such a situation. I could raise that in a few days and he knows it. If he said twenty million, I would not be suspicious but a measly two million—not a chance. Something else is going on in that devious mind and I have no idea what, or even how I might find out. Maybe I should call his bluff and agree. That might smoke out his real objective."

"But Daddy, you can't trust him."

"Don't worry, hon, I am fully aware of his dishonesty. I just need to find out his real game. To that end, why don't we do as he suggested and go up on the top deck and sun ourselves. I happen to know something he doesn't, and our being visible on deck could be important for our welfare."

"What could that be, Daddy?"

"Let's go up on his sun deck and talk about it."

14

Surprises and changes

✳ Monday, December 22, 2003 ✳

Late afternoon Monday, first officer Tomkin rushed onto the bridge. "Captain Chekhov, A fast approaching ship is coming from the east northeast on a course intersecting our own. If it continues on its present course, we should sight it in about two hours. They are running radio and radar silent as we receive no signals at any frequency from her direction."

"What does hi res Radar tell us?"

"Only that it is smaller than our ship but much faster and has a rather tall radar silhouette."

"It could be a military ship then."

"Could be but no definite ID as yet."

"Damn. I wonder who they are and what they are after. Could be trouble. Our frozen catch is not legal out here. Maintain course and speed until we can identify her."

"I tried hailing but no response. Like I said, they are running radio silent."

✳　　　✳　　　✳

Before the sun reached the horizon, the ship appeared rising slowly to starboard. After watching through binoculars for several minutes, first officer Tomkin cursed. "It's that damned Greenpeace ship Esperanza. What in hell are they doing in this part of the Pacific? Little fishing is done out here this time of year. We may be in for some harassment, Captain."

"Ready the water cannons on the stern, and tell the crew to keep all weapons out of sight. We don't want them reporting we are armed. Hail them. See if they will answer. They may tell us what they want, but I doubt it."

"Captain, they slowed to match our speed and are maintaining a separation of about a kilometer. They are interested in our ship but why? It will be night soon and they will be unable to see us to do anything. My guess is they will shadow us all night and do their mischief in the morning."

"On my mark make a course change of 15 degrees port, run on that course for one hour, and then return to our original course."

"Aye Aye, sir"

"Execute."

Fifteen minutes later, officer Tomkin reported, "They matched our change and are maintaining their same distance. Captain, when we make the next change they will be on a collision course with us. Is that wise?"

"We are a much bigger ship. Do you think they would want to tangle with us? We'd sink them."

"Captain, the Esperanza is an old Russian firefighting vessel with ice breaking capabilities. I don't think you would want them to run into your ship. The Star would most likely come out second best."

"Thank you mate Tomkin. I do appreciate your information and will run in accord. When we return to the original course, make sure we are never too close to the Esperanza."

Around ten the last course change was made and the Esperanza followed suit.

✳ Wednesday, December 24, 2003 ✳

Around two in the morning, two black clad figures crept down the passageway to Martin's room, opened the door and stepped inside in complete silence. One figure stepped to the bunk where Martin slept, leaned down and whispered cautiously in his ear.

"Martin Corso, please stay silent. We are Americans come to take you off this ship."

"Who? What?" Martin whispered.

"We are US Navy Seals. Do not turn on any lights. Please awaken your daughter and tell her to be quiet. I will now turn on a low level light so we can all see. We brought full cover black wet suits with hoods for each of you. Please put them on. Be quick and quiet as you can. My partner and I will provide help as needed."

"My God, My God. I can't believe it. You guys are incredible." Martin whispered.

"Talk later. Now we must take you two off this ship without being seen or heard."

Once they were fully enclosed in the wetsuits, the seals snapped a guide line on each of them so they wouldn't be separated.

"Now follow us out the door and down the passageway. We strung a guide line to follow which will take us back to where we got aboard. Move slowly and be as silent as possible. Stop only when and if we stop. Now, move!"

The trip through the passageway and down two flights of stairs in the companionways went without incident. When they were almost to the gunwale the seals moved against the bulkhead and froze with Jenny and Martin following suit. A seaman walked along the gunwale toward them. He passed within a meter of them but couldn't see them in their black outfits. They waited a full minute then headed for the gunwale.

"Hold onto these handles while we double snap you to our suits. We will step over the side with you on our backs and we will descend to a waiting Zodiac. Hold tight to the handles and leave all the climbing descent to us. We've practiced this maneuver many times so do not fear. Two more of our team are waiting in the Zodiac. Let them help you detach from us and snap onto the Zodiac. We don't want to lose you now that we are this far along."

The descent was swift and silent. Soon they were seated in the Zodiac and hooked to the safety ropes. One of the seals pulled down the rope they descended. He sat down and rolled up the rope as two others pushed the Zodiac away from the side of the ship.

"Now, let them figure out how we got you off the ship," the Seal who wound up the rope whispered to Jenny.

The four seals pulled out paddles and began paddling furiously away from and toward the rear of the ship. "We must be out of the range of their searchlights before we can start the engine and head for the safety of our ship, our borrowed ship," one of the seals whispered, "We're not out of the woods yet, not by a long shot."

Half an hour later, Silas, the leader of the seal team spoke out loud. "We're far enough out now. Gordy, crank up that engine, and lets start these folks on their way home. We can bring you up to date on all the goings on when we are aboard ship. It will be a bit noisy till we are aboard so hold your questions."

The roar of the big outboard all but drowned out his last few words.

15

Rescued and on Their Way Home
✳ Wednesday, December 24, 2003 ✳

After getting out of the wet suits, Martin and Jenny were escorted to the bridge and handed a satellite phone. Captain Thomas said, "You earned the privilege of contacting your family. We did not want to do so until you were safe and aboard."

"Thank you, Captain. First thing, Jenny, call your mother. This should be an unbelievable and marvelous moment for us all."

After a few minutes they were connected. "It's ringing." Jenny reported. "Hello Mom."

"Yes Susan."

"Mom, this is not Susan. It's Jenny. I'm with Dad aboard a ship west of Hawaii."

"My God - - - Jenny, is that really you. Oh (crying) I - - - can't - - - speak."

"It's OK, Mom. I can't either. - - - Here, talk to Daddy."

"Ellen - - - Ellen. - - - Damn, I am choked up myself. Where is everyone?"

"Eileen is downstairs." - calling out, "Eileen! Eileen! get on the phone. It's your Dad and Jenny. They've been found. They're all right. Hallelujah and thank God. It's a miracle. What a wonderful Christmas present. This will be a day to remember."

The phone clicked. Eileen said, "Dad? This is Eileen."

That's all she could say before a torrent of sobs and cries of joy drowned out her words.

Martin tried again. "Ellen, where are the rest. Are they at home?"

"No Martin. They are all over at the church working on - - - my goodness that will all be changed. They are working on a special Christmas eve service, a memorial for you two. I'd better call them. No, Eileen, run over to church and tell them in person. What a spectacular service it will be now. I don't know what to do first. Whom should I contact? I'll call Charlie right away. No, let Jenny do that. He's already over at the church."

"Ellen, don't rush. You sound so excited."

"Well, damn it, I am excited. My husband and my daughter who were dead a few minutes ago are alive and well. It's a miracle - - - an unbelievable miracle. Who wouldn't be excited. (More crying from Ellen and Eileen.)

"Eileen. Eileen. Are you still there?"

"Yes Daddy. I'm here."

"Your mother made a good suggestion, but the two of you should go together."

"We will. What happened? We were told about the crash and then that they had no hope. How did you survive?"

"It's a complicated and convoluted story, but we were not injured in the crash and experienced quite a series of adventures starting with when we were pulled out of the water in total darkness. We're fine now and on an American ship on our way to Hawaii. You'll have to wait awhile for the full story. You will learn about the incident in the newspaper or on TV before we are home. My God. I wonder how the news will handle this story. Just thought of that."

"Martin, I've calmed down a bit and Eileen and I will go to the church and tell them. How can we contact you after we hang up?"

"Captain, how can they contact us after we hang up?"

"Hand me the phone." Captain Thomas said. He proceeded to explain how they could reach the ship and then handed the phone back to Martin when he finished.

"Ellen, it's early morning out here and we slept only a short time. You have plenty to do and Jenny and I could use some more sleep in spite of all the excitement. You must want to ask a lot about what happened, but could we talk later after we catch up on our sleep? We're exhausted."

"Of course, dear man. I love you. Oh God how I love you. And you're back from the dead, both of you. It's fantastic. OK, go get some sleep. We'll take care of things from this end. I'm so happy I could scream."

Martin laughed. "Sweetheart, I can't wait until we're together. Then we can talk about what happened."

"Go! Go get some sleep."

"All right, Ellen. We'll talk later. Bye!"

"Good-bye dear man."

Martin handed the phone to his daughter. "Here, call your man right away."

Again, the call took a few moments to go through.

"Hello?"

"Hi, Charlie, it's Jenny. We're safe."

Silence!

"Charlie? Are you there?"

A few mumbled, unintelligible words, then a hesitant, "Jenny? Is that really you?"

"Yes, sweetheart, my dad and I are on a ship in the Pacific heading for Hawaii."

"I find it hard to believe, but wonderful."

"Yes Charlie, we really are on our way back."

"Wonderful!—What?—How?—I—I'm speechless. You're safe and that's all that matters. I can't believe how I feel. I'm overwhelmed."

"I can't wait until we are together and I can tell you everything. It was quite an experience. We were rescued, kidnaped, and headed for some port in China when Navy seals spirited us off and away from the ship that was holding us prisoners."

"I'll do a couple of cartwheels as soon as I'm off this phone. I don't know how to start asking questions. There are so many. The important thing is you are safe. Boy! Is this church service going to be different from planned."

"Charlie, we experienced quite an ordeal and my dad and I are exhausted. I can't keep my eyes open."

"Yes! Go to sleep. We can talk later. The important thing is my Jenny is back from the dead, safe and sound. Wait till I tell my folks. Yahoo! I'm so happy I can only shout, yahoo."

They spoke for a while more before hanging up. Jenny soon headed for some much needed sleep.

✳ Thursday, December 25, 2003 ✳

After finishing their interrupted night's sleep, Martin and Jenny were treated to some new clothes that almost fit and a good old-fashioned American breakfast. After breakfast, they gathered in a small room with the four seals, the captain and first mate of the Esperanza, and a man and woman in business attire.

Captain Raymond Thomas introduced everyone. "Martin and Jenny Corso, I would like to introduce you to the team that organized this entire operation. John Axelrod and Meridith Su, a ship monitoring team from Navy Intelligence, four US Navy seals, Lieutenant Silas Kitchner, team leader, Ensign Elrod Johnson, Seaman Gordon Yuba, and Seaman Carlos Santiago, My First Officer, Kamura Ito, and myself, Raymond Thomas, Captain of the Esperanza. The entire crew of the Esperanza participated of course and are represented in this meeting by me and Officer Ito.

"I'm sure you have many questions which you may ask as soon as we brief you on the operations thus far. I hope you realize today is the day before Christmas at your home. Here, west of the International Date Line, the day is Christmas Day. Your family and friends as well as the team gathered here, received a marvelous and joyful Christmas present. A present that will be remembered and talked about for years to come. Now, I will turn the meeting over to Miss Su who first noticed the things that led to this operation. Her persistence and determination in following up after starting with sketchy and indefinite information led to the success of the mission. Miss Su."

Miss Su, a tall, slender, almost frail Asiatic woman stood. "Sometimes curiosity reaps grand rewards. When the report came in about an aircraft may day near the big island, I checked our last satellite photo of the area taken a few hours before the may day. At about the position as the reported plane incident, was a small ship identified only as a probable commercial fishing craft. We were able to identify the craft as one of a small fleet serviced by a Russian mother ship, the Star of Murmansk. This ship is on the watch list of several international organizations who monitor illegal and harmful fishing practices. We share information about certain ships like the Star with those organizations, and they return the favor for us. When I followed up by examining photos of the Star for the entire next day, a very unusual scene unfolded. The rendezvous between the small ship and the Star provided photos of some unusual crane activity. We could tell two people were transferred from the small ship to the Star in a container handled by the crane on the deck of the Star. We never before photographed this type of activity.

"When I reported this to my superiors, they asked me to follow the photos of the Star to see where she went and what she did. At this point, Mr. Axelrod joined me to add another pair of eyes and use other types of surveillance with better resolution than the satellite photos. We decided to see if we could use photo drones to provide more detail. We found two were available in Hawaii but we needed a platform with which to launch and retrieve them. I will let John continue the story since he is our drone man. John?"

John Axelrod stood to address the group. "Thank you Meredith. What she did not tell you was that she was convinced that the two people barely visible in the satellite photos were you two. Her insistence that this was indeed the case is what put this entire mission in motion. I arranged for a long range surveillance drone from Hickam field on Oahu to fly out and photograph the Star which at this time was only about 200 miles north of Oahu and headed west. It was well within the range of the drone. Over the period of several hours we took many photos of the ship. Several of the photos gave us a positive identification of Martin and Jenny, walking on the deck. The mission changed into a rescue mission. We considered using a US Navy ship but soon discovered that would take far too long to be arranged. Then someone in our department mentioned that the Greenpeace ship, Esperanza was about to leave from Honolulu and that the Star of Murmansk was one of the ships they planned to shadow. Meridith and I rushed over to where the ship was berthed and arranged to meet with First mate, Kamura Ito. During our meeting we described the situation and our planned rescue mission using a Navy seal team.

"At first he did not even want to mention it to his captain. He said Captain Thomas was not on good terms with the Navy and would not consider it, with a seal team aboard. We persisted emphasizing the rescue of two American civilians from one of the ships on their hit list. After some tall talking, he gave in and asked Captain Thomas to speak with us. Captain, why don't you take the story from here. I'm sure we would all like to hear your version and why you agreed to participate."

Captain Thomas grinned as he rose to speak. "Thank you Mr. Axelrod. I've never been friendly with any of the military. I came close to brushing the whole thing off, but I would love to tweak the captain of the Star, so I decided to listen to their plans. The idea of a team of four Navy seals and two surveillance drones with their operators and all the equipment of both groups upset me a bit. The rescue part changed my mind and I agreed as long as they recognized the Esperanza is our ship and we must approve all actions originating aboard ship. Seeing you two sitting there made all of the problems seem minor. I am proud to be part of this mission and I changed my mind. I now regard the US Navy, and you seals in particular with great respect.

"Back to the story, the loading of all the equipment, the setting up of the drone launch and retrieval equipment and of the two Zodiacs in addition to our own, and then the stowing of all the additional food and supplies was a major task. I take my hat off to the Navy crew who accomplished all that in two days, an impossibility in my mind. We were underway and only two days behind the Star. With good weather we should catch her in four days, five at the most.

"We caught them in a bit less than five days.

"Those little photo drones did an amazing job. As soon as we were within range, the drone crew sent one up to take surveillance videos and learn as much about your whereabouts on the ship as possible. Now I will turn the telling over to Lieutenant Kirtchner as he and his team did the rest and by far the most dangerous part of the mission."

The lieutenant was a big man, 200 pounds and several inches more than six feet with dark curly hair and a boyish face. He spoke with authority.

"First of all I must compliment the captain and his crew. They handled their part of the mission like clockwork. It made our part much easier. The videos from several drone trips gave us the information we needed. We saw both Martin and Jenny walking in and out of the section of the ship where they were staying. That together with the detailed architectural plans of the Star which we obtained from the ship builder enabled us to plan how to find their cabins and take them off the ship. By the time we sighted the Star, our plans were ready.

"Captain Thomas pulled the Esperanza abreast of the Star and we maintained a course about a kilometer off their starboard bow. Being in plain sight and with all communications shut off, we were certain to keep their attention focused on our ship. As soon as it was completely dark, we launched one of our Zodiacs with the four of us. We were fortunate it was the dark of the moon. We used our motor to take a position well in front and on the port side of the Star. The ship plans showed several bar holds were attached near amidships. We planned to tie the Zodiac up to one of these. Catching them in the dark was a problem. Seamen Yuba and Santiago wore night vision goggles and would use a padded hook and line to catch one of these bars and tie onto it. That was a tricky maneuver since paddles were our only means for power and the ship was moving at about ten or twelve knots. They managed quite well the first time. It's a good thing because one try would be all we had—no second chance. The swells were rather small making our contact and hook up much easier.

"Once secured to the ship, we brought out a special plastic grappling hook to throw a line over the gunwale. This hook would not make the noise a steel one would. We were lucky, first that the hook caught and held until one of us could climb up and make the rope secure, and second, that no one was near enough to hear or notice it. As soon as the hook caught and held, Ensign Johnson, he's the monkey in our group, scampered up the rope and passed the end through the gunwale. This gave us two lines to use. Seaman Yuba went up next taking another line with him. We used that line to pull all of our gear aboard and as our guide line for our trip back with our charges. It all went quite well. The one tense moment when the crewman passed close by made us hold our breaths. That's about it. From then on all went well and downhill."

As soon as Lieutenant Kirtchner finished and sat down, Martin stood. "I hope I can say what I mean, but please pardon me if I am a bit disconnected. This is an emotional moment for me. The reality of what has happened is just sinking in. I'm sure Jenny feels as I do. You people are fantastic—unbelievable. This was an experience out of a movie and seemed unreal. How long were you on the ship, Lieutenant? It seemed like no more the ten or fifteen minutes."

"It took thirty-one minutes from when we tied up to the ship until we pushed off. We always time our missions. Operating swift and silent is our specialty. Speed and silence are an absolute necessity for the safety of all."

"Well I am still amazed. When you woke me, it was one of the most exhilarating moments in my life. I could not believe my eyes. I wonder what Chekhov thought when they discovered we were gone? He might go berserk when this hits the news. What about the news? Has any of this been given to the news media?"

John Axelrod answered. "We sent out a basic news release stating that a team of US Navy Seals rescued Martin and Jenny Corso from the Star of Murmansk in the open Pacific west of Hawaii. It explained they were kidnaped and held prisoner after their plane crashed into the ocean near Hilo. No details were provided other than the entire operation was carried out using the Greenpeace ship, Esperanza with the cooperation and direction of their Captain Thomas and help from their fine crew. I can guarantee we will be deluged with reporters and TV cameramen when we arrive in Honolulu, so be prepared."

16

Reunion in Honolulu and a return to normalcy

✳ Monday, December 29, 2003 ✳

Three o'clock Monday afternoon as the Esperanza approached the mooring in Honolulu, the scene was frantic. Media satellite trucks were parked everywhere any space existed and reporters crowded the dock. The police placed barricades around five minivans and a Navy bus that brought a number of family and friends to the dock. They would also be used to transport those who would be getting off the ship to their hotel and the Navy seals back to their quarters.

A podium and microphone were set up facing a roped-off area designated for reporters. Access to this area was restricted to one person from each news service and news agency. Not all who wanted into this area could be accommodated, so many were standing outside the wooden barricades and complaining. Police were standing about every five feet along the barricades trying to maintain order. Camera operators crowded against the barricades, their cameras aimed toward the Esperanza.

A shout went up as a group walked down the gangplank to the dock. Jenny and Martin followed the Navy crew down to their waiting family. Lots of hugs, kisses, and tears of joy all but overwhelmed them. Charlie got hold of Jenny.

His first words after they held each other for a long time, were , "Let's get married, soon. What do you say?"

Jenny leaned back, stared Charlie in the eyes, smiled, and replied. "You're right. Let's go tell everyone."

When the news was shared, Martin smiled at his daughter and said, "congratulations! It's about time. I was afraid you two would never chance it."

Ellen grabbed her husband. "Come on, Martin, we all knew it would happen sooner or later. In addition to celebrating a miraculous return of you two, the Corso girls will now be helping with a wedding. I'm sure Jenny will want our help."

"Of course, Mom. I would love help from all of you. First of all, I will take some time to consider a date. I don't plan to even think about it until we've returned to a normal life."

"That's Jenny, my conservative lady." Charlie said with a smile. "Now we should all go celebrate."

Charlie's parents worked their way through the throng to Charlie's side in time to learn about their new plans.

Grinning with excitement, Edith grabbed Jenny, gave her a hug and began forming words. "I am so happy for you, for both of you. What a wonderful sequel to your miraculous return from being lost."

Even Ray became emotional. He couldn't speak, but the tears of joy streaming down his face spoke volumes. "You are the daughter I always wanted but couldn't have."

Still holding Jenny, Edith said. "That's a lot for my quiet man to say. He's as happy as I've ever seen him. We thought we would never have grandchildren."

"Mom, don't go rushing things." Charlie said with a forced frown. "We might not want children."

Edith stepped back and gave the two of them a look up and down. "Oh, you'll want children all right. Mark my words. What do you say, Ellen?"

"Nothing those two do will ever surprise me." Ellen replied.

They all laughed heartily over that exchange.

✳   ✳   ✳

In a few months, things slowly returned to normal for Charlie, the Corso family, and their friends. Jenny and Charlie set their wedding date for September 4. The Gemini group were all back at their usual pursuits. They decided to discontinue the annual meetings and meet only when necessary. Meetings could be held on the Internet until the Ghost started to interact with Barnard's Star, or some new situation about the Ghost arose.

17

NASA announces a near-earth passing object
✳ Monday, May 3, 2004 ✳

On Monday at the University of Arizona, Dr. Ann Rivers met with a group of astronomers. Among the group were Jack Kershaw, Bernie Franks, and Angus's old friend, Pat Yamaguchi.

Dr. Rivers made an announcement. "Two days ago the NASA/JPL Near-Earth Object Program Office reported the finding of a new object on an intercept course with the Earth. While the exact path and time of arrival are not determined, it is clear that it will come close and might be a real menace. You three, under Pat's leadership will conduct the university's study of this object. Others already determined that it is most likely an asteroid moving in the plane of the ecliptic and coming from the asteroid belt. It appears to be 10 times the size of the object that made Meteor Crater near Winslow, Arizona, and much larger than the Tunguska object that exploded over Siberia in 1908.

"NASA began making plans to launch a research probe to meet the object they named Ohlmeg. They planned to photograph it, and try to determine its exact trajectory to see when and if it would collide with Earth. With the estimate of its closest approach a bit more than a year away, any project to intercept it even for research on its exact path is under the gun. NASA has asked for as much help to determine where the object is headed as the community of astronomers can muster. The space agencies of Europe, China, and Russia are also working on their own plans. They all agreed to share information thus will provide us lots of help.

"So you will understand the seriousness of the situation, I will refresh your memory about a few facts. Around 50,000 years ago, a meteor traveling about 20 km per second smashed into the Arizona desert. The explosion was equal to 2.5 megatons of TNT and left a crater a mile wide and 500 feet deep.

The Tunguska meteor of 1908 struck with an estimated two to twenty megatons of TNT depending on which computer simulation is used. Still, the meteor left no crater since it exploded between four and six miles above the surface. Considerable damage was inflicted over a large area with no human inhabitants. The explosion knocked down some 80 million trees over an area of 830 square miles and pulverized the earth in a circular area about a mile across while leaving the stripped trunks of trees standing vertical within the circle.

"The Berringer (Arizona) meteor was made of nickel-iron and is estimated at about 150 ft across and some 300,000 tons. First estimates of the size of the new meteor are between 350 and 500 feet in diameter and between one and three million tons. This is quite a bit larger than the estimated size of the Berringer meteor and the Tunguska object. Any collision of this object with the Earth could make for tragic consequences if it struck an inhabited area. For this reason we must determine its path and precise time of arrival to determine if measures are to be attempted to divert the object.

"There is an envelope in front of each of you containing a brief outline of important facts, data about the object and the work to be done. You will be given the highest priority access to appropriate facilities needed to pursue the goal. Please examine the work already accomplished before proceeding as we do not need to spend time duplicating work already completed and confirmed. Are there any questions?"

Jack Kershaw said, "It's a damned deja vu. The same scenario as Angus's Ghost star. Will they be working on this at Gemini?"

"I would imagine they are as concerned with this same threat as we are," Dr. Rivers said. "I have no information about any facility working on the project, but NASA will be keeping track of all those who are. We are to report any results to Greg Simmons at NASA/JPL NEOP where any results will be compiled and stored. His exact Internet and postal addresses are in the papers you have. Everyone working on this project will be able to access all the data as soon as it is available."

"One of the first things I am going to do is contact Angus." Pat said. "Our direct data line is still in operation and if he's doing anything, I'll want to know about it. We can share data."

Dr. Rivers stood and said to Pat. "I leave this project in your capable hands, Pat. Keep me posted as to your progress. I won't need the details, just generalities. Now I suggest you go to work."

The three men worked together successfully on several projects. The high regard they each had for the other's integrity and professional abilities along with their personal friendships assured positive results.

✳   ✳   ✳

Pat called Angus as soon as he could. "Hi, old buddy. How've you been and how's that old fat ugly assistant of yours? How are those twins?"

"We're all doing quite well thank you. Boy, do you have a long memory. That was almost five years ago. I'll tell her what you said. How are you? How's Beanie?"

"We're doin' great. She's still the old firebrand. I'll bet you didn't know we got married?"

"How'd that happen? As I remember she said she hated the idea of marriage. How'd she put it? 'Marriage is a sure way to ruin a friendly relationship.' What changed?"

"You know Beanie. One day about six months ago she waltzed into our apartment, grabbed my hand and said, 'Let's get married—now.' I was flabbergasted. Almost before I knew what was happening we were licensed and headed for a justice of the peace. On our way she said, 'Hurry up before I change my mind.' Afterwards she told me not to mention this to anyone. I didn't, but she let it slip at her office so they gave her a party. That led to another party here at the astronomy department. You knew she finished school and started her own practice, didn't you?"

"I expected that would be the case, but no, you never told me."

"That was More than a year ago. Dr. Sonsee Array, family dentist."

"That's her name, Sonsee-array? I thought you said it was hard to pronounce."

"Her Chiracahua family name is impossible for me to pronounce. Sonsee-array is her given name and means morning star. She changed her legal name to Sonsee Array so she is officially, Dr. Sonsee Array, easy to pronounce."

"That's clever. Now I know her real name. You didn't call me to chat, so what's up?"

"Are you doing any work on the object NASA announced the warning about?"

"When the news first came out, we talked about it, but some critical measurements of the path of the Ghost are coming up so we decided to pass. Besides, Gemini is far from ideal for spotting small, near-Earth objects. Many observatories are far better suited for those kinds of jobs than we are. I'll wager half the astronomers on the planet are working on that asteroid. We will not be missed."

"I understand. I thought if you were on it, we could share data. Anyway we had a chat. It's been a long time. If you ever come near Arizona please stop and visit us. Beanie and I would love to see you guys and meet those twins. Tell me ahead of time so we can plan your visit."

"Don't worry my friend. If we're ever in the vicinity, we will take you up on the invite. Keep me posted on what's going on with the asteroid. You never know, I might come up with an idea that could help. Now I better go back to work."

"Take care my friend. Bye."

18

Chasing the path of a threatening asteroid
✳ Monday, June, 21, 2005 ✳

Monday, June 21, Pat and his group met with Dr. Rivers to discuss the latest progress report. This was in preparation for a press briefing by the same group the next day. Pat gave each of them a copy of the report to study before the meeting. The report explained what had been done to date and the activities of the various space agencies around the globe. Unprecedented cooperation formed among the nations involved.

Tuesday, June 22 Pat, Jack, Bernie and Dr. Rivers walked into the press briefing to make public the results to date of their efforts and of others around the world.

Pat spoke. "I will make a rather long statement to cover what is contained in the papers each of you has been given as you entered the briefing room. Please hold your questions until my statement is completed. We will then deal with questions. By the present date, the path of the asteroid has been determined by computer simulation with the greatest accuracy possible from the data. The most accurate projections tell us the meteor will strike the Earth if only a glancing blow. The strike will come sometime near seven in the morning on Wednesday, June 15, 2005, north of the equator but in China, not over the ocean as many hoped. Of course, an ocean strike might create huge tsunamis which could cause great loss of life and large amounts of damage on all shores affected. The best thing would be if the object struck a sparsely settled land area.

"NASA/JPL in cooperation with ESA are readying a rocket to meet the asteroid, take photos and then reverse course and track it to its final path as it approaches Earth. Launch is scheduled for early July. The Chinese already launched their rocket diverted from another project. The Chinese rocket is well on its way to a rendezvous with the asteroid. The Russians plan to launch their own rocket late in August. Since the asteroid is coming toward us at 20,000 miles per hour and accelerating, and our rockets are traveling toward the asteroid at 22,000 to 27,000 miles per hour, the closer to Earth the asteroid comes, the less time our rockets will take to reach it. The Russians are also readying a huge rocket they hope will be able to change the path of the asteroid when it is closer. Each of the rockets has some capabilities to nudge the object into a path away from Earth contact. Until we understand the exact path of the object, it is pointless to try to move it as we could even be moving it from a safe trajectory to one more dangerous.

"The farther the object is from impact, the smaller would be the power needed to move it to a safe trajectory. This poses several knotty problems. The first is knowing how far and what direction to make a move toward safety. The second is knowing how to move it. The object could be a single cohesive mass, a number of various sized rocks held together by ice, or even a loose *pile* of rocks of many sizes held weakly together by gravity. The latter would be pulled apart and scattered by the gravitational pull of Earth as it approached. We will not know what we are dealing with until one of the rockets is close enough to send us back a high resolution photograph of the object. High enough resolution photographs will not be available for several weeks.

"Please understand, nothing like this has ever been attempted so don't ask probability questions as we will not answer those. If we have a reasonable answer to your question, we will answer. If not we will freely admit we do not know. Also, we will not speculate on any aspect of this happening so don't ask *what if* questions.

"To simplify this briefing we will select questioners from the cards you dropped in this box. From each person only one question will be addressed. Should a multiple facet question be asked, we will answer but one facet. Dr. Rivers will select a card at random and read the name. Please stand, repeat your name and the location of your organization. Please do not announce the name of your organization."

Dr. Rivers announced the first name. "Paul Waters."

Paul stood up. "Paul Waters, Des Moines, Iowa. When will the various rockets rendezvous with the asteroid? What are the dates? "

Jack Kershaw answered. "Only approximate dates are known at this time. The NASA rocket will be the first and will rendezvous around November 20, 2004. The Chinese rocket will be next arriving two weeks later on December 3. That's quite accurate because it is already on its way. The Russian rocket will arrive around January 3, 2005. The second Russian rocket, the big one, is scheduled to leave on February 3, 2005 and meet on April 2, 2005. The Russians hope to speed up their preparation of the rocket but may not be able to. The differences are because the rockets will be traveling at different speeds and leaving at different times. The NASA rocket will pass the Chinese rocket and arrive first because it is traveling 5,000 miles per hour faster than the Chinese. Those speed differences are strictly because of design differences between the rockets."

Dr. Rivers announced the next name. "Ruth Mendez."

"Ruth Mendez, San Antonio Texas. How can you pinpoint the exact place and time when and where the asteroid will hit, or can you? Isn't your projection merely an educated guess? How sure are you of your calculations?"

Pat stood to answer. "The precise path or trajectory of any object moving in space can be determined from repeated measurements of the path already taken and the gravitational effects of any nearby bodies. The exact position, rotation, and movement of the Earth are also recorded and predicted. This data can be entered in computer simulations and used to determine the precise movement of any object in space relative to the Earth. The same can be said of time. The longer we can track the path of an object the more accurate will be our calculations. Data about the gravitational effects of nearby large objects like the planets, the moon, and the sun are also well established and considered in the calculations. The closer the object comes to the Earth the more accurate our measurements and path predictions will be even though the Earth's gravity will affect the path more the closer it is. By a month before closest approach, we should be able to pinpoint where the object will pass within a mile or two and the time almost to the second. These data come from pure math and physics. They are far more than intelligent guesses. Does that answer your question?"

The press briefing went on in an orderly fashion for the entire two hours scheduled. When Pat announced no more questions would be answered, a loud objection was made by those who weren't able to ask a question.

"We will announce another press briefing if and when things change. In the mean time, we will post any new information to our website www.nuasteroid.com. Thanks for your participation." Pat said in closing.

✷ Saturday, September 4, 2004 ✷

Jenny and Charlie were married in a simple ceremony at the church the Corso family attended in Port Washington on Long Island. The ceremony was attended by both families and numerous friends to the point of overflowing. A dozen or so stood at the rear as all seats were filled. Most of the Gemini group were their including Lani and Angus who brought their twin girls. A gala reception was held at the local Shriners hall. The reception was a very upbeat and happy party until someone brought up the Ohlmeg asteroid. During the ensuing discussion, Charlie made a simple, factual observation on the subject.

"It's ironic how concerned we are with what damage the Ghost star may do in about 26 years and now we find another serious menace that could wipe life off the earth within the next year."

Jenny bristled and almost shouted, "Charlie Botkin don't you say such things, especially on our wedding day."

"I'm sorry, hon. I wasn't thinking . . . "

Lani came to his defense with a smile. "Don't fault him, Jenny. It's the nature of the beast that is the scientist. His statement was a basic pronouncement of a typical scientific observation made and said with total objectivity. Emotionally it was unthinking, poorly timed, and ill considered, but it's how the scientific mind works. I had to get used to it."

Charlie stared sheepishly, like a puppy caught chewing up a good shoe. "I'm sorry, Jenny but Lani's right. I was only thinking objectively. I see now my comment was not the coolest thing to do or say here and now."

"I understand," Jenny said to Charlie. Then she turned and said, "Thanks, Lani. Now let's go back to partying."

The rest of the party went off splendidly. The next day the Charles Botkins left for a honeymoon in the Adirondacks.

✳ Friday, October 22, 2004 ✳

In late October, the NASA rocket was close enough to provide some clear, high-resolution photos of the object. They provided quite a surprise. Pat called his group together to discuss the photos. Dr. Rivers joined them.

Pat spoke. "It's obvious from the first photos that the object is a pile of various sized pieces held weakly together by their gravity. Earth's gravity will pull them apart more and more as they approach Earth much like Jupiter did to comet Shoemaker-Levy. Since we are not dealing with a single, solid object, the plan of using rockets to move it to a safe trajectory may prove to be impossible. All of the space agencies around the world are now working on that problem. We hope there will be some answers from the many meetings like this now going on all over the world."

Dr. Rivers addressed the group. "Well, gentlemen, old mother nature has demonstrated how different things can be from our predictions. Our object is now a two-hundred-mile long string or cloud of objects being pulled further apart by Earth's gravity. There is one large piece which is a bit more than half the mass of the entire object. The rest of the pieces stringing out behind the first, range from house-sized down to gains of sand. The object appears to be made up of equal parts of rock and ice. Some possible nickel and iron content might add to the mass of the objects. We can't be sure about their composition until we have more data. As Ohlmeg nears Earth, gravity will pull the objects apart faster and faster. I don't see any way rockets could be used to move the entire mass. Any ideas?"

Bernie Franks, "The smaller objects will burn up in the atmosphere and not be a problem, but what about the biggest chunks? How big are they and should we consider trying to move them?"

Dr. Rivers, "From the photo in your papers you can see at present there is one large piece and a number of smaller ones. The large one and some of the smaller ones are large enough to do considerable damage should they strike the earth. Also, they seem to contain some ice which could cause an explosion like the Tunguska event. The Russians are suggesting we accelerate our rockets into the larger object to break it up. A dozen of the smaller pieces are large enough to inflict considerable damage. That's far too many for three or four rockets to strike. Everyone is now working on simulations on that and other prospective steps to move them to a path that misses Earth."

Bernie, "Couldn't we position the noses of our rockets against those larger pieces and nudge them into a safe trajectory without damaging the rockets? That way we could use each rocket on several pieces and might even move them all. We won't need to move them far at their current distance."

Pat, "We're getting into an area where we lack expertise. NASA engineers could answer that question. We will give any viable suggestions to NASA since they and their counterparts in the other nations will be the ones making those decisions. Our job is to come up with feasible ideas and provide them to NASA. Their job is to decide what to do and then do it."

Jack, "Are any estimates of the weights of those objects available? That would be necessary if we were to consider pushing them with rockets."

Pat, "Bernie and I worked up some preliminary estimates. If any of the pieces contain significant amounts of nickel or iron, those pieces could be heavier than our estimates. The largest one is about half a million tons and has most of the mass of the entire object. One other large piece of about 250,000 tons is near the farthest back part of the cloud. The rest start at about 65,000 tons and grow smaller. The thirteen largest of the group consisted of pieces of 50,000 tons or more estimated weight. Even some of the smaller objects will be capable of considerable local damage. Most of the pieces of less than a ton will burn up or fall to earth with only small local damage we can live with. Of course there could be thousands of those."

They worked until quite late and came up with a number of possibilities that were all variations of the first ideas. These were forwarded to their NASA contact. Because of the time required to mount a viable space project, the only other proposals were one each by China, NASA, and the ESU. These were last minute shots to be designed to break up the largest objects if it could not be diverted. They would not be launched until five or six weeks before expected impact if they could be made ready in time.

✳ Sunday, January 2, 2005 ✳

Today, the Russians and Chinese announced they were working together to divert the largest piece of Ohlmeg. They planned to place both of their rockets against the solid object and fire them to change their trajectory away from an earth path. The Russian rocket, scheduled to arrive on the third would be maneuvered to work with the Chinese rocket to push the main part of Ohlmeg into a safer path. They said they planned to use the large Russian rocket to move the other large piece after it met Ohlmeg and changed vector direction to match its path. The Chinese suggested the NASA and ESU rockets be used to move some of the other dangerous pieces.

Early Sunday afternoon Pat got this news. He called an emergency meeting of the group at Arizona. "I hope those people know what they're doing," he told the group as soon as they were all present. "NASA has the most accurate tracking of Ohlmeg, far more accurate than either the Chinese or Russians. I contacted Greg Simmons at NASA/JPL NEOP and he told me they were not even consulted. He is trying to get in touch with them to find out what thrust vectors they are using so he can check them out for accuracy. Greg told me that even a slight error could be disastrous."

Jack, "And the Russians branded us 'cowboys' for some of our 'shoot-from-the-hip' actions in the past. Those actions mostly resulted in positive results. They forget to mention that. They only recall the ones that seemed like failures at the time. The fuel in all rockets is limited. Do they contain enough to move any of those bigger objects?"

Bernie, "I don't see how there could be enough power in any of those rockets to move even the pieces smaller than the largest one far enough to miss the earth. We must rely on NASA for that information and for anything else to do with the rockets for that matter. In fact, there's almost nothing we can do except offer ideas anyway. We have no real power."

Jack, "Yeah. All we can do is say, 'I told you so,' after the damage is done."

Dr. Rivers, "That's enough sour grapes, gentlemen. We are all in the same threatened boat with the Russians, the Chinese, the Europeans, and even the Africans. This is a menace from the natural forces of nature, not an enemy, and not from any nation or people on this earth. Let's consider they are rushing to put their rockets to use in trying to make corrections as early as possible. As do we, they know a small effort now would be equivalent to a large effort a month or more from now. Pat explained that NASA is asking for their force vectors to check against NASA's data on the crossing of the trajectories of the earth and Ohlmeg. I will be surprised if our Russian and Chinese friends are not grateful and accepting of NASA's help. Let's start calculating the forces and power needed to nudge objects the sizes of the various large parts of Ohlmeg into trajectories that will miss the earth. We have all the data we need to make those calculations. All we need to do is develop applicable computer simulations that can grind out tables our Russian and Chinese friends can use with their rockets. If we could ask them about the power available from their rockets, we could develop burn time tables they could use for maximum effect."

Pat, "Thank you Dr. Rivers for the refocus. We feel deservedly chastised and will try to make amends. Jack, you're the resident computer simulation expert. Will you develop a schedule of data input we can supply that will help you in the simulation you will develop? Remember, we will provide you with as much help as we can. Bernie and I will proceed with the collection and organization of the required data."

Jack, "Dr. Rivers, you were right on the mark. First, as the one most guilty of taking us off the track, I want to apologize. Second, the input data schedule is already forming in my mind and should be in final form by tomorrow morning. Third, I will start assembling the various parts of the simulation programs. For this I will rely on each of you for input into its design and will schedule meetings with the group to obtain your input. I cannot do this alone, but with your help we will develop an accurate and useful simulation that can be used to predict and manipulate the results of rocket forces on the Ohlmeg parts. I would like our first meeting to convene tomorrow morning at eight."

Pat, "We should discuss the project and decide who will do what right now. There are still a few useable hours in the day. Let's put them to good use."

❋ Tuesday, January 11, 2005 ❋

A vital meeting was held in the auditorium of the Astronomy department of the University of Arizona, Tucson, Tuesday, January 11, 2005. The head of the Astronomy department, Dr. Ann Rivers was presiding.

Dr. Rivers opened the meeting. "Welcome participants and observers, ladies and gentlemen, members of the media and those of you from our student body and the general public. Welcome on behalf of the University of Arizona and the Astronomy Department. I am Dr. Ann Rivers of the Astronomy Department, host of this momentous meeting. Among those here on the stage with me are a number of astronomers and scientists who will report on the progress of our combined efforts to avert a major collision with a dangerous asteroid. The following scientists will give reports on the numerous actions being taken to avert a tragedy of immense proportions: Pat Yamaguchi, Jack Kershaw, and Bernie Franks, astronomers of the University of Arizona; Greg Simmons of NASA/JPL NEOP from Lewis research in Cleveland; Gael Maures of the European Space Agency; Akim Sheronovich from the Russian space agency and Chin Tzu Yang of the Chinese Space Research Center. Each of the panelists will bring us all up to date on their part of our joint effort.

"There will be a question and answer session after all the presenters finish speaking. Please write your questions on the cards provided in your folders and pass them to one of the monitors stationed throughout the audience. You can't miss them. They are ones wearing those florescent orange vests.

"In the folder you will find resumes of all participants so in the interest of getting to the meat of our subject, we will dispense with lengthy introductions. Suffice to say each one has added to the success of our project. The degree of success will not be known until Ohlmeg passes. Our first presenter is Dr. Chin Tzu Yang of China. Dr. Chin."

"Thank you, Dr. Rivers. Before I begin my presentation, I want to thank the University of Arizona, NASA, and all of the American scientists and technicians for all the valuable help and for the free access to significant data given to us. Without this help, our efforts would fail. This has given the Chinese scientific community a new and friendlier view of our American counterparts. We hope this will grow into a new spirit of cooperation between us.

"Where are we in our joint efforts at this point? In cooperation with the Russians and with the thrust vector data provided by American scientists, we moved the major portion of Ohlmeg into a new path that should miss our planet. The latest tracking data indicates this. Of course, we can't be certain of this until June 15 so our wait will be a long one. Things still look quite good for a miss. In about three weeks, a Russian rocket of tremendous power will rendezvous with Ohlmeg. Should there be any concern about the remaining pieces, that rocket could be used to move the largest piece of Ohlmeg even further. Dr. Sheronovich will direct his comments to address this possibility.

"As Ohlmeg moved closer to Earth, the increasing gravitational pull changed what started as a single object into a cloud or train of objects several hundred miles in length. This will accelerate and expand as the cloud nears Earth and Earths gravitational effect increases. This will also make more difficult our efforts to find and move the largest and most dangerous pieces. The Arizona astronomers and Dr. Maures will explain what NASA and the ESA accomplished with their rockets. Please write any question on the cards provided. We reserved a rather long period of time for this question and answer period. Dr. Akim Sheronovich will now give you information on the Russian efforts. Dr. Sheronovich."

"Thank you Dr. Chin. First I must say how honored I am to be in a panel with such distinguished scientists. I also want to echo Dr. Chin's praise for the Americans and Europeans who displayed such unprecedented cooperation. I also want to thank Dr. Chin and his colleagues for the cooperation and close coordination used to move Ohlmeg with our rockets. Of course, to use some old American sayings, we are all in the same boat and will sink or swim together.

"The coordinated effort to move Ohlmeg with our rockets was indeed unprecedented. Nothing similar had ever been attempted by anyone before. The thrust vector analysis provided by the Americans was vital to our operation which was not possible without that data. And we weren't even smart enough to ask for it. It was simply thrust upon us. We too learned a valuable lesson about sharing information. Perhaps this will lead to a new spirit of cooperation for which the world will be far better off.

"According to all the data from numerous sources, the largest piece of Ohlmeg should now miss our planet by about twenty kilometers. That will be close enough for quite a show as it will pass through the thin air of the stratosphere and heat up enough to provide some major fireworks. With luck, that will be all to occur. We will continue to monitor its trajectory to be sure it will pass at a safe distance.

"As for the entire asteroid, the pieces closest to the earth were the first to separate and are accelerating faster then the rest. The closer any piece is to Earth, the faster it will accelerate. This will continue to spread the pieces into a longer and longer train or cloud.

"The Americans and Europeans will report on their efforts to move some of the dozen or so larger pieces strung out behind the main piece. Our large rocket will rendezvous with Ohlmeg in about three weeks. We may use that to move some of the smaller pieces, or perhaps tackle the major part should it become necessary. This is a large and powerful rocket and has a large supply of fuel on board. It could be kept in reserve, just in case.

"The next presenter is Dr. Pat Yamaguchi from the University of Arizona and one of the hosts for this meeting. Dr. Yamaguchi."

"What Dr. Sheronovich neglected to mention is that he was instrumental in choosing Arizona to host the meeting. As chairman of the site selection committee, he lobbied everyone on behalf of the University of Arizona. Maybe he wanted to enjoy some of our Arizona sunshine. All of us here are most appreciative of his efforts as well as honored to be chosen to be hosts. Thank you so much Dr. Sheronovich.

"Now, down to business. Our people in cooperation with all the others involved in this divergent effort including those from ESA, moved six of the ten largest objects after the main piece into what we believe is a far safer trajectory. We are hopeful we will be able to move the remaining four as well. Unfortunately we may run out of fuel before that is accomplished. Both the NASA rocket and the one from the ESA are low on fuel. We were scared stiff when the NASA rocket apparently pushed against and broke through a soft or weak spot in the last object. The nose of the rocket was damaged when it broke through and impacted hard rock beneath the soft or fragile surface. At first we were afraid the rocket was stuck, but some clever maneuvering using the reverse thrusters broke it free. We were able to use it again, even with a crushed nose. We were fortunate in that no needed component received more than cosmetic damage.

Now, Dr. Gael Maures of the European Space Agency will tell about their part in this mission. Dr. Maures."

"Thank you Dr. Yamaguchi. I want to thank all of the participants in this presentation and all of the rest of the scientists and technicians who worked tirelessly on this important effort, and are still at it. Many of their names are listed in the booklets and papers in the material left on each of your seats. There is still much to do as the danger has not gone away but only been lessened a bit, enough to avoid a major catastrophe, one far more damaging than any that has happened since man came to be on this planet.

As Dr. Yamaguchi mentioned, The NASA and ESA rockets moved six of the largest objects following the massive one moved by the Russian and Chinese rockets. Four huge ones remain on the original trajectory. The remaining rockets contain a lessened fuel capacity. The Russians sent a large and powerful rocket on its way with a large load of fuel. When it rendezvouses in about three weeks, we will know if and where it will be needed. Decisions of where and when will not be made until just before the Russian rocket arrives. Since it's their rocket, Dr. Sheronovich and his organization will decide how to use it after a thorough discussion. Experiencing the unprecedented and friendly cooperation of all of us in this together, I assure everyone that the best possible solutions will be used.

"Now, for the question and answer portion of this meeting I return the podium back to Dr. Rivers."

"I must say we may not be able to answer some of your questions." Dr. Rivers began. "You will probably hear we can't answer now and may not be able to until June 15. New information will be released to the news media as soon as we learn anything. We request the media not speculate but report only the facts as they are released. Then the public will be well informed and less likely to panic. We will note and report on any false rumors appearing.

Lack of media speculation, as difficult as that may seem, is of paramount importance. Keep the populace well informed with facts with no guesses or speculation and they will trust us all. Now we will receive and try to answer your questions."

The Question and answer session went on for two hours with many types of questions not all of which were the panel able to answer. The "we don't know" answer to most of those unanswerable questions was accepted. The media were cooperative and asked no major speculative questions. After the meeting adjourned, glowing reports appeared in the media about the meeting and all of the participants.

✳ Wednesday, February 16, 2005 ✳

Pat Yamaguchi was interviewed by national TV about the effort to move Ohlmeg to a safe trajectory. Pete Arthur asked him, "Dr. Yamaguchi, will you give us the latest on where Ohlmeg is and how close it will come to the earth?"

"The international meeting in Tucson occurred five weeks ago. Since then, both the NASA and ESA rockets ran out of fuel while moving the seventh and eighth objects. The Russians used their big rocket to move the last two of those large enough to be dangerous and then spent the rest of their fuel moving the second largest piece farther away from an earth intersecting trajectory. All five of the rockets are now a few more small pieces of the still expanding cloud of objects accelerating toward the earth. Ohlmeg has been stretched and dispersed by gravity into a cloud of objects now about ten thousand miles long. By the time Ohlmeg reaches Earth, the cloud will be twice that length. In June when the cloud begins to arrive we may begin to learn for sure what is going to happen."

During the following months, Dr. Pat Yamaguchi gradually became the media's goto spokesperson for the community of astronomers and in particular, those following the progress of Ohlmeg.

19

Preparations for the trip to Tibet
✳ Monday, May, 16, 2005 ✳

Dr. Yamaguchi was again interviewed on TV. Pete Arthur asked him, "Doctor, Ohlmeg is supposed to arrive over Tibet at around seven in the morning on Wednesday, June 15. Is that still the case?"

"Nothing has happened to change the predicted arrival time and place. Even at twenty-thousand-miles long, the cloud of objects will take no more than an hour to race past the earth. A lot of the smaller pieces will impact earth or come into the atmosphere. A spectacular meteor shower will occur from out over the Pacific ocean east of China to the Tibetan plateau. These meteors will streak parallel to the surface. We predict most of the large, dangerous pieces will pass ten to fifty miles above the earth and not impact the surface. This is because of the efforts of several nations whose rockets moved the largest pieces into a safer trajectory. Several pieces of 50,000 tons or less may come close enough to strike the surface in western China or Tibet. About fifteen of these objects are capable of doing catastrophic damage should they strike the surface or explode in the air like the Tunguska event of 1908."

"Is there any danger for the US?"

"If Ohlmeg arrived twelve hours later, it would impact the US. For Americans and everyone on the planet except the Chinese and Tibetans, the arrival time is quite definite and predictable."

"How can you be so sure of when and where these asteroids will arrive?"

"To an astronomer it is quite simple. Any object moving in space has a definite and definable path or trajectory. That path is affected only by gravity as it moves in the vacuum of space. The force of gravity of all objects with mass is proportional to the inverse square of the distance between it and any other objects with mass. Since gravity is a rather weak force, the effects of objects much smaller than an object the size of a moon, a planet, a star, or a galaxy can almost be neglected in any calculation. The rotation and position of the earth are also known quite well. This makes calculation of the time and path of Ohlmeg an easy task for modern high speed computers. The problem is that Ohlmeg is not a single object but an ill-defined cloud of objects of many sizes spread over a bit more than ten thousand miles by Earth's gravity. By the time it passes, that same gravity will accelerate the entire cloud of objects to a velocity of forty-five thousand miles per hour relative to the earth. The entire cloud will pass by or intersect our planet during a period of about thirty minutes. We hope it will pass by with little harm done, but the chances are some of the objects will strike the earth."

"I understand rescue and health care workers from all over the world are already in or on their way to China to help in case they are needed. A number of scientists are also going to record any major events. Are any of your people from the University of Arizona going?"

"Our entire staff knows of and applauds the worldwide rescue and health care efforts. Some of the rescue and medical people here at the university are already on their way to China. Four astronomers and five technicians from our astronomy department are leaving tomorrow on a research mission. I am privileged to be among those on the mission. Our goal is the Tibetan plateau where we hope to observe and record what should be an amazing meteor shower. The Chinese were most helpful in granting us immediate permission. They will provide guides, technical assistance and transportation into what is a rather remote and mountainous region of Tibet."

The interview continued for the entire thirty minutes of the program and covered some of the details of their mission. At the end Pete said, "That's a long trip and I hope a safe one. We'd love for you to come for another interview after you return."

"Thank you, Pete. I'm certain it can be arranged."

Pat left for some hurried final preparations and packing for the long trip.

✳ Thursday, May 19, 2005 ✳

Preparations for a trip and research effort like this ordinarily take several months, or even years to collect all the required instruments, cameras, tools and computers, and pack them up for shipment. Knowing what was coming, Dr. Rivers authorized much of the preparations months ago without knowing for certain if they would be able to go. When word came late in May, there was much elation in the astronomy department. When Dr. Rivers announced she was sending the three top astronomers, Pat Yamaguchi, Jack Kershaw, and Bernie Franks, but that she was staying behind, she almost had a revolution.

"If you're not going, we're not going," the three echoed in unison.

"One of the biggest and most exciting astronomical events in history and you think we would let you miss it?" Jack said. "Not a chance, so pack your stuff."

"It's been years since I went out into the field on a project. Someone's got to stay here and mind the store."

Bernie chimed in. "The mark of a strong leader is having trained subordinates to take over in a heartbeat. And you, dear leader, are a good one. You have capable people to step in while you're away, so you're going, no argument."

The three stood like a wall, arms crossed and defiant.

"I guess if you put it that way I have no choice but to go with you."

The three cheered their leader whom they liked and respected.

Dr. Rivers smiled. "Now I have a lot of work to do. I won't sleep much for the next six weeks."

Pat said, "We're all faced with this problem. We'll be about forty hours on planes to Lhasa then another forty hours before we reach our research site in the Nyainqêntanglha Mountains. We can catch up on sleep then."

Bernie rolled his eyes. "We may be able to sleep some during the first flights, but after Beijing I doubt we'll be able to sleep much. The last ten miles from Yangbajain to the plateau where we will set up our observation camp will be on horseback. Are you all prepared?"

"I hope the horses and guides will be at the start point when our trucks arrive at the base pick up site." Jack sounded worried as he spoke.

Dr. Rivers chided, "Come on guys, Our Chinese friends promised us all would be as they said. They are so pleased with the help we gave them, I'm sure they will go all out to make our trip and stay as pleasant as possible. Let's not second guess them. Several of their astronomers will be joining us as well. That's quite good insurance. I anticipate a rather pleasant experience, providing the big Ohlmeg meteors don't come too close."

Pat said, "Most of the meteors will burn up in the atmosphere because of the flat trajectory. We will only be endangered by the large pieces the size of busses or houses. There aren't many of those."

The packing and inventorying of all their equipment took every moment they could spare. Everything except personal luggage was packed securely in a shipping container designed to fit into the cargo hold of the commercial aircraft. The container would remain intact all the way to Lhasa where it would be transferred to a truck and taken to where it would all be unpacked and then repacked on horses for the last ten miles of the trip. As it was, a few small items, last minute additions, were packed in their luggage.

20

The Long Trip to the Tibetan Highlands
✳ Tuesday, May 31, 2005 ✳

Tuesday evening they boarded USAir flight 2888 to Los Angeles. Early Wednesday they transferred to an Air China Boeing 777-300 for the flight to Beijing and Lhasa. The flight left Los Angeles at 1:40 am.

Bernie provided the happy message. "OK troops, we're on this plane until ten after midnight tomorrow. Of course, that's only 15 hours from now so sleep fast, all of you."

"Yeah, and be prepared for major jet lag. By the time we reach our destination our biological clocks will be half a day behind local time. Be prepared for a major biological adjustment. I plan to stay up all night when we'll be working and sleep all day."

Dr. Rivers said, "Jack, you forget we will be working in the daylight. The first objects should arrive around seven in the morning and the last will pass no more than an hour later."

"Damn, I did forget. Guess I'd better scratch that plan."

Pat said, "Two weeks from now when Ohlmeg arrives, our biological clocks will be completely reset. I wouldn't worry about it. With less than an hour of action to collect all our data, we'll be doing so much we'll sleep little anyway."

Bernie said, "Several days will be required to set up all of our recording equipment for the hour of action. We will need far more time to set up and tear down than to collect the data. Which reminds me, I hope our two technicians who will go ahead with the truck will pack with care all our stuff on those horses."

169

Jack said, "Bernie, you are such a worry wart. With Fred and Ramon directing things, those horses will be loaded and half way up the mountain before we are at start of the trail. They were both ranch hands before they were trained as technicians for our instruments. That's why they were chosen for this trip, double duty. Where are they? They weren't on the American flight here with us."

"Right here, Jack," a voice said from behind him. The voice was Ramon's. He, Fred, Angie, Karen, and Talbot were seated in the two rows behind them. "We took an earlier flight so we could pick up some stuff we couldn't find in Tucson."

With a chuckle Dr. Rivers said, "Don't tell them what you got. Let them worry a bit when we are on the plateau to set up our instruments."

Ramon said, "OK, boss. Mum's the word."

Bernie said, "What's going on here? Why would we be worrying?"

"Just wait. You'll find out soon enough," Dr. Rivers said with a smirk on her face.

With her singular knack for keeping a secret, it would do no good to try to work it out of her. They would wait—and wonder.

The plane took off on time and soon they were all sleeping.

✳   Thursday, June 2, 2005   ✳

After a two-hour, twenty-minute layover in Beijing airport, they took off at 7:40 a.m. for Lhasa. They arrived on time in Lhasa at 12:15 Thursday afternoon. They checked in at a hotel near the airport, all but Fred and Ramon. A car was waiting for them to whisk them off to the horses. They followed the truck with the shipping container north out of Lhasa.

They stayed two nights in the modern hotel where the service and food were both excellent. Friday, our Tibetan guide took us on a walking tour of Lhasa. The weather was wonderful, in the seventies and clear. Our guide was well informed, interesting and entertaining. He grew up and lived all his life in Lhasa.

"Enjoy the food and amenities while you can. They won't last long," Dr. Rivers announced when we arrived back at the hotel. "While we're up on the plateau, we'll be sleeping in tents and eating military type MREs for the several weeks we'll be on the plateau. Don't forget, because of the altitude you may be short of breath with even minor exertion Oh, and no showers will be available so be prepared to rough it. There will be no medical personnel with us, so be careful not to injure yourselves or others. It's a minimum 10 hour trip on horseback plus three hours by bus to the nearest hospital."

✳ Saturday, June 4, 2005, 4:30 a.m. ✳

They left Lhasa in a small bus for the trip to Yangbajain and then the base pickup point. They took an often bumpy, 150 mile, four hour drive over mountain roads that were narrow and precarious. The pickup point was a small level spot where the road came to an abrupt halt at a steep and narrow valley. Two dozen horses and several guides and porters are waiting. They will soon pack our luggage on several of the horses. Everywhere we looked, the surrounding mountains seemed to go straight up. A few minutes after they stepped out onto the pavement, the bus turned and disappeared down the road we traveled to get there .

Watching the bus leave, Bernie said, "Well, there goes our last connection to civilization."

"I don't know about the rest of you, but I'm gonna put on some cold weather gear," Pat said opening his luggage while the porters waited to load the pack animals.

"Yeah, good idea Pat," Jack said "it's down to about forty degrees already and we're headed up quite a bit higher. I understand the temperature drops down to near zero at night up on the plateau where we're headed. I hope we brought enough warm clothing."

"Yeah, what's with the guides? They don't seem to be wearing heavy clothing."

Dr. Rivers looked at Bernie. "You forget, they live here year 'round. It's summertime to them, the hottest part of the year. How'd you like to be here in January?".

"Brrrr! No thanks."

The lead guide, the only one who spoke English came over. "You are the last. Please climb on your horses quickly. We must be on the plateau before dark. The climb will take 10 hours in the absence of any problems or delays."

He and the others helped everyone mount the shaggy, short legged Tibetan horses that seemed almost too small. When pat asked the guide about them, he laughed.

"Tibetan ponies are strong in spite of their size. Notice their large chests and hindquarters. They were bred from wild stock to work high in the mountains in all kinds of weather. Their short, sturdy legs make them quite sure footed and together with their shaggy coat and heavy body, help them conserve heat in the cold. Don't worry, they will carry us up to the plateau."

"I wasn't worried, just curious. Thanks for the information."

He grinned. "You'll also notice that most of the Tibetan people are built with compact, short bodies and large chests. It's an evolutionary adaptation to the cold and altitude."

"I'm Pat Yamaguchi. What is your name?"

"Paljor Dorje. Isn't your name Japanese?"

"Yes, but I am a fifth generation American. You seem quite an educated man. How did you become a guide? Your speech seems almost American."

He laughed. "I graduated from Stanford University in your state of California. I like your country, especially the personal freedom. I worked in Palo Alto for five years after I graduated. Then I decided to come home. I have been a guide here for fifteen years. Being a guide is a desired and honorable profession."

"You are good at it. Getting us packed, mounted, and on our way so quickly was an accomplishment."

"Thank you, but the real expert is the man up on the lead horse. His name is Kunchen and he has been guiding people up into these mountains for almost forty years. He has never lost a single passenger."

"Impressive."

"I understand you are scientists here to study the coming meteor shower. We know little about the meteors. All we know is that great danger threatens us from a massive meteor that could strike nearby. How much danger will they pose?"

There is danger all right but not a lot for any one person. It's about an equal chance as being struck by lightning in the states. Does that happen often in Tibet?"

"Lightning is frequent and dangerous here. People are struck too."

"Well, that's a possibility about equal to being struck by one of the meteors that are not completely consumed by passing through the atmosphere. Of course, should a large object of hundreds of tons strike, the resulting explosion could cause untold damage and extensive injury and loss of life if it struck a populated area."

"Well, you don't seem too worried so I won't worry either. Thanks for the information. Now I am going to go up front and help Kunchen. I'd like to talk with you more, later."

"Stop by any time."

They followed a small stream up its valley. The trail wound a tortuous path between sloping cliffs on both sides of the stream. The worn floor of a path beside the stream gave evidence this was a well-used route. Right before noon we arrived at a small lake in a rather flat area where we climbed down from our horses. Those horses went directly to the lake for a drink. Paljor announced a meal would be served in a few minutes. The break was a welcome respite from the hours on horseback. All seven of us sat on the ground on a carpet Paljor and several porters rolled out for us. The carpet was chair, couch, and table for our meal and surprisingly comfortable. As soon as we finished eating, the carpet was rolled up and Paljor urged us to mount our horses. We stopped for only twenty minutes.

"We made good time so far, but the most difficult part of the trail lies ahead," Paljor warned. "Your camp is only about four miles away, but some places are quite steep. Be sure to take a good hold on the saddle horn when your horse is struggling up a steep incline. The horses never fall, but a few careless riders have. A fall from a horse in this rocky terrain could cause a serious injury. That's the reason for the high back and front of our saddles, to keep the rider from falling off when the horse climbs."

Within a few hundred yards we learned what Paljor was talking about. We rounded a bend in the stream bed and came upon what looked like an insurmountable wall of rock. Our horses reared back and climbed up the wall while we grabbed the saddle horn and held on. As the trail leveled out for a hundred feet or so I shouted to Paljor, "I see what you mean. That was quite a climb."

He turned, grinned and said, "That's a small one. We will be climbing several others much bigger before we reach the plateau."

A number of groans expressed the group's feelings. The air was getting a bit colder and the wind was picking up. This was not a pleasure jaunt.

Pat commented, "It's getting a lot windier as we climb higher."

"Wait until you reach the camp." Paljor said. "It will be even windier on the plateau. The mountain winds are always blowing. This time of year they are mild compared to winter."

"Paljor, you're full of encouraging comments."

"A kilometer ahead we will be making the longest climb of the journey. After that the trail is on the plateau and quite level for the last two kilometers to camp."

"Thanks, Paljor." Pat said. "You are so encouraging."

"Doctor, you and your group are doing quite well. We are moving at a steady pace and should reach camp in a little more than an hour, well before dark. We should have plenty of time to get comfortable before night falls."

✳   ✳   ✳

The last climb was quite an ordeal. Several times Pat thought his horse wasn't going to make it, but he did. Then they crested the climb to find a plateau covered with snow. The path was packed snow, easy to follow. They could see the colored dots of the camp tents against the white snow while still more than a kilometer away. Clouds filled the sky so bright sunlight on the white snow did not pose any problems.

By the time they reached the camp the time was 5:30. They were half an hour early. Pat mentioned this to Paljor.

"We made good time up the mountain. Our little horses performed like champions and no one fell off. Now I must help the others unload your supplies and help set up everything. Cloudy skies mean snow will probably fall tonight. We will be well prepared before the snow starts."

After Paljor left, our five technicians brought four large corrugated boxes and set them down in front of our tents. Ramon opened the first box and asked, "Do you know what is in these boxes?"

No one answered, but all of the technicians were smiling. Ramon continued.

"How cold will it be tonight?"

Jack said, "Zero?"

"It's about freezing right now, zero° Centigrade and 32° Fahrenheit. Are you all comfortable in this wind?"

Pat was a bit chilly and said, "Now that you mention it, I do feel a little chilly. How low will the temperature go tonight?"

Ramon smirked. "According to our guides the temperature will drop to minus 25° Centigrade. That's minus 13° Fahrenheit and is very cold. A strong wind is also going to blow. Do you think your cold weather gear will keep you warm?"

The three male astronomers looked a bit unnerved. Jack asked, "OK guys, we are now freezing our butts off. What's in those boxes?"

Ramon grinned as he said, "Your boss, Dr. Rivers asked us to go to an outfitter in LA who specializes in the latest in cold weather gear. That's why we flew in earlier, before you left. In the boxes you will find a complete outfit of the latest in cold weather clothing technology for each of us, names attached. In the boxes are underwear, pants, shirts, jackets, socks, gloves, and boots. Those clothes will keep you warm down to minus 60° in any wind we might encounter. They are light weight and not as restrictive of movement as what you are now wearing. These clothes will make moving about and doing our work much easier. That's not all. You will also find a special sleeping bag with equivalent specs to the clothing. We'll be sleeping in these tents on cots off the ground. These bags are the only ones guaranteed to keep us warm, even if our tents blow away. Oh yes, both the clothing and sleeping bags are equipped with special liners that absorb perspiration. At night when you are in the sleeping bag, the liners from your clothing will be drying out and during the day, the same for the sleeping bags."

Pat said, "I could not believe it. I never gave the cold a thought. I assumed our heavy outer clothing would do the job and whatever was provided for sleeping would be adequate."

Dr. Rivers said, "Well, we did provide what was needed. Now everyone, find your bag of clothes, pick up one of the sleeping bags, head for your tents and change into them. Roll call and inspection will be in front of my tent in thirty minutes. Now move."

"Yes boss" came from someone who knew Dr. Rivers did not like being called, boss. She ignored the comment.

✳ Saturday, June 4, 2005, 6:30 p.m. ✳

At six-thirty, everyone was standing in front of Dr. River's tent in the new outfits. For easy identification at a distance, the astronomers wore bright green and the technicians wore bright orange. The outfits were light weight, easy to move in, and comfortable. We could not believe such light weight clothing could be so warm in the falling temperatures. The two Chinese astronomers were wearing, what else—red.

Dr. Rivers spoke. "Remember, there are no showers or bathing facilities of any kind here. In the bag with your clothing is a toiletries case and a package of dri-shower cloths. These cloths are what their name says, a dry shower. Used once a day they should keep us clean and odor free while we're here. I understand most if not all of the men plan to let their beards grow to simplify the problem of shaving.

"Our food will consist of eight different nutritious, vacuum dried meals as well as some special meals for Miss Von Dyche who is a vegan. All we need do is add water and let the package stand for about twenty minutes. The mess tent is heated so our meals will not freeze while they are hydrating. As soon as we finish eating, we will call an organizational meeting in the mess tent which will be our place for meetings of all kinds. One word of warning, all of our equipment is to be set up, tested and operational by two days before the meteors will begin arriving. I doubt any early visitors will show up, but we can't be sure so let's be prepared. One more thing. All trash and waste materials must be placed into the recycle or trash containers. We promised to leave no evidence of our having been here. Let's be good stewards and careful to keep that promise. Now, let's head for the mess tent where those wonderful food packets await."

21

Setting up the Observation Station
✳ Wednesday, June 8, 2005, 8:00 p.m. ✳

Setting up all of our equipment took us several days to complete. The portable seismometers gave us fits. Attaching the sensors to the rocky ground was very difficult. We drilled holes in the rock and secured the sensors. Setting them up and getting them calibrated was time consuming. That took a lot of effort but was accomplished and they were all set for any quakes. The seismometers were borrowed from the geology department and we received only rudimentary instructions as to their mounting and use. Angie used them on other field trips so she assumed responsibility for their installation and use. By Monday, June 13 everything was checked out and operational including the short wave radio, our only link to the outside world.

At the morning meeting, Dr. Rivers expressed her gratitude. "I am delighted and impressed by everyone's effort. We are completely ready for the arrival of what ever comes our way, astronomically that is. We placed fourteen high speed cameras to cover the entire sky. Seven are automatic and will start running with the slightest change in sky radiation. Even the smallest meteor flash will be recorded. Seven are manual and will be operated by our camera experts in the orange jackets. The cameras use synchronized audio as we expect sonic booms to accompany some of the larger objects.

"All of our lighting and electronics are powered by two wind generators. A third one is available in reserve. The winds up here are quite fierce so plenty of electrical power will be available to run the equipment and keep the batteries charged. In fact, one generator provides enough power to run everything, The second is only on as a backup should the first one fail. All we can do now is watch over things and pray for clear skies. Today would be perfect, not a cloud in the sky. Let's hope the clear sky stays. Any questions?"

Jack asked, "When we can expect the first meteors to show up? Sitting here waiting for something to happen for two days will drive me crazy."

I answered. "The object appeared to be a single cohesive mass when first discovered more than a year ago. We cannot be sure when the earth's gravity started pulling it apart, but it did. The object was described as a large pile of various sized rocks and ice, held weakly together by gravity. Once the earth's gravity overcame that of the object, it began to pull apart. Since only the largest pieces were visible to our telescopes, a number of smaller pieces could have been separating for a long time, maybe as long as a year. The pieces closest to the earth were the first to separate and would accelerate slightly faster then the rest. The cloud of objects surrounding the large pieces has stretched out to hundreds of thousands of miles or more. We don't know. That's why we wanted to be set up two days before the date the bulk of the object will pass. It's speed approaching Earth has reached 45,000 miles per hour. The first objects would need to be a million miles in front of the main body to arrive much before seven a.m. Tomorrow. It is pure guesswork, and don't hold me to it, but I doubt we will see any activity from the parts of Ohlmeg until some time Wednesday morning."

I no sooner said those words when one of the telescope cameras signaled a photo of something had been taken. The video recording in the flash drive of the telescope camera was removed and brought to the computer on the table in front of us.

Talbot loaded the data into the laptop and brought up the video. "What is showing, Talbot? That's your baby. What showed up?" I asked.

After checking out the laptop, Talbot reported, "It was a bright meteor from the north and was not part of Ohlmeg. My guess is we will see these every few minutes unless we raise the intensity warning threshold. Dr. Rivers, what do you think? The settings on all of the automatic cameras are quite low. Should we raise them up?"

"Let's wait for a while and see if we need to raise them. If too many to handle come in, we can always change them then. I don't want to miss the first ones coming from due east. Those will most likely be from Ohlmeg."

22

The Meteor Shower begins
✳ Wednesday, June 15, 2005, 4:00 a.m. ✳

About four Wednesday morning, Talbot awakened everyone. "Hey gang, up and at 'em. Our meteors should begin arriving in a couple of hours and we need everyone alert and at their posts when that happens. The whole event will be over in about half an hour so don't blink or you'll miss it. Let's go."

Hearing those words I jumped out of my sleeping bag, quickly got into my clothes and headed outside. Within minutes everyone was out in the meal tent grabbing coffee and rolls before heading to their posts and checking their equipment.

About quarter of six Talbot warned us, "A few real ones moving west were bright enough to trigger the warning. The second one came about two minutes after the first. My guess is those are the first arrivals of Ohlmeg. A number of false alarms showed earlier before the two showed up moving west. They were the only ones with the proper trajectory . . . Come on everyone, the show has begun. We will soon be busy with lots of work to do."

Ten minutes later a bright meteor roared completely across the sky and disappeared beyond the mountains to the west. We then heard the sonic boom.

"That one was about a hundred pounds." Jack Kershaw explained. "Only one boom and not very loud. I'll wager we'll hear a lot louder ones before morning is over."

By six fifteen everyone was watching meteors fly west arriving mere seconds apart, many followed by sonic booms. Occasionally one would fly clear across the sky and disappear over the horizon. A full-blown meteor shower was well underway, and our cameras were recording everything. So far none of these were big enough to reach the earth but burned up in the atmosphere. The meteors were entering the atmosphere tangent to the surface. They were all traveling horizontally and burning up miles high. We did not hear another sonic boom. Apparently they were all too small and too high to be heard.

Dr. Rivers began issuing orders. "Listen up everyone. We've enjoyed the show for a while, but we do have much work to do. You each have your assigned duties and a schedule for operating the equipment. Be sure to check out each of the manual cameras so they will be ready to start when they are supposed to. If you find an idle moment, check your assigned instruments and make sure they are working as they should be. We will only have one shot at this rare phenomenon and we don't want to miss anything. Talbot will be monitoring the automatic cameras to make sure they are operating as they should be. Also, be prepared for the unexpected. A meteor strike within our camp is not likely, but could happen. We've had several drills on that possibility so don't forget what we trained to do.

"Everyone please understand, this mission may be quite dangerous. I will repeat some facts for you. From our tracking of Ohlmeg with the cameras on NASA's rocket we don't anticipate any of the big pieces arriving much before seven. That's only half an hour from right now. The largest part, the large first piece, should pass through the atmosphere fifteen miles above the surface just before seven. This huge object will cause some fireworks and two sonic booms, so we will know for certain when it goes past. Most of the largest pieces will follow soon after and in near identical trajectories. The unknowns include all of the pieces smaller than the largest thirteen and the second largest piece trailing behind the rest. They will be in or close to their original trajectory. Thousands of pieces large enough to wipe out this entire mission site exist. One strike here could be a disaster. The second largest piece is our main concern since the rockets we used did not move it far. This piece will come much closer to the surface and could even impact it. The consequences of that impact are unknown, but will be devastating if it hits in an inhabited area. This large object will arrive no more than half an hour after the first large one. If no strikes hit after 7:30 you can be assured the danger of serious damage has passed. I will heave a sigh of relief when the time arrives.

"If you must leave your station for anything, notify your alternate so your job will be covered. As I said before, consider the event started so no breaks until it's over. And be careful! We don't have any spare bodies so try not to hurt yourselves or anyone else. We went over all of the specifics numerous times so I won't mention any more here and now. We are blessed with a cloudless sky for the moment. Let's hope it stays that way. Our weather guru says we will have clear skies for the next hour or so. I hope he's right."

With a rumble of conversations, everyone went about his or her duties. I checked out two cameras while keeping a weather eye toward the western sky. Anticipation stilled all conversation and all eyes were watching the sky. Except for the wind sound, it was dead quiet.

"There it is!" someone shouted.

The awesome sight grew in brightness from a concentrated circle of sparks to an object appearing larger than a full moon glowing and brightening to almost as bright as the sun. At 45,000 miles per hour it soon disappeared over the western horizon. The huge meteor took less than fifteen seconds to traverse the entire sky from east to west. After it disappeared, the first of two loud sonic booms echoed and reverberated through the mountains like a continuous blast of thunder. The boom was felt as much as heard. The second boom followed less than a second later. This was followed by a dying roar as the meteor's flaming trail slowly dissipated.

No more than a minute after the meteor disappeared a pair of smaller ones flew across the sky much closer to the surface. Though they were much smaller, their closeness to the surface resulted in their booms being sharper and as loud. As they reached the eastern horizon, a large bright flash occurred. One of the objects struck a mountain in the Himalayas. That would register on the seismometers.

These same scenarios kept repeating, always on similar trajectories. At one time four large meteors were visible at once, each with its accompanying sonic booms. Among the several dozen dangerous meteors that flew across the sky during the shower were several that struck mountains in the Himalayas emitting brilliant flashes. At about twenty-five after seven the sky was quiet for a few minutes. Then the second largest piece came in. This one was much closer to the surface than the first as it appeared much larger even though it was smaller in size. The sharp and powerful twin sonic booms struck us while the meteor was still in sight. Its disappearance behind the mountains south of us was followed by a huge blinding flash that dissipated quite slowly. We could see fiery pieces flying high above the mountains to our south. The last piece of Ohlmeg struck the earth with the force equivalent of 10 megatons or about 150 times the force of the atomic bomb that destroyed Hiroshima.

Everyone was awe struck into silence realizing there was now a fresh crater about a kilometer wide and 250 meters deep the other side of the mountain where several villages and one city were situated. That's the size of the Berringer crater in Arizona which was made by an object about equal in size to this one.

Angie was the first to break the silence. "What is the name of that city on the other side of the mountain and what is its population?"

I said, "Shigatse! I believe the city has close to 90,000 inhabitants. That's what I remember from reading about the area we were going to visit. Shigatse is the second largest city in Tibet."

Fred Anglin spoke up. "Unless my sense of direction is off or I don't remember the maps I studied about this area, Shigatse is quite a bit farther west than where that meteor hit. The meteor must have created devastation wherever it struck. I am also wondering about the damage those other meteors caused when they hit the mountains and if any people were on those mountains?"

A sudden brilliant flash of light came from beyond the mountain ridge to our immediate south. This was followed by the sound of an explosion about thirty seconds later. Both came from the direction of our recent trek up to the plateau.

"Don't like that one bit." Dr. Rivers said, a worried expression on her face. "I hope that one didn't damage our way out of here. It looked to me like it hit right where we climbed up to our base here. Where is Paljor our guide? Maybe we should send a team to investigate our route back. Paljor!"

Fred said, "He's over by where the horses are. I'll go get him."

On their way to join Dr. Rivers, Paljor said, "I share your concern. I wondered about our route back when I saw that flash. It seemed to be close to our trail. I already asked Kunchen to ready horses for a trip back to see if our trail is still intact. "

When they joined Dr. Rivers, Fred said, "Paljor's on the ball. He's already preparing for a trip back down to see if the trail's still useable."

Dr. Rivers said, "That's quite a trip. How long do you think it will take to go down and come back?"

"Kunchen and I will make the trip. He's packing the horses right now. We'll stay overnight and return tomorrow. We'll use our radios to report to you what we find, unless we're out of range. These mountains sometimes make radios like ours useless for several reasons."

"Don't chance anything." Dr. Rivers warned. "If the trail is blocked or gone, come right back. The rest of us would be hard pressed without you and Kunchen."

"Don't worry, Doctor. We haven't lost a single person for many years and we plan not to lose one now. Now, if you will excuse me, I want to help Kunchen so we can leave as soon as possible. It's morning so we should be able to start back today while it is still light. Once we are back on the plateau, our radios will work. We plan to camp overnight right where the trail reaches the plateau."

"Safe travels, Paljor, and keep us posted. We still have lots to do here before we can pack up to leave. We'll all be anxious to learn what you find."

With that, Paljor turned and headed back to the horses. Half an hour later we watched the two men on horseback ride south across the plateau. It was eight o'clock.

✻   8:00 a.m.   ✻

No new meteors appeared for half an hour so at eight thirty Dr. Rivers and I decided to call a meeting in the mess tent. Our entire Arizona group and the two Chinese astronomers gathered in the tent. We did not call the Tibetan guides and their packers since they did not speak any English. Dr. Rivers asked me to address the group regarding our brief discussion of our revised plans in case our way down from the plateau was blocked or impassable.

"Dr. Rivers and I briefly discussed a plan in case our route back is blocked. I'll relate our discussion and ask for any suggestions from the group. Talbot, we want you to try to radio our one contact in Lhasa with the short wave. Tell him we are OK but are concerned about our return route down from the plateau. Ask if they learned anything about damage caused by the major meteor impacts. Then see whom else you can contact with the short wave. We'd like to learn about the other strikes and of course the huge one from that last large piece of Ohlmeg. All those strikes in the Himalayas were in remote regions so news may be a long time coming. Shigatse is another story. See if you can contact anyone in Shigatse. Some of the Chinese may speak English and can tell us of any damage from the big hit."

Talbot said, "Our man Sheng Su in Lhasa has been trying to reach us ever since the big one hit. I turned on the radio a few minutes ago and answered his call. He was relieved to hear my voice. Then he told me that the entire Yarlung Zangbo River valley above Ranbo and Gyangze was cut off from power and telephone lines. That includes the city of Shigatse. The meteor probably destroyed dams and power stations between Gyangze and Shigatse. He says news is unreliable and no one seems to have the exact location where the meteor struck or how much damage it did. The Chinese officials in Lhasa are trying to fly a reconnaissance plane over the area to give a report, but as yet there is no word. Apparently they even lost radio communication."

"That doesn't sound good. Any other news he offered?"

"He says almost no reports are coming out of the area where the meteors hit. My guess is there was a lot of damage with power and communications systems out of working order. News from the area is slow at best when things are normal. With this catastrophic incident we may not hear for a long time and I don't mean hours, I mean days. Oh yes, all commercial flights into or out of the area are cancelled. Apparently the officials don't know what happened and won't chance any flights. The railroads stopped running and the highways are blocked. The blast did a lot of damage, on a huge scale."

Then I remembered. "The seismometers. Talbot, I'm going to check the seismometers to see what they can tell us."

I needed about fifteen minutes to run a printout from the seismometers. I showed the printout to the group.

"Look at this. Those first four indications must be the meteors striking the Himalayas. Look at the latest. It's much larger and you can see numerous others overlapping each other. Those must be earthquakes triggered by the massive impact. I never considered that. I wish we had someone here who could interpret these for us. Never thought to bring a geologist."

✳   7:30 p.m.   ✳

It was almost dark when Talbot who had been monitoring our radio shouted, "It's Paljor. He's back on the plateau. Wait, let me hear his entire report. Then I can tell you all."

We waited impatiently as Talbot talked to Paljor on the radio.

Talbot reported. "He says the trail to where we mounted the horses was not damaged. . . . Here's the bad news. Some of the road to the trail base from Yangbajain has been damaged and is impassable. When the meteor hit, a bus was at the base to pick up another group at the trail head. After seeing the explosion, the driver drove back down and found the road was gone about two kilometers back. He drove back to the trail head and parked the bus. He has been trying unsuccessfully for radio contact with his base of operations for many hours when Paljor and Kunchen rode in. He was glad to see them. OK, Paljor wants to talk to one of the guides. He says he will tell them to start to pack up everything and everybody at first light in the morning. He also says for us to pack all our things including our equipment tonight so they will be ready for the packers first thing in the morning. He is assuming all of our work is done here. Is he correct?"

Dr. Rivers said, "Yes, we're done here. Ramon, go bring one of the guides so he can talk to Paljor. I believe we recorded all the data we needed and are done here unless someone has something else to do. . . . I assume the silence means we are ready. In that case, let's start packing. We can leave the wind generators, the lighting and the radio on and the tents up until the morning. We can take all that down while the packers are loading up everything else. Pack the instruments first."

23

Meteor Shower Over, We Head Back

✳ Thursday, June 16, 2005, 10:00 a.m. ✳

The packing and loading went well and we headed out across the plateau shortly after ten o'clock Thursday morning. At twelve thirty we met Paljor. Kunchen was not with him.

"Kunchen has gone back down the trail. He wants to check something out and meet us at the end of the roadway where we first got on the horses."

I remembered our original plans. "Paljor, it's almost one. Isn't it a bit late to start down? Our original plan was to camp overnight right here and start down first thing in the morning so we would be sure to reach the road before dark."

"That was the original plan, but Kunchen wants us to camp down at the base of the trail. We should be able to get there before dark if we start right now and don't stop to eat or waste any time."

I was concerned about no stops. "Will we be able to make a potty stop or should we do so right now before we start."

Paljor laughed. "Good suggestion. Let's stop and take a break right now while we are on level ground. Then we might make the bottom of the trail in six hours while it's still light."

Everyone scurried for a spot away from others and the two women took a blanket for a privacy screen. With nothing around big enough to hide behind, everyone improvised. We were all back on our horses in about ten minutes. The trip down seemed a bit slower and more dangerous. It was almost dark when we came out on the flat area where the road ended. It would be a pleasant change to set up camp without snow. The packers took care of the horses and by eight the food tent was in operation. We were all hungry. After we ate, Paljor stood up and called our attention.

"Kunchen is checking out the old trail from here to Yangbajain. For many years before the road was built, he used to travel up the old trail from the city. He left to check to find out if the trail is still usable. The trail we came down is part of an old trail running from Yangbajain clear to Baingoin some two hundred or so kilometers north. That trail was used by travelers for centuries to go north. He's sure the part down to Yangbajain is still useable. It follows the same stream bed as the upper part and does not go east like the road does and was unaffected by the meteor strike. The trip will take six to eight hours if the trail is still usable."

Jack was concerned. "If it's anything like the trail we came down and hasn't been used for years—how long ago was the road built?"

"I'm not certain, about fifteen years ago. It was opened right before I started as a guide," Paljor said. "It continued to be used by men on horseback since then, but I don't know how often. We'll wait here for Kunchen to bring us news. Believe me, he will not send us down the trail if any serious danger is present. That part of the trail is not as steep as the part you came down so it could be easier."

Talbot, who unpacked and set up the radio, shouted, "News everyone, and not good."

He reported, "I found a news report in English from Beijing about the strike. The meteor hit dead center on the Yarlung Zangbpo River about five kilometers east of Shigatse. A wall of water came up the river into the city and did a lot of damage before reversing course and resumed flowing west. Several thousand people are feared killed but the number is not confirmed.

The strike caused numerous earthquakes in this area with many faults. These quakes shut down all of the power plants in the area. This led to a complete shutdown of the other powerplants connected to the grid. No information was given about the actual damage, and that may not be known for days or even weeks. From the air they estimated the crater to be about two kilometers long and a kilometer wide. One small village on the bank of the river was obliterated. The crater is centered where the village had been and is now filling with water from the river.

"More news. Mt Everest is no longer the highest mountain on Earth. Three hundred meters were blown off of its summit by one of the meteors. The others struck less well known mountains creating strangely shaped craters. It was fortunate that none struck inhabited areas. Twenty climbers were on Mt Everest when it was hit. There has been no news about any of them or their fate as yet. That's all they reported in English.

"We were fortunate those meteors did not strike a densely populated area. That's no consolation to the people in Shigatse or of the destroyed village, but if the strike was in a major metropolis the death toll would be staggering."

Dr. Rivers spoke to the group. "That news is sad and sobering. We are all heartsick for the families of those lost in this calamity, especially in such a remote area. This will be an experience we will all remember for the rest of our lives. We were so close. We should observe a moment of silence or prayer for those who died."

The tent was silent for five minutes. Dr. Rivers interrupted the silence. "Now, we should all try for a good night's sleep. We'll be getting up early so let's hit those sleeping bags now."

We were all tired from the day's exertions and especially at the high altitude. I went to sleep within ten minutes of setting up my tent and rolling out the sleeping bag.

✷ Friday, June 17, 2005, 8:00 a.m. ✷

At Dr. Rivers' request, everyone gathered in the food tent after eating. She addressed the group which included Paljor.

"From what Paljor told us, Kunchen is following the old trail to Yangbajain to find out if we can use it. We don't know how long they will take, several days at least. There is no point in our siting around waiting so we are going to work. I want the wind generators set up and operating so we can use our equipment. The wind here is much less than on the plateau so we may need all three generators to maintain enough power. Talbot, I want you to see if you can contact anyone on the short wave, try Sheng Su in Lhasa.

Our radio is low power and we didn't plan on using it to contact the university. Maybe Sheng Su can make contact with someone at the University and provide us with a relay link so we can speak with them. I'd like to tell them we're OK and where we are. Tell me what you find out.

"The rest of you can unpack your equipment and start checking through the recordings for anything of significance. We now have time on our hands so there's no point in waiting till we are home to work on our data. You will need to pack up again, but suppose we are stuck here for a couple of weeks. I'll ask Paljor to direct his men to unpack the things packed for the horses. It's quite clear the trucks with the shipping containers will not be here for a long time after we've gone down the trail to Yangbajain. We'll pack those containers when we are back in the city."

Paljor stood. "I'm pleased you are choosing to work while we wait as it will be several days before we can leave. Two of our men will head down the trail and meet with Kunchen. One of them, Klojain, said he worked the trail two years ago and it was difficult but not impassable. He also said that was the last time the trail was used. Kunchen may need some help clearing brush out of gullies. Klojain told me debris was his worst problem."

Dr. Rivers said, "Thank you, Paljor. I'm certain you and your men will clear a way through the trail. OK troops. Let's go to work."

Before long everyone was working and the generators were humming. The one disappointing thing was that Sheng Su could not make contact with the university. Even Lhasa was having electrical problems from the meteor strike. Sheng Su was operating his radio on battery power because of the power irregularities and that cut his broadcasting power to about a third of its usual strength. He told us all commercial flights within Tibet were stopped because the flight control system was also shut down due to the power problems. Damage to the infrastructure from the meteor strike caused both transportation and communications to be negatively affected in a big way.

24

The Trail Breakers Finally Return
* Tuesday, June 21, 2005, 3:00 p.m. *

Tuesday afternoon, three weary and hungry men rode into camp on their worn out horses. After taking care of the horses, they came to the food tent. While eating the first fresh food they had seen in five days, they related their findings to Paljor. The meal took half an hour after which Paljor told us what they found.

"Kunchen said the trail is now usable. He and then the other two spent almost the entire time clearing trees and brush out of narrow sections of the trail. They burned most of the brush and used the water from the stream to flush out the ashes and remaining debris so the trail is usable. Kunchen says we should prepare to start down at first light on Friday morning. That means getting all the animals packed and ready to leave in the dark before daylight. He does not want to hurry on the way down as the trail is still a bit precarious. He plans to wait until Friday so they and their horses can get some rest. He warned us the horses would be plodding through water in the stream most of the way. The trail that used to follow the stream is mostly gone, but the stream bed is now quite clear and usable. Any questions?"

"Yes. How long does he think the trip will take?" Jack asked.

"He's hoping we can reach the trail end in twelve or thirteen hours but thinks it could take as long as eighteen. That's why he wants to make an early start. The going will be slow because of conditions in the stream. He is concerned that no one is hurt or falls from a horse. The trail is not steep but narrow, winding, and single file in many places. This will not be an easy trip."

Dr. Rivers spoke to the group. "Please continue checking and organizing the data in your assigned recordings. I doubt we will be able to send anything back to the university until we reach Beijing. Then we may not be able to blast our way through the Chinese red tape for permission to send data. My guess is we'll end up downloading our data back at Arizona. One thing we should try to do is copy all significant data onto one of those big USB drives and when completed, turn the drive over to Pat. Pat, I want you to oversee the data transfer to make sure we backup everything and catalog things so we'll know what we have and where it is. Talbot, I want you and Pat to see me right after we're finished here. There are a few more things we need to do. Now, if there are no more questions, let's go to work."

The silence was only broken by a few mumbled comments between individuals as they left the tent. Pat and Talbot joined Dr. Rivers.

"What's up?" Talbot asked Dr. Rivers.

"Grab a bench and let's sit over by the open tent flap and talk. I want to be certain no one overhears us."

I was concerned. "What's this about and why the secrecy?"

"I have a few suspicions about our Chinese astronomers and what might happen as we leave China."

"Why so?" Talbot asked.

Dr. Rivers explained, "there are several reasons. I spoke with those two Chinese for some length and asked a few telling questions. In my opinion, they are not very experienced astronomers. They do understand quite a bit about data retrieval and storage, more than most astronomers would."

"How'd you come to that conclusion?" I asked.

"For one thing, our equipment was let through Chinese customs with only some cursory checking, much less than I expected. They did pay close attention to our computers and in particular, our data storage devices. They counted them and took down the serial numbers of each item."

"So? They recorded all of our equipment. Why did that make you suspicious?" Talbot asked.

"Because they paid little attention to our telescopes, wind generators, or other equipment. The only serial numbers recorded were those of the computers and storage systems. My guess is they will impound and hold them and copy all of the data. That will give them the results of our effort without any cost to them. Talbot, you are our computer guru, what can we do to prevent them from copying our data?"

"Not much, I'm afraid. Even with 128 bit encryption their supercomputers could decipher our data if they wanted to. The alphanumeric data could be scrambled and then encrypted, but the digitized images from all those telescopes would take more computing power than is available here."

Pat, "Don't we have a lot of those brand new 128Gb flash drives we used on the cameras to collect and store images? You transferred all of that data onto the big USB drives for permanent storage didn't you? How many of those thumb drives are in your stuff and is there enough capacity to hold the most important of our data?"

"Pat, you're a genius. Because they were a last minute acquisition, I brought the entire shipment of 100 of those drives in my luggage in a small metal box. They never gave that box a second look in customs. Oh, but I can guarantee you they will look through everything when we leave. We'll need a secure place to hide them where they won't find them."

Dr. Rivers, "Those drives are small enough to store inside the metal tubes on much of our equipment. How about sticking them inside the support poles for the wind generators?"

Pat, "Those tubes are large and screw together. They might decide to open them up."

Talbot, "I know the perfect place. The frames that held all those telescopes. They are heavy aluminum and the inside of those tubes are about the right size. We could stuff a few inside each tube and pack some tissue in with them to keep them from rattling."

Pat, "They might look into one to find out what's inside. If they found any of those thumb drives they would know where to look for the rest."

Talbot, "No chance, those tubes are riveted into the sockets of both the frame that holds the telescope and the cast aluminum base. I doubt they would drill out the rivets to look in the tubes."

Dr. Rivers, "If they are riveted together, how would we be able to put the drives inside?"

Talbot laughed. "I built those frames. I can drill out the rivets in the bottom and then rivet them back in place after we stuff the drives and packing inside. I doubt they would take those bases apart. Hell, they don't even know what to look for, especially anything as small as a flash drive."

Pat, "We could pack the USB drives in a well-hidden place. If they find those and it's obvious we hid them, it will send them off the trail. They won't be looking for anything else."

Dr. Rivers, "I wondered, what about those two Chinese astronomers? They were nosing around all of our computers and data storage when we first set up. I wonder if they found we were using flash drives to transfer data from the telescopes to our PCs and USB drives?"

Talbot doubled over in laughter.

"What's so damned funny?" I asked. "If they knew we used those flash drives I'm sure they would tell their friends in customs to look for them."

Talbot controlled his laughter at last. "Those Chinese, I played a little joke on them. They were asking me how we collected the data from the telescopes. I didn't think it was any of their business so I told them our computers were connected wirelessly to the telescopes. One of them asked if that wasn't an insecure way. I laughed and asked him who could gather and steal our data out here in the middle of nowhere. That seemed to satisfy their curiosity. They seemed to be quite impressed that we were using wireless data transfer. They were not around when I picked up the flash drives and transferred the data. Here's another thought. We could stick all four of those USB drives in the metal box, pack bubble wrap around them and stick the box in my luggage. If they find them, they'll think we were trying to hide them from customs. If they don't catch the box, all of our data will be safe."

Pat, "That'll never happen. They recorded the serial numbers of those drives and will be looking for them. Aren't they password protected?"

"Of course." Talbot replied. "All of our storage devices and disks are password protected with encryption. Why do you ask?"

"What would a person do if they tried to open a file on one of those drives and did not know the password?"

"Try a few names from the group, why?"

"Couldn't you program those drives so that after a few failed attempts they would wipe the data clean? Doing so would foil their efforts to steal our data."

"I see what you are getting at. A bit of careful programming would be required, but I could do that. First I must transfer all our data to those flash drives. That will take some time. Then I would confirm the accuracy of the data on the flash drives. Once the data is on the flash drives, I'll pack them in those aluminum frame tubes where they will stay until we're back in Arizona. While I'm doing that I will also be working on that self destruct program. I already have a few ideas. I'll tell you when I have everything worked out. The program must be fool proof. The Chinese have some savvy computer people."

✳   ✳   ✳

Thursday morning Talbot came over to my tent, a huge grin on his face. "Pat, I'm having a lot of fun trying to foil our Chinese friends. My plan is all worked out. Now all we can do is hope they don't find those flash drives, and I don't think they will."

"Don't try to explain your plan to me as I wouldn't understand. I'll trust you know what you're doing."

"I only wish I could see their faces when they try to open up those data files on our computers or the USB drives. The safety key is the entire lyrics to the song, 'Mary had a Little Lamb,' all four verses. No way in Hell they can break that. They would need to know and use all of those lyrics to prevent my little worm from overwriting zeros to the entire data disc. If they miss one character including punctuation, it would trigger overwriting zeros to the entire drive."

"I'll take your word on that."

"I will explain the whole thing to you over a couple of beers when we are back in Arizona. You'll get a kick out of it. I wanted you to know before we head down the old trail."

25

After a Week Long Stop, We Hit the Trail

✳ Friday, June 24, 2005, 5:30 a.m. ✳

Friday morning we were up before dawn breaking down the generators and tents and helping the porters pack them on the horses. The first faint glow of dawn was barely showing when we crossed the road and started down the trail which was wide and flat at first. We moved along at a brisk pace.

When Paljor came close, I asked him, "Why are we going so fast? We're moving much faster then we did at any time on the upper section of the trail. Isn't it a bit dangerous to ride so fast in this trail?"

He pointed to the sky. "Kunchen is concerned about those clouds up over the mountains. Thunder storms in the mountains could mean flash floods and we will soon be riding down a stream bed that could be dangerous if it floods. We'll reach a plateau a few kilometers down where we would be safe from any flash floods. The Tibetan word for flash floods means water avalanche, and that's what these sudden floods are, water avalanches."

"Those clouds are miles away, how could they be a danger"

"In the Tibetan highlands with rugged mountains and steep valleys flash floods are quite common in the summer. Every year a number of Tibetans die in them. The water moves down the mountains from one to two hundred kilometers per hour. In some places the wall of water reaches as high as a three-story house rushing through the narrow canyons. Those flash floods can cover many miles in a few minutes and inundate unwary travelers before they reach the safety of high ground."

"If that is such a danger, why are we going now?"

Paljor laughed. "It is a serious danger of which we must constantly be aware. If we waited for a time without the danger of flash floods, we would wait until cold weather and the end of thunderstorms in the mountains. Kunchen will plan for escape routes and warn us of any floods. As long as we do as he asks we will be quite safe."

"I certainly hope so."

*   *   *

After about an hour we came to a place where the trail narrowed. The stream cut a narrow passage through a rocky ridge. We rode single file for quite a while down a gentle slope. All the twists and turns made for slow going. Kunchen urged the horses to go faster. When we came to a widening of the canyon where another canyon joined the one we were following, Kunchen and Paljor directed the horses up the side canyon to a grove of trees a hundred feet above where the two canyons joined. We were stopped no more than fifteen minutes when, with a loud roar, a wall of water crashed through the junction of the two canyons below us and rushed up the canyon we were in.

Paljor rode up to where we were standing. "Don't worry, Kunchen assured me the water would not reach us here. As you can see, we came up here just in time. Let's dismount and wait it out. We'll be stranded here for some time before the flood subsides."

Frightened by the roar of the nearby water, one of the pack horses bucked and pulled free from Rabten, the man holding him. The horse ran back down the canyon, a stampede of one. Rabten ran after him, shouting as he ran. The horse plunged into the water which by now was rather still and swam toward the raging torrent in the main canyon. He probably realized his error when he felt the strong current. He turned and started swimming back but it was too late. Rabten was up to his neck in the still water shouting at his horse. It was soon carried out of sight in the swift current in the main canyon. Kunchen ran down the canyon shouting warnings at Rabten as he stood in the water. Rabten turned and made his way slowly back up the canyon and out of the water. He looked dejected. Kunchen went to comfort him for his loss.

Paljor came over and spoke to us. "That was a tragedy for Rabten. These horses are like family to their handlers. Not only that, but the horses are their livelihood and cost more than a year's income to replace and train. You lost some equipment, but Rabten lost a friend and part of his livelihood."

"I understand," I said. "Please tell him how saddened we are by his loss."

"I'm sure he will appreciate your expression of sadness and concern. We may as well dismount. The water will take an hour to run out to where we can continue."

I was worried. "Will it be safe to continue? Won't we risk another flood?"

Jack said, "Yeh, I don't relish gettin' flushed down no arroyo. How do we know it'll be over when he says it's over?"

I smiled. "Jack, Paljor said Kunchen has never lost a traveler in many years as a guide. I for one am confident of his guidance. He got us up this canyon away from the flood before any of us got wet. What a terrific testimonial."

"We were only up here ten or fifteen minutes before the flood came crashing down. As far as I'm concerned, that was calling things a bit close."

Paljor explained, "Kunchen knew we would get to this safe spot. He saw the flood coming down the mountain and realized there was time to reach this safe place."

"He saw it? How in Hell did he see that?" Jack asked.

Paljor replied, "Kunchen has been guiding in these mountains for forty years. He can see and follow a flash flood by the water it sprays up into the air. He knew the flood would reach the trail after we moved to safety. After fifteen years guiding, I am beginning to be able to recognize the telltale spray or rising mist. I too can follow the progress of a flash flood, but I have yet to learn the timing of its passage down the mountains. For that I still rely on Kunchen. He tells me no more floods are coming our way so it will be safe to continue once the water slows to a safe flow."

❋   ❋   ❋

Two hours later Paljor shouted, "Mount up. Kunchen wants to go now so we can reach Yangbajain before dark. Water is still coming down the stream, but it's slow enough the horses will be all right."

Within half an hour we were back on the trail, albeit riding through a foot or so of moving water. The horses didn't seem to be bothered so I didn't worry. After no more than a quarter mile on the trail we rounded an outcropping at a turn in the stream bed and saw an amazing sight. Standing on a flat area about twenty feet above the stream was a battered and bedraggled Tibetan horse. All remaining of the load he carried was a tattered cinch strap and a bit of badly torn canvas. Rabten bounded up the slope to where he stood, overjoyed to find him alive. After a quick examination, he shouted down to Kunchen who shouted back. Rabten then led the horse down the steep slope to where the caravan stopped. He walked the horse over to Kunchen who gave him a thorough examination with Paljor standing close by.

After about ten minutes Paljor came to talk to us. "Other than a number of cuts and abrasions, the horse fared quite well in spite of his ordeal. Rabten is overwhelmed with joy at finding him alive. He was certain he was killed. His survival is quite miraculous."

I agreed. "Indeed. I was quite amazed when we saw him standing on that rocky hill and even more so when we learned his injuries were not serious. Tell Rabten how happy we are for him and for his horse."

"I'll do so right away. He will be pleased."

❋ Friday, June 24, 2005, 5:30 p.m. ❋

The rest of the decent was uneventful. We arrived in Yangbajain while the sun was still above the horizon. By the time we unloaded the horses and said goodbye to the guides and handlers, the trucks with our shipping containers arrived to pick up all of our luggage and equipment. An inventory disclosed that the only things we lost when the horse panicked were some folding chairs, tables, the tents and tent poles, items we no longer needed. We were fortunate that was all that was lost. When we made out the list, I added the box with the USB drives, just in case.

As we walked into the hotel, Angie remarked, "It will be wonderful climbing into a real bed with sheets, after a long hot shower of course."

Her remark was followed by expressions of agreement from everyone. At this time, Paljor, who came to the hotel with us, called us together.

"I want to thank you all for being such wonderful guests on a tiresome and even dangerous adventure. Every one of the handlers and guides expressed their thanks for the way you treated them, more as equals and not as servants the way so many foreign travelers do. They appreciated that as did I."

Dr. Rivers responded. "On behalf of our entire group, I want to thank you and your group for keeping us safe for the entire journey in spite of some real dangers. Our lives were truly in your hands and you all performed faithfully and wonderfully. I will write a letter of commendation from the University of Arizona to your organization telling of the thoughtful and excellent way you all performed. You were a very important part of our expedition. We could not have accomplished what we did without you."

"Thank you, Dr. Rivers. I will relay your words to the group. They will be quite appreciative. Now, I must bid you all farewell and wish you a safe and pleasant journey home. Good bye."

After our goodbyes we all headed for showers and a good night's sleep in a real bed.

26

Chinese Officials Delay our Flight
✳ Sunday, June 26, 2005, 7:30 a.m. ✳

Sunday early, we took a bus from Yangbajain to Lhasa where we boarded our flight to Beijing. While we were on the bus, our equipment traveled to Lhasa by truck in the airline shipping container. Both trips were comfortable and uneventful. We were scheduled for three hours between flights in Beijing but that was not to be. About an hour after our arrival, all we Americans were herded to a large room in customs. All of our equipment, supplies, and luggage were spread out on the floor in neat groups. A uniformed customs agent was standing by five of the groups. Another agent, by his uniform a superior officer of some sort approached us. He appeared to be rather upset.

"Who is in charge?" he asked brusquely.

"I believe that would be me." Dr. Rivers answered.

"And who are you, and what are all these things you are trying to take out of China?"

"I'm Dr. Ann Rivers, head of the department of astronomy of the University of Arizona. These things are the property of the University of Arizona. The luggage is the individual property of the members of our scientific expedition. All are things we brought into China when we arrived here several weeks ago. I believe you have a manifest listing our property. The expedition was encouraged and approved by the Chinese government. Is there a problem?"

"Yes, you pose a problem. I have no authorization for you to remove any of this equipment from China and without written authorization it is

201

considered the property of the Chinese government and will remain here. You may go and take your luggage with you, but the equipment stays here."

"I'm certain there must be a mistake. We were granted permission by the highest level of authority to bring this equipment into China, to conduct a scientific investigation of the meteors in Tibet, and return with our equipment to Arizona. My documents to prove that are in my briefcase with my luggage. And by the way, who are you and what gives you the authority to take our equipment."

"I am Mr. Dow Chin, Chief officer of the Beijing Customs Department of the Republic of China and I have no papers on your expedition as you called it. I would like to know what papers are in your possession. Please give them to me."

Dr. Rivers went over to the pile of our luggage and retrieved her briefcase. She soon produced a file folder of papers and handed them to Mr. Dow. After examining the folder for ten minutes, he turned to Dr. Rivers.

"These seem to be in order but my people will compare the manifest with what is here. Our officers will take some time to do this. Go into the waiting room next to the entrance," he said pointing. "There are seats. I suggest you wait while we check your list against what is here."

He turned to his officers, instructed them, then walked out of the room. We did as he suggested and were soon seated on several hard, wooden benches in the waiting room decorated with typical customs drab colors and no decorations of any kind. The lone wall hanging was a picture of Mao Tse Tung. The flight to LAX was to leave at 1:00 p.m. and it was already past ten. When the examination was still continuing at 11:30, I spoke to Dr. Rivers.

"I'm beginning to be concerned. We can see through the window in the door that they are still looking through our stuff. If they don't finish soon, we will miss our flight. That would not be good."

Dr. Rivers looked through the window in the door. "Mr. Dow is back. I'll go ask him how long it will be."

We watched her talk to Mr. Dow. They carried on a long, animated conversation. After twenty minutes, Dr. Rivers threw up her hands in an obvious sign of frustration, turned and walked back to the waiting room.

As soon as she entered, she said in disgust, "That pompous ass said it would be another hour for them to check our manifest against our incoming records and with all of the items on the floor. He says they already found some serious discrepancies. When I pressed him for the details, he told me they could not find a number of items from both the arrival list and the manifest. I pointed out the note on the manifest describing the loss of a number of items when the horse was swept away in the flash flood that caught us on the trail to Yangbajain. He completely ignored the list and insisted we were hiding something. He pointed out that we agreed not to leave anything behind for any reason. I repeated what I said before about the loss in the flash flood and it seemed not to make a bit of difference. What an ass."

"What will we do now?" Talbot asked.

"We'll need rooms in a hotel and to take our luggage." Karen said angrily. "I hope we can change our flight."

Dr. Rivers marched back out to ask Dow for help in changing our flight and getting a hotel. When she returned, she was livid which was unusual for the even-tempered doctor.

"That bastard won't lift a finger to help. I suppose we should go find a taxi and . . . no, I'll find a phone first and call our embassy. He did give me entry forms so we can leave customs. He's not going to force us to stay here all night."

✳ Sunday, June 26, 2005, 2:30 p.m. ✳

About an hour and a half later we were picked up by two SUVs from our embassy and taken to a hotel they recommended. Dr. Rivers spoke to the embassy staff member who came in the SUV we were in, a Miss Janice Latrobe.

"I'd like to file a complaint about this if it's possible. She told her. How can I do that?"

Miss Latrobe said, "I can write up the details for you once you are in your hotel room. You might need to come to the embassy tomorrow to sign some papers, but that is easy to arrange. I'll call you as soon as I am back and find out if you need to come to the embassy. I'll also call some of our Chinese government contacts and find out if they can help. I collected all of your names and reservations and would be glad to change your flight for you. We are here to help Americans when problems arise."

Everyone in the SUV thanked her profusely.

About four in the afternoon Miss Latrobe called Dr. Rivers and told her she changed our flight and contacted her Chinese counterpart to explain our problem. She also said for us to stay put until she straightened everything out so we could leave with our equipment. She promised to call us in the morning and tell us when we will be able to leave.

✳ Monday, June 27, 2005, 11:00 a.m. ✳

She called about eleven the next morning and Dr. Rivers relayed her message. "Miss Latrobe made the contacts she promised, and said there was still a problem. She said she would be down in less than an hour to talk to us about it. She said she might bring a Chinese official with her—one who would be able to help."

"Damn, that doesn't sound encouraging," Jack said.

"Jack, you're such a pessimist," Angie said. "Miss Latrobe is a helpful friend. Let's look on the brighter side and be appreciative of her help. At least wait until we learn what she has to say before jumping to conclusions. I for one am glad they are coming here to talk to us. I'd be afraid any phone conversation would be listened to."

"Maybe our hotel room is bugged." Jack said. "Did you ever think of that?"

"Oh for Christs's sake, Jack," I said. Our embassy arranged for our rooms. I'm sure if a chance existed of them being bugged they would tell us."

"How would they know?" Jack said.

Dr. Rivers was getting angry. "Will you please stop? If you are afraid you'll be overheard, don't say anything you don't want others to know. That's an easy thing to do and solves real or imaginary overhearing problems. I don't think we should rush to judgement. Let's wait until Miss Latrobe and the others are here and can answer our questions. And Jack, please do not ask if the room is bugged. We will assume not."

✳   Noon   ✳

When they arrived, we met them in a conference room off the hotel lobby where we were seated around a long table. Miss Latrobe introduced her companion.

"This is Miss Soo Lee, a member of the Chinese diplomatic corps here in Beijing. Miss Soo has worked in the Chinese Diplomatic Corps for the last fifteen years after receiving her Masters Degree from the university here in Beijing. She received her Bachelor's Degree from the University of Arizona some years ago. I trust that will give you all confidence in her efforts to straighten this all out so we can be on our way. She is also a good friend of mine. Lee would like to say a few words as we start, Lee?"

"Thank you Janice. We will all feel better if we keep this informal. This was a lesson I learned at Arizona that I have few chances to use here in Beijing. Diplomacy, and especially Chinese diplomacy, tends to be formal, so this is a pleasure for me and I hope for you as well."

A murmur of consent and agreement came from all. Miss Soo continued.

"I hope our efforts here will help you to return home with memories of a friendly Chinese experience. I am quite sorry for the delay and unpleasantness you experienced yesterday. I am working to straighten things out as quickly as possible. Several unfortunate events brought about the incident. The first was our error in not warning customs who you were and when you were arriving as well as your flight connections. That was the result of the confusion caused by the events connected with the meteor strike and the resulting disruption of our electric grid in Tibet. Another error involved the items you lost in the flash flood. Again, the break down in our communications systems caused by the meteor strike is why Customs was not informed of this. In checking with the guides in Yangbajain we obtained the details of your loss. The guides had no itemized list of the items lost, only that everything being carried by that one unfortunate horse was lost. Here is a complete list of those items brought in that were not accounted for among the items you were to take back with you. If you would check the list and confirm those were indeed the items lost we can approve the removal of the items you do have. The Chinese government is especially concerned that nothing is left behind. You acknowledged and agreed to our policy as part of your expedition agreement. Once the list of items is approved and signed by your representative and me, the items will be packed in the shipping container and moved to the plane for your flight. I must tell you that for this to be done in time for your flight is impossible so you will be delayed one more day. To provide some compensation we would like to invite you all to be the guests of the Chinese government for dinner this evening at one of Beijing's finest restaurants, Najia Xiaoguan. We will also pick up the costs of your unplanned hotel stay. I hope you will accept these gifts along with our sincere apologies for your inconveniences. At this time I will be pleased to answer any questions you may have."

As Miss Soo sat, Miss Latrobe stood. "I'm sure I can speak for all of us Americans when I say how saddened we were to learn of the great loss of life and injuries caused by the meteor strike. We are also sympathetic to the terrible damage to property and the disruption of so many lives. There will be a huge amount of work undertaken to return Tibet to full functionality. Many lives damaged by the strikes will not be fixable at all. For those people, we understand the tragedy and loss of life they experienced. We hope they will recover quickly. Now, Dr. Rivers, of the University of Arizona would like to say a few words."

"Miss Soo, our loss was indeed tiny in comparison to what so many of your people suffered. For our group, I want to thank you for your kindness and say we are pleased to accept your gracious offer. I for one would like to talk with you about your time at Arizona. I was at the University when you attended so I'm sure there are people we know in common and even some experiences. Several others here may have been at Arizona then as well. All of our members will come to you and introduce themselves and offer their own thanks. And Miss Latrobe, I want to thank you for all the ways you helped us. I will write a letter to the embassy telling how attentive to our needs you were on such short notice. What about our luggage? Must we take it through customs once more?"

Miss Soo smiled as she stood. "As I understand it, your luggage has already been checked through customs. They would appreciate you telling them what, if anything, you purchased since you went through customs and that you are taking with you. You will each be given a form for this purpose as you check your luggage for the flight. This may be a bit irregular but is being done to better accommodate your needs. The usual customs charges will be applied of course. Since I doubt any of you will be buying any high value items in your remaining time, those forms will not be needed."

The group stood around chatting with the two ladies for about half an hour before retiring to their rooms to prepare for the evening out.

The dinner was an elegant and friendly event. We each felt good about our Chinese hosts and did indeed, "return home with memories of a friendly Chinese experience."

27

At Last We Go Home

✳ Wednesday, June 29, 2005, 6:00 p.m. ✳

The rest of the trip was anticlimactic. We were greeted at the Tucson airport with great enthusiasm by friends and relatives. The news media were in force. Their stories would dominate TV and print media news for some time under variations of the theme, "Astronomers return from harrowing experiences with meteors in the mountains of Tibet."

Beanie came running to greet me, grabbed and held me saying, "Next time you go off on an adventure you're going to take me with you. I was upset with all the news of catastrophe and being unable to hear from you. Do you have any idea what not hearing anything from you for three weeks is like?"

"Well, I had the other side of the same coin. I certainly missed you. Now I'm home safe and none the worse for wear. From my standpoint, not to be able to communicate with you till we were in Beijing was just as painful."

"Your call made my day and relieved a lot of tension. Now I want to hear all about your experiences. Were you really trapped in a gorge by a flash flood like the media reported? They also said you had some problems with Chinese officials when you were trying to leave. Is that true?"

"Slow down, Hon. Can't that wait till we are home? It's late, after six, and my severe case of jet lag is getting to me. After jumping fourteen time zones it's a bear. I'd like to kick back in my chair, relax, drink a beer and then tell you what happened. There are quite a few stories and some of them are still playing out. How about it?"

"Oh, all right. I momentarily forgot about jet lag. I'll try not to press you. Would you like me to fix you something to eat when we get home?"

"Would I ever. I'm hungry for any of your cooking after all the strange food and MREs. Your Japanese cooking with Chiricahua modifications sounds fantastic to me. Then we can spend the evening sharing the last month's happening."

"Sounds like a plan."

*   *   *

Early the next morning, I found Jack Kershaw at work on our PCs. He dug them all out of the shipping container and took them to his lab where I joined him and two technicians.

"There is no point in trying to recover anything on any of these hard drives after the Chinese had their hands on them," he told Angie and Ramon, two of our technicians he asked to help him with the computers. "Between the USB drives and the flash drives we kept all of our data safe and in duplicate. Because our Chinese friends may have left some unwanted presents hiding on the hard discs, I want you to format all of them using our special scrub format that replaces even the boot sectors. Then do a standard reinstall of our network and operating systems so we can return them to service. OK guys, move it. I need to start organizing the data from Tibet for NASA."

Organizing all the data from so many sources took Jack more than a month of steady work. While he was organizing our data, I was communicating with Crazy Charlie and Angus to find out what was happening with the Ghost. Little had changed. Angus informed me the latest data on the path of the Ghost indicated it would pass quite close to Barnard's Star.

"In fact," Angus said, "The most likely path is a collision course with Barnard's Star. The likelihood of an actual collision is quite remote of course. Our measurements show a probability range of half a light year at the current distances involved. As the time to passage shrinks, our projections of the path past Barnard's and then the Sun will become more accurate. We won't have accurate details until almost the time of passage. We'll wait and see."

By the way, we pinned down a more accurate speed for the Ghost. According to calculations based on our latest measurements, the Ghost is moving at 91.4% of the speed of light. That's a bit faster than our first calculations and quite a bit more accurate."

"What does this change do to our time table?"

"Pat, the timing did not change at all. The accuracy of our parallax distance measurement has only been reduced to a range which is more than the change in the estimated speed. By the time the Ghost is nearing Barnard's we will be able to obtain much more accurate figures on everything."

"Are any more meetings of your group scheduled?"

"We decided all future meetings would be held on the Internet until and unless a physical meeting becomes a necessity. There's not much we can do other than examine the data anyway. We'll meet when the Ghost passes Barnard's which won't be until June 2024. That's nineteen years from now. A lot can change in nineteen years."

"You got that right, old buddy. Keep in touch, will you?"

"Sure will. Lani and I hope to visit Arizona before the twins are in high school. We'll bring them with us."

"Don't wait too long. Beanie and I would love to see you."

"We'll try. So long!"

"Bye, Angus."

28

A New Twist in the Ghost's 's Story
✳ Tuesday, July 5, 2005, 9:00 a.m. ✳

Angus received a call from his friend, Professor Hans Schuman from the neighboring Keck telescope.

"Hello Hans How are you?"

"I'm fine, thank you Angus. How are you doing?

"Great, Hans. How long has it been since we talked?"

"About three years if my memory serves me, right before I returned to Cal Tech. This is the first time I have been back to Hawaii since."

"What brings you back here now?"

"For the last two years I worked with the K2 mission of NASA's Kepler space telescope searching for exoplanets, mostly around class M dwarfs from about half the mass of our sun to two times its mass. I'm sure you are familiar with that program."

"It's a bit away from my area of research, but I am familiar with it."

"Well, Angus, I believe you will now become a lot more involved. NASA reported they found a planetary system around your Ghost star. I am bringing the details for you to look at. The information has not been confirmed as yet so I did not want to announce my visit. I'd like to sit down with you at your earliest convenience. Until we can arrange a meeting, I'll be working at my old office at the Keck. You will, of course, keep this confidential?

"I'm flabbergasted. Never thought about the possibility of objects orbiting the Ghost. That's amazing. Some time will be required for me to get my head around this. Give me your number and I'll see how quickly I can rearrange my schedule so we can meet. Where would you like to meet?"

"At Gemini would be my choice. I already worked up a draft proposal I'd like to go through with you. Let's find out if we can work together on this. We worked quite well together on our last cooperative effort if you remember."

"Do I? I'll bet those OSI jerks are still smarting over what we did. I still smile when I remember. I'll try to get back to you today, but maybe tomorrow. I can't say off the top of my head."

"That's fine. I must finish a week's work first, so I'll be busy. Before I forget, bring anyone else you think might want to be at our meeting, if only for the introduction. I'm sure Lani and John would like to be included. They are both still involved, aren't they."

"Of course they are and will! Planets around the Ghost? That will take some time and effort to understand. I already thought of some questions. By the time of our meeting I'll have a ton of them."

Dr. Schuman laughed. "They will most likely be the same questions I am wrestling with. It's a real challenge. They told me it was quite unusual to find a planetary system around such a small star. They also said it was 0.72 solar mass, quite a bit larger than I remember you telling me. Let's hope we find the answers. I'll await your call."

"I'd like to know how they calculated its mass. That's a lot more than our 0.54 solar mass figure. A variation that large is more than I could expect. Something doesn't make sense. I'd like to check their method and see their calculations."

"I'll see if I can obtain the information you want by the time we meet."

"I'll appreciate it. If we've been using the wrong data, it could affect most of our predictions. That would not be good. I suppose we'll eventually learn the correct number. It's good to talk to you, Hans. I'll call as soon as I have a meeting date. Bye."

The first thing Angus did was call John Carroll and ask if he and Lani could see him right away.

"Give me half an hour, Angus. It sounds important."

"It is, and half an hour will be fine, 9:45."

Angus stepped into Lani's office. "Am I interrupting anything?"

"No, sweety, what is it?"

"I just talked with Hans Schuman, remember him?"

"Sure do. He's the guy from Cal Tech who was at Keck, isn't he?"

"Yep! Guess what he learned about the Ghost?"

"That it's reversed direction and is now moving the other way?"

"Yes! Right!"

"All right, tell me."

"NASA people found a planetary system around our Ghost star. Can you believe it?"

"Nothing about that star surprises me. Has anyone confirmed it?"

"No, Hans wants us to do that. You and I are going to John's office in a few minutes to set up a meeting with Hans. Can you join us?"

"I'm not doing anything I can't put off for a few hours. Let me tidy my desk and I'll be with you."

"No rush. We've plenty of time."

✳   ✳   ✳

John's secretary, Ani'i Pohaku, sent us right in as soon as she saw us.

"He said to expect you."

"Thanks, Ani'i," Lani said as we walked by.

"Grab a chair and let's learn about what's so important," John said.

Angus repeated his conversation with Dr. Schuman.

John leaned forward in his chair. "That could be troubling news. It's going to force us to rethink our theories about how the Ghost came to be moving so fast," John said.

"It's going to make us rethink a lot of things, past, present and future," Lani said as she sat.

Angus shook his head. "Yes, and the NASA information about the mass of the Ghost has got to be in error. Our measurement of 0.54 has been confirmed over and over. I asked Dr. Schuman to find out how they reached such a figure before we meet. He said he would try."

"When can you show us a clear view of the Ghost? I'd like you to set Gemini up to look for those planets and the dust cloud. We're quite good at spectral analysis and will be looking for small variations in the radiation from the cloud cause by its Doppler effect."

"I don't know, John, We haven't anywhere near the resolution Kepler does. Their satellite has discovered most of the known exoplanets."

"We don't need high resolution," John said. "We won't be looking for planets, All we will be after are spectra of the two farthest reaches of the dust cloud.

Lani asked, "Couldn't we link with Gemini South? That would give us a huge base and improve our resolution. I don't believe we ever tried looking for evidence of planets or blue shifted dust, only distant red shifted galaxies"

"Lani's right," John said. "Angus, do it. Use the direct line to Cerra Pachon and see how soon we could be set up. The Ghost is near it's highest in the night sky right now so it's a good time."

"OK, John. I'll call you as soon as I learn anything. Come on, Lani. We've got work to do. I'm between projects at the moment."

Lani looked at John. "Can I put my current project on hold? I'll need your OK to do so."

"Let me think . . . Sure, Lani. It's an important project but is not time sensitive. I'll reassign you to this new Ghost project along with Angus. Stay on it till you find the answers and revise our predictions if necessary. I'm sure you will keep me posted. Oh, and check with me when you work out a meeting date with Schuman. I'll make certain I have no conflicts."

✱ Friday, July 15, 2005, 2:00 p.m. ✱

The meeting in John's office was underway. In the interim, Angus contacted Gemini South and arranged the hookup. Because of the urgency of the project, several others were postponed so they could start right away. The first attempt would be Monday, July 18. Dr. Schuman moved to Hilo and Jack Mercer found an empty office with computer access for him to use. He brought with him the findings of Kepler on the Ghost, the records of NASA's mass calculations of the Ghost and other data and records. Early in the meeting he gave everyone a copy of the draft proposal. They all took time to look through it.

John leaned back in his chair. "Dr. Schuman, I see no problems with any part of this. As far as I am concerned, it's OK as written. Any questions you two?"

Dr. Schuman stood and said. "Not from me. I much prefer we are casual and not use formal protocol. Please call me Hans. I believe we are all on a first name basis here. I'd like to feel like one of the crew."

John stuck out his hand and said, "Welcome to the Gemini crew, Hans."

A round of friendly laughter set the stage for warm cooperation.

Angus spoke. "Hans, I'm quite sure why the huge difference between NASA's mass estimate and our own. I checked the procedures they used and discovered no indication NASA took into account the increase in luminosity caused by the high speed of the star toward us. As the spectrum shifts far into the blue, it causes the luminosity to rise. Normally this is but a minor effect and can be ignored, but with the exceedingly high speed of the Ghost, this effect becomes a significant factor. Your people at NASA will find that to be the problem."

"Sounds logical to me. Scientists hate to be corrected. I'll send them your information, gently."

Hans passed around copies of a high resolution photo of the Ghost NASA provided obtained from Kepler. They were taken in both visible and ultra violet light two weeks earlier.

"The photo is shown as it looks from Earth," Hans said. "Examine the photo. You'll see it shows a faint blue cloud around the star oriented vertical to our position. That is the dust cloud of particles we believe range from sand grain to basketball size, the Oort cloud of the star so to speak. Although the cloud is radiating in the infrared, we see it as blue because of the blue shift of its radiation caused by its high velocity toward us. We theorize that cloud was created by larger bodies colliding and breaking up. Because of the clear area around the star, we believe there are planets orbiting that are too small for us to resolve at this distance. Gravity of the planets or planet has cleared all of the smaller bodies out as far as four AU from the star. A close examination will show that the cloud is somewhat doughnut-shaped and oriented almost in the vertical from our point of view. The Doppler variation between the spectra of the dust above and below the star tell us the material is orbiting. The pattern of the variation and of the dust indicates possible existence of one planet, maybe two."

Angus said, "That brings an entirely new set of possibilities to the system passing through the solar system. How large is that cloud and what other data do you have?"

"The exoplanetary system we studied the most is the one around Formalhaut. At 25 light years, it is close enough for Kepler to provide quite a bit of high resolution information, including images. Formalhaut has four times the mass of the Ghost so the entire system is much larger and has three confirmed planets. This makes detailed comparisons chancy at best. However, the shape and appearance of both systems are quite similar. If we use the same relative measurements for the Ghost as for Formalhaut, the cloud should be between 100 AU and 150 AU across and the clear area around the star about fifty AU across. It may be like the Kuiper belt around the sun in composition and about of equal relative size. The cloud will pass the solar system edge on, a giant doughnut passing near or through another doughnut about twice its size. Not much more information is available and what is available will largely be conjecture. Where we go from here is up to our group, of which I am pleased to be part."

John spoke, "This is a tremendous challenge that has already involved several revisions of our priorities and will doubtless involve even more. First of all we must list the various new parts of the problem. I'd like us to do that today. It can be tweaked later to fit new information. Then I want you three to divide those parts among you according to your knowledge and experience. If you need any other astronomers, I'll see what I can do. Also, as soon as you can, list your needs as to technicians, special equipment, and access to telescope time. I can't guarantee you'll get what you want when you want because a number of other high priority projects are in process that will be needing resources as well. My job is to determine who gets what and when. Don't be petulant if you must wait when you think you shouldn't. Yes Angus?"

"John, those are the rules we always went by. I think we can handle them with a minimum of discord. Hans, You've not worked like this with John, but I can assure you he is excellent at keeping things running smoothly and usually with complete harmony. It's why he has that position and also why the entire Gemini organization not only respects him but cares very much for him as well. He is the heart of Gemini."

"I'm almost embarrassed with such praise. I do appreciate it. To me, the biggest and most important help in my job is having such a competent and efficient staff here at all levels. Your loyalty to the organization and to our purpose is our greatest asset. We are a team, a well organized, cooperative team. That makes my job so much easier. Hans, you will fit in well. You did when we worked together a few years ago. Now let's stop patting each other on the back and go to work."

An in concert, "Yes boss," brought chuckles from all.

They worked on organizing the project and discussing some of the new considerations until almost seven. They decided that the most demanding work ahead would be determining what conceivable dangers and damage could come from a cloud of objects from microscopic to basketball size passing through at 91% of the speed of light.

Lani seemed a bit shaken as she pointed out, "We will need to calculate the energy of the various sized particles striking Earth at near light speed, just in case. Off the top of my head, $e = mv^2/2$ means we could experience a number of small to medium nuclear sized explosions if the cloud passes too close. A golf ball-sized object would lose almost no energy passing through the atmosphere and strike the Earth releasing the amount of energy of several medium sized atomic bombs. The particles in the cloud would be moving at the speed of particles in the CERN super collider. You all know the kind of energy those collisions release. They would also be millions of times heavier. I have a hard time visualizing one of those strikes, let alone a cloud of them."

"You're right, Lani," Angus said. "It's a whole new set of problems we'll work on. We'd better do some ground work before some idiot with a little bit of knowledge scares the entire world to death. It's the original problem with the Ghost all over again. I hope we won't fight those battles again. Let's try to keep this quiet until we have some real answers. Hans, who at NASA has this information?"

"The entire Kepler group know about the cloud, but I don't think they put that together with the Ghost coming at the Solar system. They are so fixated on finding exoplanets with possible life that they don't look at much else. They won't see the Ghost as promising or exciting. I doubt they will work on it anymore, or even think about it for that matter. We're quite safe here. My guess is that no one outside this room has a clue about this. Let's try to keep it that way, for the time being anyway."

John shook his head. "It's deja vu for sure. We have some experience to work with. We now need some ideas on how to handle sensitive information. We should schedule a meeting of the old Gemini group before too long. I'll take care of that today or tomorrow . . . OK, tomorrow," he said as Lani pointed to the clock. "I'll also call Crazy Charlie for his input. He'll understand more about this than all of us put together. I'll try and reach him tomorrow. Right now it's past seven. We've been at this for five hours. Why don't we call it a day and start in tomorrow? We can use the morning to cover our individual chores and then eat lunch at eleven thirty. We can start our meeting during lunch, OK?"

Angus grinned and said to John, jokingly, "Easy for you to say. I've scheduled several hours work on the telescope. I hope we can obtain some good photos of the Ghost and have a clearer look at the dust cloud. With Gemini's high capabilities in obtaining spectra, we might find something

Kepler missed. It's going to be a long night, several nights in fact. I assume everyone plans on working through the weekend, right?"

John said, "I forgot today was Friday. I guess we will be working straight through. Why don't we each prepare our responsibilities and plan a short organizational meeting at lunch tomorrow?"

A nodding of heads in agreement was all that was needed. They quickly broke up and went their individual ways. With what they each needed to do, none of them would sleep much this weekend.

29

The Ghost and its Dust Cloud

✳ Saturday, July 16, 2005, 8:00 a.m. ✳

Angus, Lani and Hans sat down in Angus's office to go through the results of their night's work. They worked together to obtain photos and spectra from the Ghost. Most of the photographs were disappointments. Only the ones with the light of the star blocked out and with long exposure times showed even a hint of the cloud.

"Angus, you did the spectra," Hans said. "Did you have any better luck than we did with the photographs?"

"Not much. At this distance the dust cloud gave us barely enough light to capture one spectrum of the brightest section of the cloud above and below the star. The results indicate the cloud is rotating much slower than the cloud around Formalhaut. Because of the smaller size of the system we expected it would be rotating much faster. Then Lani reminded me that I should take into account the high velocity of the system. I made the same kind of mistake NASA made in calculating the mass of the star.

"We all agreed it was difficult getting our heads wrapped around all the calculations that were affected in any math involving a star-sized object moving so fast. With an object moving at normal speeds, the relativistic factor would be so tiny as to be irrelevant. This is far from true for any object moving as fast as the Ghost. We must never forget that."

Lani looked at Hans. "I am wondering about your friends at NASA who are working with the Kepler instrument. Could you find out if they would be able to provide us with a high resolution image of the Ghost and its cloud of dust? It would be best if they could make several images in the near and far ultra violet. That's where the infra red glow of the dust would be blue shifted."

"I can try. They operate with a busy schedule, or did when I was working with them. It's too bad the Transiting Exoplanet Survey Satellite (TESS) won't be launched until 2017. That instrument could give us a much higher resolution image of the dust cloud."

Angus said, "I doubt that would be any better. Since the cloud would be back lit by the Ghost, and we would be viewing through the thinnest part of the cloud, it might not show as much as we see with Kepler. Besides that, TESS will not be in service for two years. Let's concentrate on what data we have right now."

"I'll contact them and see if they can obtain the images you want. I'm sure they would provide them if they could. Because of the way those bodies in the dust cloud reflect light, it is possible to approximate the size of the particles and density of the cloud. That information should be quite helpful. That is important if the cloud contains golf ball size objects or larger as Lani pointed out. At the speed the star and its dust cloud are moving, even small objects could pose a serious threat if they impact the Earth. We never had to consider that before. Let's keep that to ourselves until we better understand the makeup of the cloud and how close it will come to the Earth."

Angus agreed. "Let's keep any information about the cloud confidential. We'll need a better handle on its contents, extent and the path the whole thing is going to take. Media people love to speculate about possible dangers. They would have a field day with this information. Mili can handle it for us. She's an expert at handling media people. As long as we follow her instructions, the lid will stay on tightly."

They continued their discussion, broke for lunch, and then worked on their plans for dealing with the dust cloud for several hours. They agreed a lot more data would be needed before they could even begin to formulate a comprehensive plan. They decided to meet again only after Hans obtained the images and data they would request from the Kepler group at NASA. That request would take a lot longer than they hoped.

30

Kepler Views and Data Come Hard

✳ Wednesday, September 14, 2005, 4:00 p.m. ✳

The Kepler group at NASA took two months to find the required information. Hans went to visit with Kepler people after talking with them so he could help with the project. For them it was not a high priority since it had nothing to do with exoplanets. Hans used his considerable negotiating talents to persuade them to schedule time on the Kepler telescope for making the required images. When they made time for him, they collected almost a hundred photographic images at several blue shifted wavelengths. They also took a number of spectral readings. With the digital images and spectra in his possession, Hans returned to Hawaii late on Wednesday afternoon.

✳ Thursday, September 15, 2005, 9:00 a.m. ✳

The following morning, Lani, Angus and John eagerly awaited Hans's arrival at Gemini. They met in John's office. Hans spread the photos and spectra out on John's desk in organized piles.

"This is the most significant photo," Hans said as he placed one on top. "It was taken near the middle of the far ultra violet which agrees with the known velocity of the Ghost. We blocked the light from the star, but the dust could still not be seen. It was also made at near the limit of resolution. The cloud is quite uniform and smooth because the dust particles are uniform and very tiny. The cloud doesn't seem to contain many objects larger than the dust particles embedded within. My opinion is because of the cloud's slow rotation, the light of the star has overcome its gravity for those microscopic particles. This keeps them suspended in their present position. All larger particles were drawn into the star by gravity a long time ago. I don't think we need to worry about impacts from particles in the cloud. Of course, that is merely my opinion, my conclusion if you will.

"The smoothness of the spectra between the part of the cloud moving away from us and the part moving toward us relative to the star confirms that opinion in my mind. As I said, that is merely my opinion. I want to know what the rest of you think, and take your time. Examine the photos and the spectra in detail and decide what conclusions you can draw from that information."

After a quick examination of the photos and spectra, John said, "Your conclusions are quite sound, but let's see if we can shoot them down . . . play the devils advocate. No offence intended, Hans."

"No offence taken, John. I've had time to examine the data, and you are just starting. Four heads are better than one so I will patiently await your opinions. Any discussion or questions are welcome. Go to it, guys . . . and gal."

The three spent the next few hours examining the data and discussing many ideas. While they were busy, Hans was in his office catching up after being gone.

Angus stood up. "I don't know about the rest of you, but I can't find fault with anything Hans said, and we all tried. He hit it right on the money. That means the cloud poses no additional threat. I'm also thinking its close encounter with Barnard's star could blow that cloud completely apart. Right now it's in a delicate balance between gravity pulling it in and the electromagnetic energy from the Ghost forcing it away. The combination of gravity and light force from Barnard's might destroy that balance and the cloud. Of course, it will be twenty years before we know for certain."

"I hope the media doesn't go off the deep end speculating about that," Lani said.

John smiled. "The media people seem to be tired of the Ghost. We are talking about twenty-six years in the future. They'll not be exercised about the Ghost's distant future actions until a rather short time before it passes by. That's the nature of the beast. If we publish our recent findings and realizations as a scientific report in our usual journals, I'll bet the media will miss it completely."

Angus added, "Especially with the broad implications of no harm to come. It is nothing like as sensational as the first revelation, or even Charlie's new theory for that matter. That one did create quite a stir."

Angus was right on both counts, Hans's interpretation of the Kepler results and his prediction about media attention. For the next twenty years things would seem quite normal, whatever normal is.

31

Drastic Changes After Nearly two Decades

✳ Tuesday, January 9, 2024 ✳

Nearly nineteen years passed since the meteor strike in Tibet. The greatest changes are in technology and how people make a living . . . The jobs people do. Much of this is driven by changes in the power structure of the world. China is now the most powerful nation in the world with the biggest economy and the most powerful military. New personal freedoms and a new kind of capitalism for the Chinese raised their standard of living to the highest in the world. This was not without some painful adjustments and a good deal of inner strife. In spite of the problems, the Chinese began to excel in everything. Many other oriental nations are also doing quite well.

While every European nation save Norway, Sweden and Germany were overwhelmed by Islamic extremists, these three alone resisted the Islamic onslaught by shutting down their borders and becoming world leaders in automation and robotics. Their efforts were aided by what happened in America almost overnight.

Just when most of the world delegated the US to relative obscurity, an amazing thing happened. An unheralded, little known company specializing in drilling geothermal wells to generate electric power completed several hundred successful geothermal well power plants in the US. A group of their researchers developed a revolutionary system for creating hydrocarbon fuels, diesel, gasoline and jet fuel in their deepest wells.

They pump a mixture of water and carbon dioxide down into these wells along with a complex catalyst powder at high pressure. The extreme heat plus the high pressure at the bottom of the wells provides the energy to dissociate the water and carbon dioxide and recombine them into hydrocarbon molecules releasing oxygen in the process. The process is related to the one used in catalytic crackers in refineries for many years. The complex catalyst drives the chemical reaction producing the hydrocarbons. The powdered metal catalyst is removed from the high pressure mixture of water and hydrocarbons. The remaining mixture is flashed through turbine generators in the manner of high pressure steam. After the huge pressure drop across the turbines, the remaining mixture of water and hydrocarbons is fed to a separator to remove the water. The hydrocarbons are then fed into a typical refinery distillation column where the various types of fuel are separated. The fuels from the various "cuts" from the column included methane, LP gas, gasoline, jet fuel, diesel and some heavier oils. The process is like the one oil refineries used for many years.

The water and catalyst powder are recycled back into the well with more carbon dioxide taken from the atmosphere. Since the fuels are a byproduct of the generation of power, they add little to the cost of the operation. The oxygen could be compressed and used in other industrial process but because there is so much, most is expelled into the atmosphere. The rapid expansion of the process resulted in a number of huge changes.

1. The price of hydrocarbon fuels came down to a fraction of what they were a few years earlier. This dropped the bottom out of the mined petroleum market. The funding for middle eastern terrorists dried up almost overnight as wells became economic disasters and were shut down everywhere. Natural petroleum products could not compete in price.

2. The US was catapulted into being the world's largest supplier of fuels of all kinds. The resulting boom in our economy put us on a fast track to catch the Chinese economy.

3. The anthropogenic global warming movement came to a sudden end because every carbon dioxide molecule from the use of these fuels came out of the atmosphere. It was constantly being recycled.

4. Liquid fuels in America dropped to less than a dollar gallon and most of that is tax. To satisfy the demand, many new geothermal well power plants were hastily drilled, built, and put into service producing liquid fuels. The only negative effect of this process was the escape of hydrocarbons into the atmosphere. That was kept low by technology developed for petroleum refineries.

5. Because of these dramatic changes, the Ghost is seldom in the news and never on the front page. Most of the public seems to have forgotten it.

✳ Wednesday, January 10, 2024 ✳

Crazy Charlie calls Angus at Gemini to ask about the Ghost.

"Hey you old rascal, what's cooking. I haven't heard a peep out of you for years."

"Well, I could say so as well. Communication goes two ways you know."

"Yes, the last time it was you who called. As I remember, the twins were just starting college. How long ago was that?"

"They both graduate this year, so it was four years ago. Angela earns her degree as a chemical engineer from Cal Poly and Star graduates from the University of Hawaii. She's the astronomer."

"So they both stuck to their original choices. Isn't that rather unusual these days? How about Jesse what's he doing? As I remember, he was a good athlete like his dad."

"He's at Michigan State on a football scholarship, but he's also an honors student. His major is math. He wants to be a math teacher, college level. I am so proud of all three. They are hard workers and it shows."

"Sounds like they take after their parents. Those twins were spectacular young ladies the last time I saw them. I suppose they are even more gorgeous by now. They take after their mother."

"That's a good thing except for all the guys after them. How are Jenny and your two? The kids were in junior high the last time I saw them."

"Jenny is still the joy of my life., bright, happy, and competent. C started at Stanford in computer science after graduating high school at 16, not too long after you were here. Jessie is an artsie one. She has discussed so many different careers, all in art, I have no idea where she is headed. She is a well adjusted, happy young lady. She has a delightful personality, much like her mother.

"I'm sure you called with more to discuss than our families, not to downplay the important things in life of course. What's with the Ghost and Barnard's? I received your message with the latest and accurate path of the

Ghost past Barnard's and the exact time of the passing. So it's going to pass almost as close as the moon is to Earth, too close for comfort as the saying goes."

"The chances of such a close encounter are infinitively tiny, almost an impossibility. In a day or so I'll send you all of the precise data we recorded so you can run some simulations. I'll be interested in what you come up with. Of course, there's nothing we can do but watch and record."

"Makes one feel a bit impotent, doesn't it? I thought a lot about what might happen and developed an interesting theory."

"Oh? What's that?"

"I'm in the process of writing a paper on the Ghost passing Bernard's and will use the results of the upcoming simulations in that paper. I'll send you a copy as soon as it's ready for publication. Until my work is complete, I'd rather not release any information to anyone. I'm sure you understand."

"Wow, it's that important? I do understand fully and will be interested in reading your paper."

"I don't know that it's so important, but it does provide a new slant on the physics of extreme velocities. It's been bouncing around in my mind ever since I first learned of the Ghost. You said something about how different it must be for me than those tiny particles I specialize in. That got me to thinking, not about the differences but the similarities. Working on that led me to this different concept. So I must thank you . . . or curse you as it may be."

Angus laughed. "Now you charged up my curiosity. Hurry up and write that paper so I can feed my curiosity."

"As soon as I finish the simulations with your data I'll be able to complete it. No more than a month from now I will email the paper to you. You'll be given the first opportunity to see it. Now, are you planning any meetings of the group around the time our stars cross paths? If so, I'd like to be invited."

"We haven't discussed that yet. We're sort of waiting for your simulations to talk about it. You're welcome to come for a visit at that time. You might even be able to watch the passing as it happens. It's in early June, our best guess is the sixth, unless our calculations are off or something unusual happens. Tell me if you decide to come. And bring your family. All the old timers here would love to see Jenny."

"I'll make a point of scheduling a visit and will be sure to bring Jenny. She would love a visit. I'll bring Jessie too if she can get away. She was only ten the last time we visited the islands and always begged to return."

"I'll look forward to it. Now I had better send the data off to you ASAP so you can run those simulations. We'll talk more after you send me that important paper."

"Say hi to Lani for me. Bye for now."

"Likewise from me to Jenny. So long,"

✳ Tuesday, February 6, 2024 ✳

Charlie publishes his paper titled, ***Super Velocities of Large Objects and Their Relation to Gravity***, and sends Angus a copy by email. The next day Angus calls.

"I'm still digesting your paper. I'm having some problems with understanding the math. Particle physics is not my strong point, but the logic is right on and understandable. So you think that because of the extreme speed of the Ghost, it will not interact gravitationally with other stars at all? That's hard to believe."

"No, it will have an effect and cause some reaction, but the reaction will be so small as to be negligible. The particle motion in all of the matter is so slowed by the speed of the entire object, it generates no more than half a percent of the at-rest force of gravity. The gravity of any object at rest will affect the moving object an equal amount. It would take a massive object moving at that speed to cause much gravitational effect, an object like a neutron star or black hole. The Ghost is not massive enough. It has tremendous kinetic energy but only a tiny gravitational force at that speed. It should cause no problems even passing right through the solar system."

"If you're right, we have nothing to worry about. What a relief that should be to humanity. God, do I hope your theory is on the money."

"There is a unique opportunity for us to check the math when the Ghost passes Barnard's. We are close enough to measure the actual deflection. That measurement should confirm my hypothesis. Your long baseline telescope is ideally suited to make such a measurement. If we can work things out, I'll be spending the next four months working with you setting up for the minute or so when the Ghost passes closest to Barnard's. What do you think?"

"I think it's fantastic. I'll start the ball rolling at this end and give John a copy of your paper. I'm sure he'll be able to make the necessary arrangements. There are only four months to prepare. How soon can you come out here?"

"There are preparations to make here that will take two or three weeks. During that time we will keep in touch via the Internet. I don't think that will slow things up at all. Can anyone at Gemini help find me a place to live? Two bedrooms and an office would be nice. Three bedrooms would work if we could use one as an office. Jenny will be coming with me and our daughter. She would never forgive me if we left her home. I could send them out early to search for a place. They would be much happier and would certainly be better at deciding on a place than I would. Scratch my earlier request."

"Lani has some friends, connections that could help. Why don't you ask Jenny to contact her?"

"Wonderful idea. I'm sure your home number is in our book. Jenny could call her tonight. You should warn Lani. Would seven your time this evening be OK?"

"OK. Better yet, I'll ask Lani to call her this afternoon then it won't be so late there."

"With those two on the phone it could be for hours. Having Lani call is the best idea. Jenny will be home from late afternoon on. Now, I'd better start. I have lots of preparations to make, and no idea how long it will take my ladies to be ready to go. It could take days."

"Okay old friend. We'll be on the phone together a lot the next two weeks. Bye for now."

"So long."

32

The Ghost Passes Barnard's Star
✳ Thursday, May 30, 2024 ✳

John Carroll is talking to Angus, Charlie and the technicians. "Preparations for the measurements of the Ghost as it passes Barnard's are almost complete. The links to the Gemini in Cerra Pachon are tested and ready. The Ghost will pass Barnard's one week from today. If Charlie's theory is correct, our measurements of the positional change of the Ghost and movement of Barnard's will be imperceptible. This goes against all the accepted physics of gravity. If Charlie's theory is not correct, and the previous understanding of gravitational forces holds true, both measurements will be almost a degree.

"We will have only one chance that will last less than a minute so we better be careful. We will be running a number of test sessions all week to hone our skills for that minute. Angus will be managing the operation of both telescopes, and Charlie will be managing the computers. Do as they say. Once we record the passage, we will be able to make repeated measurements using the recorded data. That's why it is so important that the recording is flawless. Now, practice, practice, practice. One more thing. PRAY FOR CLEAR SKIES."

Everyone went to their stations for the test run. They ran a hundred tests during the next six days. They finished the last test Wednesday at eleven in the morning. Angus spoke.

"Be back here and at your station no later than two-thirty in the morning. The close passing will occur at 3:06 am. We will start recording at three and shut down at three-twelve. Right now it looks like clear skies. We are lucky with the weather. I hope we will be accurate with our recording with no glitches. This is a one chance only opportunity as has been drilled into you for the last few weeks. Don't be nervous, just do your job. Now, go get some sleep."

✳   2:50 a.m.   ✳

The image on the display screen in the computer room showed an overlapping image of the two stars. Even at the highest resolution the images on the display are larger than actual size. The blue one is partially covered by the orange one. The Ghost is behind Barnard's. In sixteen minutes their positions will reverse. Each person involved is at their station, attentive and waiting. The telescope on Mauna Kea is poised and ready, as is the distant one in Cerra Pachon. Everything is ready to begin in ten minutes.

At six minutes and eight seconds past three, the images reverse. The blue one is now in front of the orange. At twelve minutes after three the recordings are finished. As soon as they finish, Angus downloads the data and plugs it into his computer. After a preliminary check of the measurements he turns to Charlie who is anxiously waiting.

"Would you like to hear what the measurements are?" he says, looking at Charlie with a grin. "Would you really?"

"Well, are you going to tell me?"

"You'd like me to say no deviation, wouldn't you?"

"Come on Angus, tell me before I burst a blood vessel."

Angus grins from ear to ear. "Well, your theory is right on the money. There was no measurable deviation, none at all."

Everyone cheers and Charlie does a cartwheel right in the computer room.

Charlie is ecstatic. "That means we are in almost no danger from the Ghost. We will be able to watch the Ghost fly by with no damage, no fear, no loss of life. Thank God." Charlie says as he hugs everyone in the room.

"There's one more thing you are going to deal with." Angus says with a huge grin.

"Oh? What's that?"

"Your theory that we confirmed. Before it will be accepted, it must be duplicated by a lot of physicists. First they must figure out how to confirm it and there will be no more Ghost passing to do so. The chance it could pass close enough to the sun in six years is remote and that's the only possibility I can see. Confirmation is going to be the biggest problem. It overturns some long accepted physics of gravity, light speed, and even relativity. It raises more questions than it solves. Many physicists will be unhappy. Years of work will be required for your theory to be confirmed and until then, you will have lots of detractors. Be prepared."

"Oh my God. I never even considered such a development. I guess I'll grin and bear it."

✳   ✳   ✳

The entire of humanity celebrated the news about the Ghost for weeks. The news media treated Charlie as if he saved the world. The messenger was looked at as though he were the creator, the savior. The harder he tried to distance himself and disclaim all the adulation, the more intense it became. Those seeking an audience with him became so numerous and persistent that he did everything he could to avoid them. He went into hiding with Jenny and their children.

His doubters and detractors among the community of scientists were vocal and persistent. He was even accused of doctoring the measurements to prove his theory. No one could come up with a way to confirm the theory or the data obtained from Gemini. The only known possibility would not come up for the next six and a half years. Even then, the Ghost would have to come close enough to the sun or one of the giant planets that measurements could be made and his confirmation duplicated. So this controversy would continue for several years. Uncharacteristically, Charlie withdrew from the world which was difficult for him to deal with.

✳ Monday, August 10, 2026 ✳

It was a year before Charlie changed tactics at Jenny's suggestion.

"They are still after you because you are running away from them and hiding. Why don't you open up and make yourself available? Make those TV appearances and radio interviews. The only reason they are still bothering you is because you are trying to avoid them. Forbidding things makes people want them more. It's human nature."

Within two months the furor died down enough that Charlie could resume his former life. His hiatus from the university ended and he returned to his former position in August 2026. Jenny and the children were busy resuming their former lives in the community and at school. In but a few months they were settled in.

A subdued Charlie Botkin walked into the HEP department at Cal Tech. Everyone greeted him joyfully. The other faculty members joined the office staff to welcome him back.

Diedra greeted him first. "Dr. Botkin, it's wonderful to have you back. We all missed you a lot."

This sentiment was voiced by everyone. Charlie went to each person and expressed personal thanks. He also greeted the new members of the department.

"Thank you all for your support and encouragement. It's been difficult and I missed you all big time. I also missed my work. I hope it doesn't take me too long to get back into the swing of things. Dr. Herbert has done a commendable job of filling in for me. I thank you for that, Ed. Thanks to Ed and Diedra and their communications, I kept up with most of the action here. You each are part of that. Now I better go back to work. I will need a while to catch up so please bear with me."

Diedra and Ed walked into my office with me. My desk was clear. Not a paper in sight. They both grinned.

"We decided a fresh, clean desk would be helpful for you to start with." Ed said. "Diedra will bring things to you one at a time so you aren't overwhelmed."

"Hey guys, don't baby me. I can take it. Bring it on."

Ed laughed. "I remember how your place was always organized chaos. I'm sure that state will return before long. I'll be glad to bring a large stack of stuff from my desk to yours as quickly as you want. The tasks you handed me when you departed were and are formidable."

"Ed, you've done an excellent job filling in. I can't thank you enough."

"Taking over the stack of things on my desk will be the best thanks you can give me. A number of projects await your return. You'll be quite busy for some time."

"That's just what I need. Something to keep me busy so I can soon be back in the saddle working here again. Give it to me. I'm ready."

"I promise to keep things coming as fast as you want. I made a list for you to prioritize. That's the first thing. I did some preliminary organizing of the list, but you must complete it. After you finish that, the fur will fly." Diedra promises as she hands me a few papers.

The number one item on her list is to run simulations using the latest data from Gemini on the Ghost. I leave that as the first priority.

33

The Ghost's Path is Defined

✳ Friday, September 4, 2026 ✳

The results of the latest simulations are on my desk. The path of the Ghost through our solar system is now quite clearly defined. It will pass quite close to the earth. I call Angus as soon as I read the results.

"Do you think it will do any damage to us?" he asks as soon as I tell him how close.

"No, I don't think so."

"You don't sound convincing. I can tell you're not sure."

"Well, I'm certain, but, damn it, we won't find out what happens until it passes. I'm not comfortable saying there is no possible chance for damage."

"According to your Super Velocity theory, no damage should occur. No gravity, no damage. Is that not the case?"

"Yes, that's so, but some gravity will still be present. It's not quite down to zero. Gravity would only reach zero at the speed of light. The Ghost is moving at slightly less than that, about 9% less. That works out to a gravitational force of around 1% of normal. I've been trying to figure out if it will affect ocean tides and if so, by how much. It requires a complex simulation and I still must find a way to put one together."

"I see what you mean. You're a long way from any of my areas of expertise so I can't be of much help. Of course, there is no precedent for this event in either theory or practice. You, my friend, are the only one on this earth with any kind of expertise in the area."

"I tried to find out if anyone has worked on a method to confirm my SV theory. So far, no luck. That's a tough problem. Using the passage through the solar system will be too late, like locking the barn door after the horse has been stolen."

"Why don't you make a public request? Pose the problem of confirmation of your SV theory. Someone might come up with a solution. Do not mention anything about possible tidal change or effects of the passing. Lots of scientists are out searching for difficult problems to solve. With all those minds searching, one of them might come up with an answer."

"Good idea. I'll give it a try. By the way, today is our twenty-second anniversary. I plan on leaving a bit early and taking Jenny out to a special dinner at our favorite restaurant, just the two of us."

"I cannot believe it's been that long. I still remember Jenny telling us about some crazy guy who proposed to her over the phone the first time she talked to you. That made quite an introduction."

"She reminds me of that every once in a while. We chuckle over it. I always tell her how I know a good thing when I first find it. I certainly did well with that one."

"Congratulations and pass that onto Jenny. She brightened up our reception room when she was here. She's one in a million."

"Yep, I am one lucky dude. Now, I'd better hurry so as not to be late for our night out. I'll keep you posted on things. Bye old buddy."

✳ Monday, September 21, 2026 ✳

Dr. Robert Chen Yu from our physics department stopped in to see me. He called Diedra and made an appointment. She brought him to my office and introduced us.

"Dr. Botkin, I read your recent public request and it piqued my curiosity. Then I read your papers describing your SV theory and the results of the confirmation using the close passage of the two stars and I was fascinated. I thought a lot about it and decided to come up with a simple test. I put together a proposal for you. I would like to run a joint experiment with you, an experimental test that might confirm your theory."

"That's music to my ears. Tell me about your test. If it sounds reasonable, I will be pleased and honored to join with you in a corroborative effort."

"The test involves some unusual apparatus using some tiny and sensitive motion and gravity sensors. These sensors are a recent development of our instrument specialists. The apparatus involves dense weights mounted at the ends of counter rotating arms pivoting on a vertical shaft. Remember the centrifuges used to test pilots for g-forces?"

"That was a long time ago, but I am familiar with those centrifuges. I see where you are headed."

He laughed. "That does not surprise me. In my proposed apparatus are two arms with dense weights attached to both ends of each arm and balanced so they can be rotated at high speeds in relative safety. The balanced arms will rotate in the opposite direction so the weights will pass close to each other at an extreme speed. Each weight will be a hemisphere of spent uranium or other strong, dense material. The hemispheres will pass with their flat surfaces as close together as is possible. Each hemisphere will hold two sensors firmly in the center of the flat surfaces. The sensors will need wireless capability for sending data."

"I'm right with you. It sounds plausible so far."

"The entire centrifuge must be in a vacuum chamber to remove the effects of air friction and turbulence. At rest measurements will be recorded with the weights at their closest possible position. As the weights rotate and pass each other faster and faster, measurements will be taken of both gravitational force and any deviation from the at rest positions. The measurements will be taken at the precise moment the hemispheres are at their closest. It's true that the relative velocity of the hemispheres will be tiny compared with the speed of light but according to the math described in your paper, it should be fast enough to make a tiny change in the two properties. This change will be enough to be detected by the sensors. The centrifuge must be very strong and delicately balanced or it will tear itself apart at the speeds of rotation required. This will not be an inexpensive system or procedure."

"You are right on with that comment. How will we obtain the necessary funding?"

"I finished detailed requests for grants from the university and the government. I will need your permission and your name with mine on the requests. Your reputation and prestige will be an important and necessary part of such requests. I also included NASA as they own several of the centrifuges I mentioned. The centrifuges will require considerable modification, but the containment ring, motors and drive shafts will require only minimal changes. That should reduce the cost. NASA also has a suitable vacuum facility at Plumbrook in Ohio."

"I see you did quite a lot of work on the project already. I must compliment you on your thoroughness. I will study your proposals and unless I discover a glaring error I can say I'll be aboard. In fact, I am already quite excited about your project. I must thank you for bringing it to me and giving me the opportunity to participate."

"Several of your friends in the physics department told me you would be excited. I must admit as a new member of the department I was a bit intimidated by your professional reputation. My colleagues assured me you would be easy to approach and easy to get along with. They were quite correct. Dr. Botkin, I am impressed."

"Just call me Charlie. Everyone else does. Except at formal professional occasions where titles are used, I much prefer to be called Charlie. How should I call you?"

"Rob or Bob usually does the job. Like you I am not much on formality except at formal, professional activities."

"We'll work well together. What is your specialty, or do you have one?"

"I teach undergraduate physics. If I have a specialty it would be the physics of exotic materials, mostly related to metallurgy and magnets. My undergrad degree was metallurgical engineering. I switched to physics for my MS and doctorate. So I'm a mixed bag."

"That's interesting. We have something in common. I went to engineering school myself, Purdue. My majors were math and physics but I started in engineering school and took many engineering courses as electives when I switched to the science school for my last two years."

"No wonder we understand each other. I'll be interested in your opinion after you read my proposal. I'll leave it with you until I hear from you."

As he got up to leave, I asked a question. "It's obvious you are of Chinese ancestry. I'm curious about your background."

Rob laughed. "I'm a many generation American. My great grandparents escaped China and came to this country during the start of the Boxer rebellion. We are part of a rather large and close family for which I am grateful. My grandfather fought in the first world war and two of my uncles were pilots in the second."

"That's interesting. Your family has been in this country about as long as mine."

I am able to make his project priority number one.

34

Theory Confirmation Experiments
✳ Friday, March 12, 2027 ✳

Obtaining the approval and funding of the project took three months with virtually everyone's support in pushing it through rapidly. During that time the NASA centrifuge was examined and modifications engineered. With NASA's support and cooperation it was moved to the vacuum chamber at Plumbrook where Rob and Charlie were working in concert with NASA engineers to design the many changes that would be required. NASA agreed to fund this preliminary part of the project. Their principals were quite interested in Charlie's theory. The project was titled: GELOS, The Gravitational Effects of Large Objects at Super Velocities.

Once funding was approved, Charlie, Rob, and NASA engineers, worked with several manufacturers to produce the counter rotating shafts, the balanced arms, and massive hemispheres. The existing electric motors were easily adapted to drive the concentric shafts. The body of the centrifuge was usable as it was. Three more months were required to ready the apparatus for the first operational test of the entire system.

✳ Friday, March 12, 2027, 9:00 a.m. ✳

Charlie spoke to the group gathered in the control room. "We ran the system several times to balance both arm systems. We tested the electronics and sensors and they work. The air has been pumped out of the sphere and the vacuum is holding. At this point the at-rest or base measurements are made and recorded.

"The system will now be started and the speed slowly advanced in small increments. As the speed is increased, the hemispheres will be slowly brought as close together as is practical. We only tested the balance up to one hundred

RPM. As the speed is increased, the slightest off balance our sensors detect will trigger an automatic stop in the increase. At this point, we will measure the imbalance and determine what is required to correct it. The system will be stopped, corrections made, and the system balance refined. We will then run another test, repeating the test cycle.

"This will continue until we near the speed at which the system is predicted to fail, where the arms will break or the hemispheres will detach from centrifugal force. We are using a factor of safety of 1.5 as any failure of this type will destroy the apparatus, an unacceptable event. If the readings are not consistently different from the base or at rest readings, the system will need to be strengthened to handle even higher speed. Theoretically, the system is strong enough to attain the speed needed to cause measurable changes in the two properties and confirm the gravitational change in large objects moving at super velocities.

"Most of you will be monitoring readings of individual sensors. Should any of you notice anything out of the ordinary, please hit the panic button at your station. If that happens, the system will be held at that speed. The system will then be examined for any sign of trouble. Once we determine it is safe to continue, the test and the speed increase will be continued. Remember, it is better to be safe than sorry. Should the data at any point confirm the gravitational changes, the test will fulfill its purpose. Repeated runs with confirming data will establish the accuracy of the theory."

Rob added, "I must emphasize how important it is for you to hit the panic button and stop the system if you have any question of any kind. I added my words to what Charlie said. It is better to be safe than to *chance* being sorry. No one will be faulted if they pause the system for any reason. Continuing after the system is checked against your concern is easy enough. We will now start the first run."

* Friday, March 12, 2027, 11:30 a.m. *

There were two stops. One because of a glitch in one of the readings requiring an adjustment of a sensor position. The other one for a minor change to balance the entire system. When the test was completed, they found a measurable change in both properties was detected. At this point, the readings were recorded. The speed was then increased in specific steps and the new readings recorded. These steps were repeated as the speed increased up to the safety limit. The entire series was repeated twice each day during the next two weeks for a total of 30 sets of readings. The readings were shared with NASA and taken back to Cal Tech where Rob and Charlie could examine them using the university's supercomputer.

✳ Monday, March 15, 2027 ✳

Rob and Charlie received the results of the compilation of data from the supercomputer and are looking at the information.

"I must hand it to you, Charlie, the results match the calculations in your theory. That's positive confirmation. You did it, man, congratulations!"

"We did it you mean. Without your support, collaboration and your clever test, I couldn't have done it. The paper and the theory it proclaims will carry both of our names. That means you will participate in creating the definitive paper on the theory." I added with a grin. "That's going to require a major effort."

"It will be a pleasure, a labor of love. I am looking forward to it. I understand NASA has made the equipment available to any qualified individual or organization who want to use the system to run a confirmation. I know a number of confirming tests will be made by groups of scientists. That should bring acceptance of your theory."

"What do you suppose the absolute best result of the confirmation is?"

"Of course, we can now announce in complete honesty that the passage of the Ghost poses little danger to the Earth."

"I will call Angus and tell him ASAP. He'll be amazed and quite pleased. Everyone will be pleased. God, it's rewarding to be the bearer of good news for a change."

✳ Monday, March 15, 2027 ✳

The good news hits the world media. Charlie and Rob become instant celebrities. Charlie is prepared for the onslaught because of his previous experience. Rob is not. Charlie takes Rob under his protection and together they make the rounds of TV interviews, talk shows and social media exposures. Because they did not try to hide, but made themselves available, the furor soon died down. After one of their last TV appearances, they were having lunch together in a small restaurant in downtown LA.

"Charlie, I find it hard to believe things quieted down so quickly. You were so correct. Telling me to stay open and put up with all the craziness worked."

"It's going along with human nature, that's the key. I learned the hard way after trying to hide for almost a year. This only stimulated the clamor of the public. The harder I made it for them to find me, the harder they tried and the more aggressive they became. When, after Jenny's suggestion, my family and I made ourselves available, it took less than two months for the clamor to die down. It was amazing."

"OK. Now that things are quiet again, we can go back to work. I must do a lot of catching up and so must you."

"Yea, it's back to research, teaching, and waiting for the Ghost. We've got almost four years to wait and prepare for the event. I hope it doesn't come with any surprises"

"We'll wait and see, Charlie, wait and see."

"Yes old friend, this will be a long and hectic wait."